PLAN OF
NEW ORLEANS

SINS OF THE NIGHT

Also by Sherrilyn Kenyon

THE DARK-HUNTERS

Fantasy Lover	*Acheron*
Night Pleasures	*One Silent Night*
Night Embrace	*Dream Warrior*
Dance with the Devil	*Bad Moon Rising*
Kiss of the Night	*No Mercy*
Night Play	*Retribution*
Seize the Night	*The Guardian*
Sins of the Night	*The Dark-Hunter Companion*
Unleash the Night	*Time Untime*
Dark Side of the Moon	*Styxx*
The Dream-Hunter	*Dark Bites*
Devil May Cry	*Son of No One*
Upon the Midnight Clear	*Dragonbane*
Dream Chaser	*Dragonmark*

THE LEAGUE

Born of Night	*Born of Fury*
Born of Fire	*Born of Defiance*
Born of Ice	*Born of Betrayal*
Born of Legend	

CHRONICLES OF NICK

Infinity	*Inferno*
Invincible	*Illusion*
Infamous	*Instinct*
Invision	

Sins of
the Night

SHERRILYN KENYON

St. Martin's Press
New York

SINS OF THE NIGHT. Copyright © 2005
by Sherrilyn Kenyon. All rights reserved. Printed in
the United States of America. For information address
St. Martin's Press, 175 Fifth Avenue, New York, N.Y. 10010.

www.stmartins.com

The Library of Congress Cataloging-in-Publication Data
is available upon request.

ISBN 978-1-250-10494-6 (hardcover)
ISBN 978-1-4299-0608-1 (e-book)

Our books may be purchased in bulk for promotional, educational, or
business use. Please contact your local bookseller or the Macmillan
Corporate and Premium Sales Department at 1-800-221-7945, extension 5442,
or by e-mail at MacmillanSpecialMarkets@macmillan.com.

Originally published by St. Martin's Paperbacks in 2005

First St. Martin's Press Hardcover Edition: November 2016

10 9 8 7 6 5 4 3 2 1

For my mother. Thank you so much for giving me the love of vampires and of all things paranormal. I owe you more than can ever be repaid and there's not a day in my life that goes by where I don't feel the loss of you deep inside my heart. I miss you, Mom.
I always will.

Sins of the Night

PROLOGUE

Mississippi University for Women
Columbus, Mississippi

She was dead.

Melissa's heart was pounding from her rushing adrenaline as she scrambled to reach the safety of Grossnickle Hall. Two hours ago, she'd foolishly told her friends to leave her at the library while she finished researching her English paper.

Lost in the misadventures of Christopher Marlowe's life, she'd spent more time there than she'd meant to. The next thing she'd known, it was late and time for her to head back to her apartment-style residence hall. She'd briefly considered calling her boyfriend to come get her, but since he was working tonight on the stocking crew, that seemed a moot issue.

Without another thought about the stupidity of a twenty-one-year-old woman walking alone, she'd gathered her books and headed home. But now as she ran across campus being chased by four unknown men, she realized just how idiotic she'd been.

How could someone lose their life over one bad decision?

And yet it happened to people every day.

It wasn't supposed to happen to me!

"Please help me," she screamed as she ran as fast as she could. Surely there was someone who saw her? Someone who would call security out to help her.

She rounded a hedge and ran straight into something. She looked up at the man in front of her.

"Please—" The words died as she realized he was one of the four blond men chasing her.

He laughed evilly, showing her a set of fangs.

Screaming, Melissa fought his hold. She threw her books against him, and shoved with every ounce of strength she possessed.

He let go.

She darted toward the street only to find another blond man waiting there. She drew up short, looking for somewhere else to run to.

But there was nowhere to go that one of them couldn't catch her.

Dressed all in black, the newcomer stood as if completely nonchalant to the danger or her terror. His long blond hair was pulled back into a ponytail. He wore a pair of dark sunglasses that completely shielded his eyes from her and it made her wonder how he could even see in the darkness.

There was something timeless about him. Something all-powerful and frightening. He seemed to be cut from the same cloth as her pursuers and yet there was something about him that was entirely different. Something more powerful. More ancient.

More frightening.

"Are you one of them?" she choked.

One corner of his mouth twisted up. "No, precious, I'm not one of them."

She heard the others closing in on her. Turning her head, she watched them slow down as they neared her and caught sight of the man she was standing with.

Fear was etched plainly on their handsome faces as one of them whispered the word "Dark-Hunter."

They stayed back as if debating what they should do now that the other man was there.

The newcomer held his hand out to her.

Grateful her nightmare was over and that this man had finally stopped them from hunting or hurting her, Melissa took his hand. He sneered at the ones who had been chasing her as he pulled her closer to him.

Every piece of her was trembling in relief that he had come to her rescue. "Thank you."

He smiled at that. "No, precious, thank you."

Before she could move, he grabbed her into his arms and sank his fangs into her neck.

The Dark-Hunter tasted the life and emotions of the co-ed as he drank her life's essence into his body. It was pure and untainted. . . . She was a scholarship student who'd had a bright future ahead of her.

C'est la vie.

Reveling in the taste of her, he waited until he could hear and feel those last few faint heartbeats that would cease when she died. She went completely limp against him. Poor child. But there was nothing sweeter than the taste of innocence.

Nothing.

He picked her body up in his arms and walked slowly toward the Daimons who had been chasing her.

He gave her over to the one who appeared to be their leader. "There's not much blood left, guys, but her soul is still intact. *Bon appétit.*"

1

Katoteros

Death was ever swirling through the halls of this nether realm that existed far beyond the reach of mankind. It didn't haunt here. It lived here. In fact, it was a natural state of being. As the Alexion for Katoteros, he had long grown accustomed to its constant presence. To the sight, sound, scent, and taste of death.

Everything mortal died.

For that matter, Alexion himself had died twice only to be reborn to his current state. But as he stared into the eerie red mists of the sfora—an ancient Atlantean orb that could see into the past, present, and future—he felt an unfamiliar twinge of emotion.

That poor woman-child. Her life had been too abbreviated. No one deserved to die by the hands of the Daimons who sucked the souls out of humans so that they could artificially elongate their short lives. And certainly no human deserved to die at the hands of the Dark-Hunters who had been created solely to kill the Daimons before those stolen souls perished from the universe forever.

It was the job of all Dark-Hunters to protect life, not to take it.

As Alexion sat quietly in the dim light of his room he wanted to feel outraged by her death. Indignant.

But he felt nothing. He always felt nothing. Just a cold, horrifying logic that bore no emotions whatsoever. He could only observe life, he couldn't live it.

Time would march on and nothing would change.

It was the way of things.

But her death was a catalyst for something greater. With Marco's actions, he had set into motion his own demise, just as the girl had the moment she'd decided to study late.

And just like the girl, Marco wouldn't see his own death coming until it was too late for him to avert it.

Alexion shook his head at the irony. It was time for him to return to the dimension of the living and do his duty once more. Marco and Kyros were drawing together Dark-Hunters and trying to convert them to their misbegotten cause and they wouldn't stop until he forced them to.

Their plan was to rebel against Artemis and Acheron. And Alexion's job was to kill any who refused to see reason.

Standing up, he started away from the orb when he saw the images on the wall around him change. Gone were the Daimons and Marco.

In their place was *her*.

Alexion paused as he saw the French Dark-Huntress fighting another group of Daimons not far from her own home in Tupelo. She was intrepid and quick as she danced around the male Daimons who were trying to kill her. Her movements were beautiful and swift, like a frenetic dance.

She laughed defiantly at them, and for an instant he could almost feel her passion. Her conviction. She reveled in her life so greatly that her feelings were able to reach out across the dimensions that separated them and almost warm him.

Closing his eyes, he savored that fleeting twinge of humanity.

Her name was Danger and there was something about her that almost touched him.

And for some reason he didn't comprehend, he didn't want to see her die.

But that was foolish. Nothing could ever touch the Alexion.

Even so, he could hear Acheron's voice in his head.

Some of them might be saved and those were the ones Acheron wanted him to focus on. *Save what you can, my brother. You can't decide for anyone. Let them choose their own fates. There is nothing to be done for the ones who won't listen—but for the one who does . . .*

It's worth it.

Perhaps, but what concerned him most was how little he cared whether or not they lived anymore. Duty. Honor. Existing. Those were the things he knew.

He was becoming unsalvageable. How much longer until he refused to even render a choice? It would be easy, really. Pop in, strike them down, and come home.

Why go through the motions of trying to save anyone when the Dark-Hunters were the ones who damned themselves to begin with?

No, he wasn't Acheron after all. His patience had run out long ago. He no longer cared what happened to any of them.

But as he watched Danger slay the last of her Daimons, he did feel something. It was quick and fluttering, like a dull spasm.

For the first time in centuries, he wanted to change what was to come—he just didn't know why. Why should he care?

Holding his hand up, he banished the images from his walls.

Even so, he continued to see the future clearly in his mind. If Danger continued on her course, she, like her friends, would die during the Krisi—the judgment Alexion would soon deliver. Her loyalty to them would be her death.

But she wasn't the only one who could perish by Alexion's hand. Alexion closed his eyes and summoned another Dark-Hunter into his mind.

Kyros.

He was setting the course for the downfall of not only himself but for all the others too.

This time, there was no mistaking the pain Alexion felt. It was so unexpected that it actually made him flinch. It was the last remnant of his humanity and he was relieved that he still held even a tiny ounce of it.

No, he couldn't just stand by and see the man die. Not if he could help it.

"Nothing is ever truly set by fate. In one blink, everything changes. Even though it should be a clear, sunny day, the softest whisper into the wind can became a hurricane that destroys everything it touches."

How many times had Acheron told him that?

Everything was coming to a head again and Alexion wanted to change what was meant to be.

It was odd to have such vivid feelings now after all these centuries of experiencing absolutely nothing.

There's always hope.

Yeah, right. He'd long forgotten the sensation of hope. Life went on. People went on. Death went on. Tragedy. Success. It all cycled through there and here. Nothing ever changed.

And yet he felt different for once. Marco had gone Rogue and aided the Daimons. There was nothing to be done for him. And even worse, there were others who were quickly following his lead. Others who were allowing him and Kyros to turn their minds away from the truth. The Dark-Hunters in Northern Mississippi were coming together to rebel against Acheron and Artemis.

It was something that had to be stopped.

His resolve set, he made his way out of his room in the southernmost point of Acheron's palace and headed down the gilded back hallway that ran from his elaborate chambers to the centrally located throne room. The black-veined marble floor was somewhat cold against his bare feet. Had he still been human, that cold would be absolutely biting. As it was, he could only acknowledge the temperature, he couldn't really feel it. And yet that coldness seemed to seep all the way through him.

Reaching the twelve-foot door that was made of gold, he pushed it open to find Acheron on his throne while Acheron's demon, Simi, was lying on her stomach in the far corner of the room, watching QVC.

The demon, who appeared to be a human woman around the age of twenty, was dressed in red vinyl. Her ever-changing horns matched her clothes perfectly and her long black hair was braided down her back. She had a giant, half-empty bowl of popcorn cradled in her arms while her tail whipped around her head as if swishing in time to the countdown clock.

"*Akri?*" the she-demon demanded. "Where's my plastic?"

As he always did while at home in Katoteros, Acheron wore his black formesta—a long robelike garment that was left open in front, baring his chest and black leather pants. It was made of heavy silk that was embroidered on the back with a gold sun pierced by three silver lightning bolts—a mark that had been branded onto Alexion's shoulder.

Acheron's long black hair was left unbound, hanging about his shoulders. He sat on the gilded throne strumming a solid black electric guitar that played perfectly without the benefit of an amplifier. The wall to his left was a series of television monitors all of which showed the cartoon *Johnny Bravo*.

"I don't know, Sim," Acheron said distractedly. "Ask Alexion."

Before Alexion could reach Acheron's throne, the demon appeared before him, hovering in midair while her large red and black wings flapped to support her weight. Her wings, like her horns and eyes, were ever-changing in their color to fit her mood and momentary taste. Her hair color changed too, but it was linked to Acheron, therefore her hair color was always identical to his.

"Where's my plastic, Lexie?"

He gave her a patient but strict stare. Simi had been nothing more than a very small child nine thousand years ago when Acheron had brought him here to live. One of the duties Acheron had assigned to him was to help watch over her and to keep her out of trouble.

Yeah. That was next to impossible.

Not to mention, he was every bit as guilty of spoiling her as Acheron was. Like his boss, he couldn't seem to help himself. There was something innately compelling, endearing, and ultimately sweet about the demon. Something that made him love her like a daughter. In all the worlds, she and Acheron were the only two things that still made him feel any human emotion. He loved them both and he would die to protect them.

But as her "other" father, he knew he owed it to Simi and to the world to try and teach her some restraint.

"You don't need to buy anything else, Simi."

Her singsongy response was quick and automatic. "Yes I do."

"No," he insisted. "You don't. You already have more than enough baubles to keep you occupied."

She pouted at him while her eyes flamed red and her tail flicked around. "Gimme my plastic, Lexie. Now!"

"No."

She wailed, then spun around toward Acheron and flew to his throne. Suddenly QVC appeared on his monitors.

"Simi . . ." Acheron said. "I was watching something."

"Oh, pooh, it's a stupid cartoon. The Simi wants her Diamonique, *akri,* and she wants it now!"

Acheron passed an exasperated look toward Alexion. "Give her the credit cards."

Alexion glared at him. "She's so spoiled, she's rotten. She must learn to control her impulses."

Acheron cocked a brow at him. "And how long have you been trying to teach her restraint, Alexion?"

That didn't bear commenting on. There were some things in life that were indeed futile. But immortality was boring enough. Trying to control Simi often added a lot of spark to it. "I finally got her to sit in front of the television quietly . . . sort of."

Acheron rolled his eyes. "Yeah, after five thousand years of trying. She's a demon, Lex. Restraint isn't in her makeup."

Before Alexion could argue, the box where he kept Simi's credit cards appeared in the air before her.

"Ha!" Simi said to him in a delighted tone before she seized the box and rocked with it in her arms. Her happiness died as she realized it was locked. She pinned Alexion with a menacing glare. "Open it."

Before he could refuse, it popped open.

"Thank you, *akri*!" Simi shouted as she grabbed her cards, then fluttered away and headed for her cell phone.

Alexion made a sound of disgust at Acheron as the box vanished. "I can't believe you just did that."

The monitors returned to the cartoon. Acheron didn't say anything as he reached down to feed his black guitar pick to the tiny pterygsauras that was perched on the arm of his throne. The small, orange dragonlike creature chirped before it swallowed the plastic whole. Alexion wasn't sure where the pterygsauri came from. For the last nine thousand years, there had always been six of them here in the throne room.

Alexion still wasn't sure if they were the same six or not. All he knew for certain was that Acheron loved and pampered his pets and as the Alexion, he did too.

Acheron patted the creature's scaly head as it preened and sang happily, then looked back down at his guitar.

"I know why you're here, Alexion," he said, as another pick appeared in his hand. He strummed a melodious chord. "The answer is no."

Alexion feigned a frown he didn't feel. "Why?"

"Because you can't help them. Kyros made his choices long ago and now he has to—"

"Bullshit!"

Acheron paused his hand in mid-strum, then gave him an angry stare. The swirling silver eyes turned red, warning that the destroyer side of Acheron was coming to the forefront.

Alexion didn't care. He'd served Acheron long enough to know his master wouldn't kill him for insubordination. At least none that was this mild. "I know you know everything, boss. I got that a long time ago. But you've also taught me the value of free will. True, Kyros has made some bad choices, but if I go to him as me, I know I can talk him out of this."

"Alexion . . ."

"C'mon, *akri*. In over nine thousand years, I have never once asked you for a favor. Never. But I can't just go in and let him die like the others. I have to try. Don't you understand? We were human together. Brothers in arms and in spirit. Our children played together. He died saving my life. I owe him one last chance."

Acheron gave a heavy sigh as he began playing "Every Rose Has Its Thorn." "Fine. Go. But know that as you do this, whatever he decides, it's not your fault. I knew this moment was coming from the day he was created. His choices are his own. You can't accept responsibility for his mistakes."

Alexion understood. "How long do you give me?"

"You know the limits of your existence. You can have no more than ten days before you have to return. At the end of the month, you must render my judgment to them."

Alexion nodded. "Thank you, *akri*."

"Don't thank me, Alexion. This is distasteful work I'm sending you to do."

"I know."

Acheron looked up to stare at him. There was something in his swirling silver gaze that was different this time. Something . . .

He didn't know, but it sent a raw chill over him. "What?" he asked.

"Nothing." Acheron went back to playing the guitar.

Alexion's stomach knotted in apprehension. What did the boss know that he wasn't sharing?

"I really hate it when you don't tell me things."

Acheron gave a lopsided grin at that. "I know."

Alexion stepped back, intending to return to his room, but before he could turn around, he felt himself slipping. One minute he was in the throne room at Katoteros and, in the next, he was lying facedown on a cold, dark street.

Pain slammed into him with resounding waves of agony that

took his breath as he felt the rough, pungent asphalt against his face and hands.

As a Shade in Katoteros, he didn't really feel or experience anything this real. Food had no taste, his senses were all muted. But now that Acheron had placed him in the human world . . .

Ow! Everything hurt. His body, his skin. Most of all his skinned-up knees.

Alexion rolled over and waited for his body to fully transition into his control again. There was always a burn when he came to earth, a brief period for him to get used to breathing and "living" again. As his senses awoke, Alexion realized he could hear people fighting around him. Was it a battle?

Acheron had done that to him a few times in the past. It was sometimes easier to drop him unnoticed into the middle of the chaos. But this didn't look like a war zone. It looked like . . .

A back street.

Alexion pushed himself to his feet and then froze as he realized what was happening. There were six Daimons and a human fighting in the alley. He tried to focus his sight to be sure, but everything around him was still fuzzy.

"Okay, boss," Alexion said under his breath. "If I need glasses, fix it, 'cause I can hardly see shit right now."

His sight cleared instantly. "Thanks. But you know, a little warning before you dumped my ass out here would have been nice." He straightened his long, white cashmere coat with a tug. "By the way, couldn't you, just once, drop me either in a La-Z-Boy or on a bed?"

All he heard was the sound of Acheron's short, evil laugh in his head. Acheron and his sick sense of humor. He could be one serious bastard when he wanted to. *"Thanks a lot."* Alexion let out a long, irritated breath.

Turning his attention to the fight, he focused on the group. The human was a short man, probably no taller than five five or five six and appeared to be in his mid-twenties. As the man turned toward him and Alexion saw his face, he realized who he was. Keller Mallory, a Dark-Hunter Squire—one of the people who helped to shield and protect a Dark-Hunter's identity from the humans.

Squires weren't supposed to engage Daimons, but since Squires were integral to the Dark-Hunter world, they were prone to be targeted.

Apparently, tonight was Keller's turn to get his butt kicked.

Alexion rushed toward the Daimon who was headed at Keller from his back. He grabbed the Daimon and flung him away from the Squire.

"Run!" Keller said to him.

No doubt the Squire thought he was a human too. Alexion kicked a discarded dagger up from the street and caught it in his fist. Enjoying the "realness" of the fight, he tossed it straight into the heart of the Daimon, who quickly exploded into a golden powder. The dagger fell to the street with a clatter. Alexion held his hand out for the dagger, which immediately shot up from the ground and returned to his grip.

Keller turned to gape at him.

The distraction cost Alexion as one of the Daimons came running up to him from behind to bury a dagger deep between his shoulder blades. Curling his lip in disgust, Alexion felt his body burst apart. He hated it when that happened. It wasn't painful so much as it was irritating and disorienting.

Two seconds later, his body rematerialized.

His expression terrified, Keller stumbled away from him.

Playtime was over.

The remaining Daimons took off at a dead run but they had only a few seconds before they, too, exploded. Only they weren't about to be put back together again.

Still not appeased over the aggravation they had caused, Alexion straightened his coat with a tug at the lapels.

Daimons . . . they never learned.

The Squire's face blanched as he backed up and stared in horror. "What the hell are you?"

Alexion sauntered up to Keller and handed him the dagger. "I'm Acheron's Squire." It was kind of true. Okay, not really. It was a lie, but Alexion had no intention of letting anyone know his real relationship with Acheron.

Not that it mattered. Keller didn't buy it. "Like hell. Everyone knows Acheron doesn't have a Squire."

Yeah, right. If everyone on earth put together all the correct information they had about Acheron, it wouldn't fill a fairy's thimble. Alexion tried not to laugh at the poor man who thought he understood the world around him while the truth was he didn't know jack about shit.

"Apparently everyone's wrong since here I am, sent to you by the head honcho himself."

The athletically built young man scanned him from head to toe. "Why are you here?"

"Your Dark-Huntress, Danger, called for Acheron and since he's busy, I was sent to check things out and report back to him on what's happening. So here I am. Joy, oh joy of my life."

That didn't seem to soothe the man at all, but then sarcasm was seldom soothing. Although, to be honest, Alexion found a great deal of entertainment from it. Which was probably a good thing since sarcasm was Acheron's native tongue.

"And how do I know you're not lying?" Keller asked, his eyes still filled with doubt.

Alexion forced himself not to laugh. The man was smart. It was all a lie. Acheron knew exactly what was happening . . . at all times. But it was true that his boss couldn't come here in person. Not while all the Dark-Hunters in the area were suspicious of him. They would never believe the truth from Acheron's lips.

If they were to choose wisely and live through this, they needed to hear the truth from an "impartial" third party, and that was why he'd come. His goal was to save them from their own stupidity.

Provided they weren't all terminally stupid.

Alexion pulled a small cell phone out of his pocket. "Call Acheron yourself and hear the truth."

2

"I'm telling you the truth, Danger, Acheron is going to kill all of us. We know too much about him and he won't suffer us to live."

Dangereuse St. Richard stood in the receiving room of Kyros's antebellum mansion outside of Aberdeen, Mississippi, with her arms folded over her chest. She'd never been on the best of terms with the ancient Greek Dark-Hunter. Tonight, she wasn't in the mood for his bull, especially not after the stories she'd heard that said Kyros had turned Rogue and was allowing Daimons to live— and this from the lips of the Daimons she'd dusted earlier tonight.

She had no patience with anyone who betrayed the Dark-Hunter Code.

The sole job of a Dark-Hunter was to kill Daimons who were former members of the cursed Apollite race—children of Apollo who had offended him and been cursed to live in the night, and to die at age twenty-seven. If Apollites chose to start sucking human souls before that birthday, they became Daimons who could live indefinitely. But for every Daimon who lived, countless human souls died.

It was something she refused to tolerate. If she could kill Kyros for it, she would. But for one Dark-Hunter to kill another was instant death. She couldn't even attack him. Whatever she did to him, she would experience ten times worse.

Thanks, Artemis, for *that* particular gift.

Until Acheron answered her call for help, there was nothing she could do to stop Kyros from his madness.

In fact, she could feel the drain on her powers just from being in the same room as Kyros. Dark-Hunters weren't allowed to spend any significant amount of time together without draining each other's powers.

The room she and Kyros stood in was dark and musty, and should have been decorated with antiques instead of the modern furniture that clashed with the neoclassical design of the house. The walls were painted a deep, antebellum gold while the ceilings held exquisite white medallions. The hardwood, pine floors under her feet were scuffed and in bad need of repair. How odd for a Squire not to take better care of his Dark-Hunter's property.

But that was neither here nor there. Right now she had much more pressing business with Kyros than the fact that he had no taste and his Squire had no clear understanding of his job description.

"Okay, Kyros." She spoke slowly, choosing her words carefully. "Acheron is a Daimon who feeds off humans and all of us were created solely so that he could fight a war with his mother, the Daimon queen, who no Dark-Hunter has ever heard of. Uh-huh."

He slammed his hand down on the cherrywood desk he sat behind. "Dammit, woman, listen to me. I'm more than nine thousand years old. I was there in the beginning—one of the first Dark-Hunters ever created—and I remember stories of Apollymi from my childhood. She was called the Destroyer and she was Atlantean . . . just like Acheron."

So it was a coincidence. Two Atlanteans did not a family make. She most certainly wasn't the only French Dark-Hunter, she wasn't even the only one to come out of the French Revolution, and none of them were related by a long shot.

Kyros would need a lot more proof than that to convince her that Acheron was the son of this Atlantean god-queen.

She gave him a bored stare. "And this Atlantean Destroyer is now leading the Daimons and sending them out to battle against Acheron, who is just using us and the humans as cannon fodder to protect himself? Really, Kyros, put down the crack pipe . . . or go write children's fantasy novels." She leaned forward and whispered loudly. "I'll bet you even know exactly who conspired to kill Kennedy, huh? I'm sure the money from D. B. Cooper is what financed your stunning collection of furniture."

He bolted to his feet and approached her. "Don't patronize me. I know I'm right. Have you ever seen Acheron eat food? We all know he's a lot more powerful than the rest of us. Didn't you ever wonder why?"

That was a no-brainer in her book. "He's the oldest and has had his powers a lot longer than the rest of us. You know the saying 'practice makes perfect,' and that man has had a *lot* of practice. As for food, I haven't been around him enough to notice."

"Yeah, well, I was around him a lot once upon a time ago, and while Brax and I ate, he never did. After we were created, Acheron wrote down his bullshit rules and the rest of us have been blindly following them for centuries without questioning them or him. It's time now that we started thinking for ourselves."

She made a noise of sarcastic amusement. "And what has suddenly brought on this grand epiphany of yours?"

Kyros laughed at that as an evil, spooky look came over him. "Do you really want to know?"

"*Pourquoi pas?* Why not?"

"Stryker!"

Danger frowned at his shout. Half a minute later, something flashed so bright in the room, she had to turn away to keep her light-sensitive Dark-Hunter eyes from burning. But the hair on the back of her neck rose as she sensed a Daimon's sudden presence in the room. Hissing in anger, she pulled the dagger out of her boot and straightened to confront it.

Kyros grabbed her arm. "No. Don't."

Her temper raged at his actions. "You would invite a filthy Daimon into your house?"

The question had barely left her lips before the Daimon sensation ceased. The newcomer still stood there, but he no longer cast that warning beacon that announced a Daimon presence to a Dark-Hunter.

A bad feeling went through Danger as she looked at the newcomer. Like Acheron, he stood a dead six feet eight, with long black hair that flowed around his shoulders, and he wore a pair of opaque sunglasses over his eyes.

"What's going on here?" she asked Kyros.

Kyros let go of her. "Yeah. I didn't believe it, either, at first. But he can mask the Daimon in him so that we can't feel his presence."

"How?" she asked.

The Daimon laughed, flashing her a set of fangs. "It's a trait that runs in my family. My mother can do it. I can do it and my brother can do it."

Scowling at the two men, she didn't understand what he was talking about.

Not until he removed the sunglasses and revealed a set of swirling silver eyes that she had only seen on one man before. . . .

Acheron Parthenopaeus.

"He's Acheron's brother," Kyros said as if he could hear her thoughts. "And he's told me lots of things about our fearless leader that have left me cold. Acheron isn't who or what you think he is and neither are we."

So how did you do that thing that made all them Daimons explode?"

Sitting next to the Squire who was driving him back to Danger's home, Alexion winced as Keller continued to ramble on with questions and comments. The man had three speech speeds: fast, faster, and "shut up before my brain explodes from trying to follow you." He'd always been told that Southern Americans spoke slowly.

That was apparently a myth.

He hadn't had a headache since he'd been human, but for the first time in nine thousand years, he was beginning to feel throbbing pain between his temples.

Much like an irritating toddler, Keller kept going, picking up speed with every word. "Now, you haven't answered me and I gotta know. You know, if we could all think them Daimons into pieces it would sure be a whole lot easier. Can you imagine all of us just looking at them—and boom! They're dead. You got to tell me how you do that. C'mon. I have got to know, you know?"

Alexion flexed his jaw before he answered. "It's a trade secret."

"Yeah, but I'm in the trade. Squires need to know, too. We're not the ones who are immortal so it seems we should know first, you know? C'mon, tell me how you did it."

Alexion stared at him in warning. "I would show you, but it would kill you to use it."

Come to think of it, that wasn't such a bad idea. . . .

He opened his mouth to tell him.

"Don't."

Alexion growled at Acheron's voice in his mind. *"Either do this yourself, or stay out of my head."*

"Fine, you're on your own from now on. I'm outta here. I'm going to go play solitaire or something."

Yeah, right. Acheron playing a game. As if he had a minute to spare.

Keller pulled into the driveway of a small mansion in north-west Tupelo, which was Dangereuse's domain. The Dark-Huntress had been assigned to the area for the last fifty or so years. Her home was designed after a French chateau complete with a court-yard that was set off to the left side of the house.

Keller pressed the control in his dark green Mountaineer for the garage door to open. "Fine, be that way. Don't share, but when I get killed, I'm going to haunt you for not telling me did-dly when you had the chance to save me. You know, that's just not right. Not right at all." He whipped the dark green SUV into the garage, then shut the garage door behind them.

Even though it was a three-car garage, there was no other car inside. He had assumed that Dangereuse would have returned be-fore now. "Where is your mistress tonight?"

"I dunno. She took off about an hour after sundown and I ain't heard nothing since. Wish she'd been here, though, to get those Daimons. I thought I was toast until you popped into the alley. And speaking of popping in, how did you do that, anyway? Where did you come from? I know you had to have some way to get here, you know?"

Alexion got out of the car slowly as he tried to get his bear-ings. He'd only seen her house a time or two in the sfora. But things looked very different in person than they did through the mist's distortion.

"Hey?" Keller snapped his fingers as he came around the SUV. "Did you hear me? How did you get to Tupelo without your own car?"

"I have special talents."

"Are you one of them teleporters?"

Alexion took a deep breath for patience, which was wearing thin in this new body. That was the hardest part about the Krisi— the judgment—and coming to earth. He wasn't used to all the bright colors, sounds, and emotions that were filtered through a real body. At times, he was like an overstimulated toddler—one who had the ability to level a city if he got pissed enough.

Keller was even more inquisitive and annoying than Simi on her worst day. And that was quite an accomplishment. "Don't ask me any more questions, Keller. I'm just going to lie to you and I'd rather not have the stress of trying to remember what lie I handed you."

Scoffing at that, Keller took him into the house, which was done in contemporary retro decor. The small foyer that led from the garage to the kitchen was a dark purple color.

Keller dropped his keys in a basket on the counter. "Why you want to lie to me?"

"I don't want to," he said drolly, "which is why I said not to ask me anything else."

The Squire snorted. "You hungry? You want something to eat or drink?"

Alexion sighed at the man's repetition. Keller tended to ask everything at least twice.

"No." Alexion looked about the dark yellow kitchen. There was a lot to be done and he needed Danger to return home so that he could begin this. Kyros was already following the usual game plan of the Dark-Hunters in the past. About a week ago, he'd started calling for Dark-Hunters to congregate in and around his

Aberdeen, Mississippi, location so that he could convince them to his way of thinking.

It was a familiar cycle. Every few centuries a lot of Dark-Hunters would find love and go free from their service to Artemis. Inevitably, one of the older remaining Dark-Hunters would think he had figured out why and somehow Acheron always got blamed for tricking them. Jealousy and boredom were a lethal mixture that could cause the most bizarre delusions. Convinced of his reasoning, the Dark-Hunter would contact the others, trying to lead them to freedom too, which meant they would all turn on Acheron.

Alexion would be sent in to either save them or judge them Rogue and kill them.

In the beginning, while he was in a human body in this realm, he'd felt like a traitor to his own kind, and yet he understood why it was necessary. Order must be maintained at all costs. The Dark-Hunters had way too much power over humanity for them to start abusing it.

There were few beings in the universe who could battle a Dark-Hunter and live, and humans weren't one of them.

But this time . . . this time something was different. He could feel it deep inside him, and it wasn't just because Kyros was involved. There was something else here.

Something evil.

Keller was still talking, though to be honest, Alexion wasn't listening. His thoughts were on other things. He paused as he walked into the living room and saw an old painting above the mantel. It was a family portrait of an older man, a young woman, and two small children—a boy and an infant girl. Painted outdoors in what appeared to be a courtyard very similar to the one he'd seen beside this house, it was obvious the portrait was from the late eighteenth century.

It must have been Danger's human family.

Dangereuse had become a Dark-Hunter during the French Revolution. Her husband had betrayed her father and her father's noble children to the Committee. She had been trying to smuggle them out of Paris, to Germany, when they had all been captured. He shuddered at the fate that had befallen all of them.

"What are you going to do for clothes tomorrow?" Keller asked as he moved to stand in front of him. "You don't got none, do you?"

Arching a brow, Alexion looked down at the clothes on his body.

"I mean other clothes," Keller snapped. "Jeez. Don't be so literal."

Alexion met the Squire's gaze. Keller was an odd but likable man. For a nuisance. "They'll be delivered."

"By who? You got you a Squire or something? Now that'd be something, wouldn't it? A Squire for a Squire?"

One corner of Alexion's mouth quirked up as he thought of Simi, who constantly brought things to him because she thought he might want or need them. "I definitely have something."

Keller frowned at him. "Yeah, okay. If you'll follow me, I'll show you to a room upstairs where you can sleep. It's real nice. Acheron has used it a few times whenever he was here in the past, but it's been a while since we last saw him. Well, okay, I've never seen him here, personally, but I know from Danger that he's been here before. I think the last time was before I was born. Or maybe not. Sometimes I get Danger's stories mixed up. Do you ever do that with Acheron? I bet he has a lot of stories to tell, being that he's older than dirt. His house must be really cool, huh?"

Rolling his eyes, Alexion rubbed his thumb against his temple while Keller rambled on.

As they left the living room and headed toward the stairs, Alexion caught a faint trace of magnolias in the air. It was mixed with something else . . . something definitely feminine. It must be the Dark-Huntress's scent and his body reacted to it instantly.

He was hot and heavy with sudden need. At his home in Katoteros, there was no one to have sex with. Nothing but long lonely nights that left him edgy and hard. The only benefit to being sent in to judge was that he usually had a day or two to find himself a woman and ease the deep-seated ache.

You have much more pressing concerns than getting laid.

That was one theory anyway, but judging by the throbbing erection he had at the moment, he would definitely argue it.

"How long have you served Dangereuse?" he asked the Squire. It was unusual for a male to be Squired to a female. Usually the humans who made up the Squires' Council forbade a Squire to serve a Dark-Hunter if the Squire might be sexually attractive to the Dark-Hunter. Since Dark-Hunters and Squires were supposed to have a platonic relationship, the Council always tried to give the Dark-Hunter a Squire who was the opposite of what sexually attracted him or her.

It made him wonder if Dangereuse might be attracted to women, as opposed to men.

"About three years. My dad is the current Squire for Maxx Campbell over in Scotland, and after I graduated college, I thought I'd like to join the family business, you know?"

The man seemed to love to end sentences with those two words.

Keller continued on without pause. "I wish I'd grown up over there, but when I was a kid, Dad was stationed in Little Rock, serving this Dark-Hunter named Viktor Russenko who got killed a few years back. Did you know him?"

"Yes."

"Damned shame what they did to him. Some Daimons caught him alone and jumped him. Poor guy. He didn't stand a chance. It was awful, you know, so the Council thought my dad needed a change of scenery. I think Scotland was a good move for him. Maxx seems to be a really laid-back Dark-Hunter. Do you know him too?"

Alexion nodded at the name. He knew much about the Highlander Dark-Hunter who had been recently relocated from London to Glasgow. "How does your father like it over there?"

"It's all right, but he misses home. They talk funny over there and not many can understand his accent. He's real Southern sounding."

Now there was the pot describing the kettle.

Keller continued to ramble on as he led the way into a medium-sized bedroom that had an adjoining bathroom. Alexion cocked his head as he felt something strange go through him. It was cold, almost sinister, and he couldn't place it.

If he didn't know better, he'd think it was . . .

"*Acheron?*" He sent the mental call out through the dimensions.

His boss didn't answer him.

Then as soon as the sensation had come, it was gone.

How strange . . .

3

Danger didn't know what to believe as she headed home from Aberdeen to Tupelo. She'd stayed too long with Kyros and her powers had waned a lot more than she should have allowed. She felt weak and sick, and in truth, she wanted nothing more than to lie down for a while and give herself time to recover.

Most of all, she needed time to think through everything they had told her tonight. To be honest, Stryker had made some rather convincing arguments.

"You have been trained that all Daimons are evil and out to prey on humans. Well, newsflash, we're not the ones who are in

the wrong. Acheron is. He was cast out of our home realm, Kalosis, because even our mother could no longer abide his rampant killing. It's why he uses you to kill us now. He wants revenge on us.

"*Your powers wane when you're together because Acheron took your souls and has devoured them. That's why the first Dark-Hunters were allowed to stay together. In the beginning, their souls weren't dead. He actually did have them. But after Acheron ate the souls of Kyros and Callabrax . . . then they were like the rest of you and could no longer be together without it draining their powers.*"

Still, that hadn't made sense to her.

"*Whether you like it or not, little girl, your souls are dead. That's why you can't be in a room with another soulless being. The energy that sustains you, that keeps you animated, begins to clash with the energy of the other soulless being. Why do you think you don't lose your powers around a Daimon? We have a soul inside us, and it allows us to be together without harm. That's why you can be with Acheron and not feel the drain and why Acheron can go into a cemetery and not be possessed. He, unlike you, has a stolen soul inside him.*"

Danger had still been skeptical. "*That doesn't make sense. What about Kyrian and the other Dark-Hunters who have gotten their souls back?*"

Stryker's answer had been automatic. "*They didn't get their souls back, they got someone else's.*"

That had been the most ludicrous thought of all. "*Yeah, right. We all know that any time a soul enters a body that it's not meant for, the soul withers and dies in a matter of weeks. Kyrian has had his soul back for years now.*"

Stryker had laughed evilly at that. *"That's not true if the soul comes from an unborn baby. That's why Daimons covet pregnant women so much. If you take the soul of the unborn, it can sustain you until the body dies."*

Those words had left her cold. To do such a thing was an abomination.

She still wasn't sure if it was possible.

"How could Acheron get such a soul?" she'd asked.

"Where do you think the medallions come from that he uses to restore a Dark-Hunter to his or her previous human state? Our mother is the keeper of souls." He had looked at Kyros. *"The Greek word for 'Destroyer' is the Atlantean word for 'soul.' Your people made the assumption that Apollymi was a god of destruction, but in truth, she is a guardian of souls. My brother uses a demon to steal those souls from her whenever he needs one. He then returns the souls to a handful of you every so often so that the rest of you will continue to obey him. He knows you have to have hope in order to not turn on him and become disgusted with your existence and duties. It's why you must go to him whenever you want to be free. He does this whole 'I have to petition Artemis' bullshit when in truth what he has to do is break into our mother's temple and steal a new soul. Trust me, there is no Artemis to petition."*

It all sounded so preposterous.

Truth is stranger than fiction . . .

That was true enough, and she couldn't get past the eyes. No one had those mystical, swirling silver eyes except for Acheron . . . and Stryker. They both had black hair, which Stryker had turned blond before her eyes.

"*Why do you think you never see Acheron with blond hair? He's afraid that you'll see it and then you'll know him for the Daimon that he is.*"

Danger turned her car down the street to head home. Everything she had ever believed about the Dark-Hunter world and her place in it was now uncertain. She hated Kyros for that. As a human, she'd allowed one man to lie to her and destroy everything she held dear.

Had she allowed another man to do the same thing?

Just who could she trust? Who wasn't lying to her?

"*Why didn't you have Stryker try to kill me for betraying you?*" she'd asked Kyros after he told her that they knew she had called Acheron to report his questionable activities with the Daimons.

He'd laughed at her. "*I wanted you to tell him. That's why I had my Squire tell your Squire about my going Rogue. Trust me, Danger,*" Kyros had said. "*Acheron won't come here and face us himself. He'll be too afraid to.*"

Stryker had agreed. "*He's right. You called Acheron because you were concerned about the fact that you'd heard Kyros was working with Daimons and not killing them. Now Acheron will send in his pawn to supposedly 'investigate.' The blond man will be someone claiming to be Acheron's Squire, even though everyone knows Acheron doesn't have one. Instead of a Squire, he's Acheron's assassin. You'll know him instantly. He'll show up wearing a white coat.*"

She had rolled her eyes at them. "*White coat? Yeah, right. That's not only tacky, that's stupid.*"

"*No,*" Kyros had said. "*White is the Greek and Atlantean color for mourning.*"

Stryker nodded. *"This so-called Squire is essentially Acheron's angel of death and he will kill all of you who know the truth about Acheron unless we kill both of them first."*

Kill Acheron.

That had made her gut tighten to the point of pain. Acheron had never been anything but friendly to her. He'd been the one who had come to her after she'd sold her soul to Artemis for vengeance against her husband. He had taught her how to fight and how to survive. Acheron had introduced her into this world with a great deal of care.

Or so it seemed.

"How do you know it was Artemis you sold your soul to?" Stryker had asked. *"Acheron could pass off any redheaded bitch as the goddess and who would know? It's not like any of you have met her before or since the moment you sold your soul. Trust me. Artemis is long dead and the woman who comes to the Dark-Hunters is whatever whore Acheron is currently doing at the time."*

But if Stryker was right, Acheron was behind it all. Acheron had designed them so that he would have his own army to fight the Daimons who were out to kill him for declaring war on them.

That just didn't seem like the Acheron she knew.

But then the Acheron she knew was extremely secretive to the point of being paranoid. No one knew anything at all about him. No one.

He wouldn't even give his true age when she asked it.

Then Kyros had disclosed the one bit that couldn't be argued with.

The piece of evidence that was the most damning . . .

"*In all the centuries I have lived I've only known Acheron to have one friend—that New Orleans Squire Nick Gautier who used to serve Kyrian of Thrace before Kyrian became human again. Everyone assumed that because of his friendship with Acheron, Nick was completely untouchable. Then a few months ago, out of the blue, some Daimon brutally kills Nick's mother and Nick vanishes without a trace never to be seen or heard from again. I know it was Acheron who did it, Danger. Nick must have found out about him and Ash killed them both to cover his tracks.*"

It was hard to refute that. Nick's disappearance had gone through their community like a death knell. He'd been well known and well liked for the most part.

And the way his mother had died . . .

It had been brutal and harsh, as if someone were trying to get back at someone.

Danger shook her head, trying to make sense of everything. "What do I believe?" she asked herself.

The problem was, she didn't know. And it wasn't exactly something she could call Acheron up and ask. "*Hi, Ash, this is Danger. I was wondering if you had sucked the soul out of Cherise Gautier and then murdered Nick out of spite? You don't mind answering me, eh?*"

Yeah, even if Acheron was innocent, he might get just a tad upset over that one.

Kyros was already sending out calls to Dark-Hunters he thought were trustworthy. He and Stryker planned on gathering them here in Mississippi to train them to take souls of evil humans, which according to Stryker was what the true Daimon mandate was.

"*We never killed innocent humans until Acheron forced us to it. In the beginning, we preyed solely on the dregs of society. Men and women who destroyed or plagued their own kind and who deserved to die. Now there are many times when we have no choice except to kill whoever we can get to, regardless of who or what they are.*

"*As soon as we show ourselves, one of Acheron's people comes in and tries to shove a knife in our hearts. We have to move fast to feed before one of you kills us. We don't want to hurt anyone, especially not the innocent Dark-Hunters. Why do you think we run most of the time when we see you, instead of fighting you? We know that the Dark-Hunters are innocent in this and none of us want to kill you for being blind and foolish. It's Acheron we're after, not his hapless minions.*

"*All of you have been programmed by him to ask no questions about us. You blindly kill on the assumption that we deserve it, and yet here I stand before you, not a monster trying to kill you. I'm only a person, same as you. I love and I need. All I want is to live in peace and to not be forced to kill the innocent.*

"*And why has Acheron lied to you? He's afraid one day that you'll all figure out the truth about him. The truth about being a Dark-Hunter. If you kill humans and ingest their souls, you can have the same powers that Acheron does. You can have the powers of a god.*"

Surely he was lying. It just couldn't be that easy.

Sighing, Danger pulled into her driveway and did her best to clear her thoughts. There wouldn't be a clear cut answer tonight. Most likely there wouldn't be one tomorrow either.

She saw Keller's green SUV in the garage. Damn. She really

wasn't in the mood for his five thousand questions tonight. Not while she was trying to sort through this.

After getting out of the car, she made her way into her house and dropped her keys on the counter. It was eerily quiet. How unlike Keller not to have a radio blasting or be in the middle of a boisterous phone conversation with a friend.

"Keller?" she called, feeling a little nervous as she headed for the living room.

She paused in the doorway to find her Squire sitting in an uneasy slump on the couch across from an unknown man who was seated in her armchair. All she could see was the back of his blond head. Even so, she could tell he was sitting very stiff and formal. It was a pose of command.

"Hey, Danger," Keller said in a nervous greeting as he saw her in the doorway. "We have a guest. He's, um . . . he's Ash's Squire."

She went cold at his words. Her heart started thumping as adrenaline rushed through her.

The man stood up slowly and turned to face her. Danger's gaze quickly fell to the white coat he wore over his solid black clothes. To the way he stood there in all his arrogance as if he dared her or anyone else to question him.

Everything he wore was black, except the coat . . . and it belonged to Ash's Squire who was blond like a Daimon. . . .

4

Danger's reaction to her "guest" was swift and automatic, and it happened without any premeditation on her part. She pulled out her dagger and threw it straight into the man's heart.

To her shock, he burst apart into a golden dust just like any good Daimon would.

"*Mère de Dieu,*" she breathed.

Kyros had been right. The man was . . .

Entering the room from the doorway on her right!

Her jaw dropped as he sauntered into the room with an arrogant swagger and a less-than-amused smirk. He pinned her with a droll stare as he moved to stand in front of her. Her dagger shot from the floor, where it had fallen after he exploded into dust, and into his hand.

He held it out to her, hilt first. It was painfully obvious that he wasn't the least bit afraid she'd use it on him again. "Could you please refrain from the theatrics? I really hate doing that. It seriously pisses me off and it ruins a perfectly good shirt."

Danger continued to gape as she stared at the hole in his black turtleneck where the dagger had gone in. There was no blood. No wound. Nothing. Not even a red mark. It was as if he hadn't been stabbed at all.

I'm dreaming . . .

"What are you?" she breathed.

He gave her a dry, almost bored stare. "Well, had you listened before you stabbed me, you would have heard the 'I'm Acheron's Squire' part. Apparently that somehow escaped your hearing and you mistook me for a pin cushion."

He was certainly a snotty bastard. Not that she didn't deserve a degree of snottiness seeing how she'd just tried to kill him. Still, he could be a little more understanding, especially since, if Stryker and Kyros were to be believed, he'd been sent here to kill her.

"He has some really sweet talents, Danger," Keller said from the couch. "He made all the Daimons explode without touching them, but he won't tell me how he did it."

Danger took her dagger from Alexion's hand, then, without thought, touched the ragged tear in his black turtleneck. He felt solid underneath. Real. There was cold skin beneath the silk and wool fabric and it was hard and masculine.

Yet human beings didn't shatter like Daimons and no Daimon reappeared after death. . . .

In that moment, she was terrified of him and terror wasn't something Danger St. Richard felt. Ever.

Alexion ground his teeth at the sensation of her soft fingers on his flesh. His body roared to life as he watched her examine him like a scientist with a lab experiment that had gone tragically wrong. She was very short for a Dark-Hunter, which meant Artemis must have taken an unusual liking for the woman. The goddess preferred to create Dark-Hunters who were equal in height to the Daimons they fought.

No more than five two or three, Dangereuse was petite and athletic. He'd seen her many times lately in the sfora as he kept watch on what the Mississippi Dark-Hunters were up to.

There had been something about her that caught his interest. An innocence that still seemed to be inside her. Most Dark-Hunters were jaded by their human betrayals and deaths, and by their duties. But this one . . . She appeared to have avoided the cynicism that eternal life often brought.

Of course, she was young by Dark-Hunter years.

Still, it would be a shame to see her lose that inner glow that continued to allow her to enjoy her immortality. How he wished he could feel it too. But too much time and lack of hope had long robbed him of it.

Her dark, chestnut-colored hair was worn in a long braid, hanging down her back, but pieces of it had escaped to curl becomingly around her pale face. Her features were angelic and delicate. If not for her carriage and self-assuredness, she would have appeared fragile.

And yet there was nothing fragile about her. Dangereuse could more than take care of herself and well he knew it. As one of the newer Dark-Hunters, she was only a couple of hundred years old and had died while trying to save the noble half of her family from the guillotine in France during their revolution. It had been a monumental task she had set for herself, and had she not been betrayed, she would have succeeded.

Not to mention that the woman had the most kissable mouth he'd ever seen. Full and lush, her lips were the kind that a man dreamed of tasting at night. That mouth beckoned him now with temptation and the promise of pure unadulterated heaven.

She also smelled of sweet magnolias and woman.

It had been over two hundred years since he'd last had the pleasure of a woman's body. And it was all he could do not to bend his head and bury his face against her soft, tender neck and inhale the scent of her. Feel the softness of her skin against his hungry lips as he tasted the supple flesh there.

Oh, to have her lithe body pressed up against his, preferably while they were both naked . . .

But then—given her first reaction to his presence—he didn't think she'd react much better to being mauled by him.

Pity.

Danger swallowed in sudden trepidation as she looked at the man before her. He was just as Stryker had foretold . . . right down to the white cashmere coat.

It's all true. All of it.

He was Acheron's personal destroyer who had come to kill them for questioning Acheron's authority. She felt the sudden need to cross herself, but caught herself just in time. The last thing she needed to do was to let him know she feared him.

Her extremely superstitious and Catholic mother had always told her as a child that the devil wore the face of an angel. In this case, it was most certainly true. The man before her was without a doubt one of the choicest examples of his gender. His dark blond hair held golden highlights and brushed the top of his collar. He wore it in a casual style that was swept back from a perfectly masculine face. His well-sculpted cheeks were covered with two days' growth of whiskers that added a savage, fierce look to him.

Like hers, his eyes were the midnight-black of a Dark-Hunter and yet she sensed that he wasn't one of them. For one thing, he didn't drain her Dark-Hunter abilities.

There was an aura of extreme power and lethal danger emanating from him. It rippled and sizzled in the air around them and made the hair on the back of her neck rise.

"What are you doing here?" she asked, forcing herself not to betray anything other than nonchalance. Although the earlier dagger throw had most likely tipped him off that she wasn't exactly ambivalent to his presence.

Yeah, that had been a really smart move. It was all she could do not to roll her eyes at her swiftness in betraying her knowledge of him. She only hoped she didn't live or die to regret it.

His smile was wicked and disturbing. "You invited me."

Was that a play on Ash's being a Daimon? No Daimon could enter someone's home without an invitation.

Or was he just making an idle comment?

Either way, she wasn't ready to welcome him . . . not yet. "I invited *Ash* here. Not you. I don't even know who you are."

He didn't hesitate to answer. "Alexion." His voice was deep and well cultured. There was only the faintest trace of some foreign accent, but she didn't know what nationality it came from.

"Alexion . . . ?" she prompted, wondering what his surname was.

He wasn't forthcoming with it. "Just Alexion."

Keller rose from his chair and joined them. "Ash sent him here for a couple of weeks to check into what you were saying about a Rogue Dark-Hunter."

She arched a brow at Keller. "Is that what Alexion told you?"

He tensed as if he realized he might have done something wrong. "Well, yeah, but then I called Ash myself and he corroborated it."

Good boy that he hadn't taken the man's word. "Did Ash say anything else?"

"Just to trust Alexion."

Yeah, right. Like she'd trust an agitated cobra at her bare feet.

Danger sheathed her dagger before she addressed Alexion again. "Well, it appears I spoke too soon. I was checking into the Rogue thing myself tonight and everything's fine so you can feel free to return to Ash now."

Alexion's dark eyes narrowed on her. "Why are you lying to me?"

"I'm not lying."

He dipped his head so that he could speak in a low tone just for her hearing. His nearness was disturbing and intense. It actually raised chills over her body as his breath fell against her skin. "For the record, Dangereuse, I can smell a lie from nine miles off."

She looked up to see the deep curiosity in those . . . She frowned.

No longer black, his eyes had turned to a peculiar hazel green that practically glowed.

Just what the hell was he?

Alexion pinned her with a fierce stare he no doubt hoped would intimidate her. It wasn't working. Danger refused to be intimidated by anyone or anything. She lived her immortality just as she had lived her human life and it would take more than this . . . person to make her shiver in fear. The worst thing he could do was kill her, and since she was already dead . . .

Well, there were worse things, she supposed.

When he spoke again, his voice was scarcely more than a primal growl. "My only real question is, why would you protect your Rogue?"

She moved away without answering. "Keller? Can I have a word with you in private?"

Alexion gave a short laugh at that. "I will leave the two of you alone so that you can tell him just how unhappy you are that he let me in." He headed for the hallway that led to the guest rooms.

Danger ground her teeth. *Don't tell me Keller already set him up in my house!*

He should know better than that. How could he do such a thing without consulting her? *That's it, he's toast, and I mean it this time.*

She waited until she was sure Alexion had left them alone and lowered her voice so that he couldn't overhear them. "What the hell happened tonight? You look like someone beat you."

"They did. I ran into a group of Daimons, and when I told them to back off, they said they were untouchable now. They said that they were working with the Dark-Hunters and that if they wanted to eat a Squire, that was fine."

Anger whipped through her that they would dare to beat her Squire. "They attacked you?"

He gave her a snide look. "No, I beat my own self up. What do you think?"

She ignored his sarcasm as she realized why the plasma TV hadn't been blaring when she came in. It was shattered.

"What happened to the TV?"

Keller looked at it and shrugged. "I don't know. Alexion doesn't say much, so I was flipping channels after we got back so that there'd be some noise in the house. Everything was fine until I paused on QVC to see this cool camcorder they were advertising, and the next thing I knew, it blew up. I'm not sure if it was the TV or if Alexion has a thing against QVC."

Thank the Lord and his saints that her Squire hadn't blown up as well.

"And where did Alexion just head off to?" she asked.

"I put him in the guest suite that you said Ash uses whenever he visits."

She clenched her fist to keep from choking him. "I see."

He gave her a worried frown. "I didn't do anything wrong, did I? I thought I was doing what you'd want me to do. You weren't here so I could ask you. Are you mad at me?"

Yes, but she didn't want to get into it with him. If he stayed ignorant of all this, maybe Alexion would spare him.

Either way, she refused to put Keller in any danger. Unlike her, he was mortal with a family who loved him dearly.

"You're fine, sweetie. Why don't you head on home before it gets any later?"

Luckily her Squire didn't argue and he was too dense to recognize the slight tremor of fear for him in her voice. In case Alexion intended to fight, she wanted Keller out of here and tucked safely away at home.

"Okay, Danger. I'll see you tomorrow night."

"Ahh . . ." Danger hedged at that. "Why don't you take a few days off? Go see your sister in Montana."

His frown deepened. "Why?"

She offered him a smile she didn't feel. "I have Acheron's Squire here. I'm sure he can—"

"I don't know," he said, wrinkling his nose. "He seems all right, but I think I'll hang close to home, just in case. You never know what can happen."

"Keller . . ."

"Don't mess with me, Danger. My number one mandate is to protect you. I may be human, but I'm your Squire and that includes all the inherent risks that come with the position. Okay? I was raised in this world and I know all the freaky shit it sometimes entails. I'm not going to leave you when we don't know what's going on other than someone is working with the Daimons. I've heard too much weirdness lately to just hightail it for no real reason."

She couldn't argue with any part of that. His loyalty warmed her greatly, and that was why when all this was over, she would request a new Squire to replace him. The last thing she wanted was to become emotionally attached to anyone, especially someone who would die of old age and wreck her.

She'd lost way too many people she cared about in her life to lose any more. The Squire's Council knew it, and since the day she'd joined the Dark-Hunter ranks, she'd never had a Squire for more than five years.

And never one with a child. There were some wounds that just didn't need to be probed.

"All right," she said quietly to him. "Go home and I'll keep in touch."

Keller nodded, then gathered up his lightweight jacket and left.

Grateful he'd listened for once, Danger took a deep breath as she headed for Alexion's room. She really didn't want him here, but what else could she do?

Keep your friends close and your enemies closer.

So long as he was in her house, she could monitor his activity and see what he was doing. Not to mention, she still wasn't thoroughly convinced by Kyros and his agenda. She'd heard a lot of weird things lately, including the rumor that some of the local Dark-Hunters were drinking human blood. For all she knew, Kyros was one of them and was currently setting her up for reasons only he knew.

Until she had more information about all of this, she would play it cooly and see for herself what was going on. But even as she thought that, a chill went over her. Alexion had some incredible powers that she wasn't sure she could fight.

How could a woman kill a man who didn't bleed?

5

At the end of the hallway on her upper floor, Danger pushed open the door to the guest room to find Alexion studying one of the Fabergé eggs that she collected. She'd started the collection about forty years ago because they reminded her of the Malowanki eggs her father always brought back for her from his annual trips to Prussia to visit his grandmother. Until the year she died, Babcia would always make sure that she'd created the Malowanki eggs for all of them to remind them of their Prussian heritage and the beauty of Easter.

None of those precious, colored eggs that Danger had guarded so carefully as a human had survived. Calling them the frivolous waste of the aristocracy, her husband had taken great pleasure in destroying them after she'd died.

How she hated that man. But most of all, she hated herself for putting her trust in someone and allowing him to deceive her so completely.

She would never be so stupid again.

Narrowing her eyes on Alexion, she opened the door wider to watch him. His modern clothes looked rather out of place in a room she had fashioned into an exact copy of the one she'd grown up in. The hand-carved Baroque bed had been imported from Paris and was decked out in bloodred and gold pillows and comforter. Gold draperies fell from the padded half-tester. She'd spent a lot of time choosing the antiques for this room.

It was the last of her world and in many ways a time capsule. In here she sometimes thought that she could glimpse sight of her father . . . hear the faint laughter of her siblings.

Mon Dieu, how she missed them all.

Grief swelled inside her, but she held it back. There was no need in crying. She'd shed enough tears over the centuries to fill the Atlantic.

The past was the past and this was the present. Tears would not bring her family back and they would not alter her life in any way. All she could do was move onward and upward, and make sure that no one ever deceived her again.

For now, Alexion was the present and he was her enemy.

He stood before the small Neoclassical-style dressing table, holding the egg carefully in his large hand as if he understood how much she loved her collectibles. In spite of herself, she was struck by the gentleness of his touch as he closed it and returned it to its stand.

He was incredibly handsome standing there and her body reacted to him with an intensity that surprised her. It wasn't like her to be attracted to someone she had just met. Hot Hollywood actors in movies and magazines notwithstanding, she normally had to be around a guy a long time before she felt such a strong, potent desire for his body. *If* she ever felt desire for him. Most of the time, she could take or leave any man.

But she actually wanted to reach out and touch him. And *that* never happened.

Alexion felt her presence like a sizzling caress. It was as if she made contact with his soul every time she drew near him. Something that was completely impossible since he hadn't owned a soul in more than nine thousand years.

He didn't know what it was about her, but his body reacted wildly to her presence. Turning, he found her in the doorway, watching him with a wary, almost angry expression.

She was afraid of him and pissed at herself for that fear, he could feel it deep inside himself. But she was trying hard to disguise it.

He could respect her for that.

In the end, she was wise to fear him. He could kill her as easily as he blinked. Yet he didn't want to hurt her.

For some strange reason, he didn't even want her to fear him, and that was something he'd never experienced before. Usually when he was in human form, he used that fear to his advantage to intimidate the Dark-Hunters and bring them back in line. He had the powers of a full god within him. The ability to take any life he chose . . .

He could hear and see things that were far beyond the comprehension of man, Apollite, or Dark-Hunter.

And yet as he stood there, only one thing echoed in his head—the sound of her laughter. He'd heard her laughing earlier this very evening as she fought with the Daimons. It was a lush, musical sound that rolled out from her. Hearty.

He wanted to hear it again.

"I mean you no harm, Dangereuse."

She stiffened defiantly. "The name's Danger," she corrected. "I haven't gone by Dangereuse in a long time."

He inclined his head to her. He knew from his research into her background that she'd been named for the grandmother of Eleanor of Aquitaine whom her mother had adored. A great duchess who'd lived life solely on her own terms and who had flouted societal rules. It was a name that suited the petite woman in front of him. "Forgive me."

His apology did nothing to soothe her. "And just so you know, I'm not afraid of you."

He smiled at her brave words. She was a tough, no-nonsense woman and he wondered if she had been like that as a human. But he somehow doubted it. The world she had been born into wouldn't have tolerated such a whirlwind personality from the fairer sex.

No doubt they would have quashed her rebelliousness, not embraced it.

She took a step into the room. Her dark eyes were piercing as they searched him for some weakness.

Good luck, ma petite. *I haven't any.*

"So, what's your story?" she asked. "You say you're Ash's Squire. Are you a Blue Blood, Blood Rites, or what?"

Alexion bit back a smile at her question. Blue Bloods were Squires who came from long generations of Squires. Blood Rites were the Squires who were charged with assuring that the rules of their world were followed. They protected the Dark-Hunters and were a police force for other Squires. Of course, he had been serving Acheron since before the Squires' Council had existed. He wasn't a true Squire. He was Acheron's Alexion, an Atlantean term that had no real translation into English.

Basically, he would do whatever was necessary to protect Acheron and Simi. And he truly meant "whatever."

He had no conscience. No morals. In his world, the only right was Acheron's will. It governed everything about him. Yes, he could and did argue with Acheron at times, but at the end of it all, he was Acheron's protector. He would always do what was in Acheron's best interest no matter the personal or physical cost to himself.

Yet he couldn't tell her the truth of his status. Only he, Simi, Artemis, and Acheron would ever know of his real relationship to the boss.

"I'm a barnacle chip," he answered in Squire slang, meaning that Acheron had recruited him to be his Squire. In a way, it was almost true.

"How long have you served him?"

He gave a short laugh at that. "It seems like forever most days."

Her dark eyes flashed suspicion and intelligence at him. She was far too bright for her own good. And far too sexy for his.

She still wasn't through interrogating him as she moved closer to him . . . so close he could now smell her. Her sweet scent permeated his head and created images of her naked and pliant in his bed.

"How is it that you did that little trick with the dagger where you reappeared after I stabbed you?"

One side of his mouth quirked up at her question and he leaned even closer so that he could smell the fragrance of her hair and skin. It went through him like a warm whiskey, shocking and invigorating.

It made his blood hot, his cock hard.

"Ask me what's really on your mind, Danger," he said, his voice deepened by his lust. "I don't like to play games. We both know that I'm not human so let's not do the polite song and dance while you tiptoe around me trying to figure me out."

Danger seemed to appreciate his frankness even as she shivered at his nearness. She looked up at him from under her lashes. That look made him feel things that he hadn't felt in a long time. He actually cared that she was confused and uncertain. He wanted to soothe her and that was beyond shocking to him.

"Are you here to spy for Acheron?"

He laughed at the very thought. "No. Trust me, he doesn't need anyone to spy for him. If he wants to know something, he does."

"How so?"

It took all of his willpower not to reach out and touch her cheek to see if it was as soft as it appeared. Her skin was flawless and tempting. No doubt it would be even softer against his tongue . . .

"I meant what I said, Danger. Acheron is able to find things out on his own. Spying is the last thing he needs me for."

Danger was getting extremely irritated by her attraction to this man and his own inability to answer her questions. She wasn't sure if she should kiss him or kick him.

The heat of his look was searing. Unnerving. It was so intense that she could almost feel his hands on her.

She had the most inexplicable desire to nuzzle him. Breathless, she decided to use his own hunger against him. She stood up on her tiptoes and moved so close to him that their cheeks were almost touching. She watched as he closed his eyes and drew in a sharp breath.

When he didn't pull back, she whispered in his ear. "Why are you really here?"

His voice was deep and thick when he answered. "To protect you."

Danger couldn't have been more surprised had he come right out and admitted to being Acheron's destroyer. She moved away from him to put more distance between them. It was hard to think straight while a man was staring at her as if he were picturing her naked. "Protect me from what?"

Still those eerie green eyes pierced her with their intense hunger. "Those who would see you dead. You are in a precarious place, Danger. The one who has gone Rogue will kill you instantly if he learns you have betrayed him."

Funny, Kyros had been remarkably understanding about that.

"He can't kill me and you know it. No Dark-Hunter can harm another."

He arched a brow at her. "You really believe that? There's

nothing that says a Dark-Hunter couldn't handcuff another to a gate, car, or anything else, and leave them outside for the sunrise. You can't hurt each other, true. But there are many ways to expose your enemy to the day without endangering yourself."

Oh, now there was one hell of a loophole she'd never thought about. But obviously he had.

"And how did you acquire this information? How many Dark-Hunters have you exposed to daylight after they trusted you?"

He laughed bitterly. "If I wanted you or anyone else dead, Danger, I hardly have to wait for the sun."

"Then what do you want to protect me from?"

He looked away from her. "I can't tell you that."

"Try me."

"No," he said from between gritted teeth. "Even if I did, you wouldn't believe me."

They were at an impasse. She wasn't about to trust him until he gave her a reason to—and probably not even then—and the last thing she wanted was a guy in her house she couldn't trust. "In that case, you'll understand if I ask you to stay in a hotel while you're here spying for Acheron?"

His expression amused, he gave a short, sinister laugh. "You met with Kyros tonight and he tried to sway you to his rebellious cause. Did you believe him?"

How did he know that? That wasn't exactly something she had broadcast. Sheez. He seemed every bit as omniscient as Acheron and it was starting to piss her off. "I don't know what you're talking about."

He closed the distance between them. His presence was

mammoth in the room, overpowering and yet strangely comforting. It was as if something inside him was putting off soothing vibes. Not to mention he had pheromones that should be bottled and sold. He was extremely compelling in a most sexual way. Acheron was the only other person she knew who had that strange "do me" factor that enticed everyone who came near him to strip his clothes off and throw him down for a wicked night of play.

What is wrong with me?

She'd never felt lust like this.

"You know," Alexion said in a deep tone that actually made her shiver, "for an actress you certainly can't lie worth a damn."

She stiffened at his words. "I beg your pardon?"

"You heard me. So what lie did Kyros tell you? I hope he was at least more creative than the 'old Acheron is a Daimon' standby."

She didn't know what surprised her more. The fact that he knew what they'd said about Acheron or the fact that he spoke of Kyros as if he knew the man personally. "How do you know about Kyros?"

"Believe me, I know everything about him."

Danger was even more confused now. Was Alexion telling her the truth? Or was he using the truth about Acheron being a Daimon to distract her? What better way to throw her off than to ridicule what could very well be fact.

Who did she believe? Kyros who seemed delusional or the man before her who seemed homicidal.

She crossed her arms over her chest and watched him closely. "So tell me, *is* Acheron a Daimon?"

Those eerie green hazel eyes narrowed on her. "What do you think?"

"I don't know." And that was the honest truth. "It makes sense. He is from Atlantis and we all know that the Daimons are from there originally."

Alexion scoffed at her. "Acheron was born in Greece and grew up in Atlantis. That hardly makes him a Daimon or an Apollite."

Still, there was more evidence to be considered. "He never eats food."

"Are you sure?" he taunted. "Just because he doesn't eat in front of you, doesn't mean he doesn't eat at all."

Okay, so he made her own point for her. It made her feel somewhat better to know that Kyros might be an idiot.

But there was still one piece in all this that didn't make sense. One piece Alexion had yet to explain. "Then what about you? If Kyros is so wrong, how did he know that you were going to come in here wearing your white coat and trying to pass judgment on all of us, huh?"

Alexion froze at her question. It went through him like shards of glass. "Pardon?"

A smug look came over her face. "You have no answer for that one, do you?"

No, he didn't. It was impossible that Kyros had learned of him. "How could he know about me? No one knows I exist."

"Then he's right," she said accusingly. "You are lying to me about your purpose. You're here to kill us all. You are Acheron's assassin."

Alexion couldn't breathe as her words went through him.

How could anyone know that? It wasn't possible. Acheron had taken great care to make sure no one knew he existed. "No I'm not. I'm here to save as many of you as I can."

"And I'm supposed to believe you, why?"

"Because I'm telling you the truth."

Doubt stared out from the dark depths of her eyes. "Then prove it."

That was easier said than done. "Prove it how? The only way to prove to you that I'm not out to kill you is to not kill you. Last I checked you were the one throwing daggers, not me."

Danger gave him a hostile glare. "What was I supposed to think? I come into my house to see my normally ebullient Squire cowed on my couch, looking beat up, and my TV blown to kingdom come. Then this blond man, and I use the term 'man' loosely, who I was told would come to kill me, stands up wearing the exact white coat that I was told he'd have on. What would you have done?"

"I would have said, hello, can I help you?"

She rolled her eyes at him. "Sure, you would."

Actually, he would have, but then he had one distinct advantage over her. He couldn't die. At least not from something born of this earth.

"Look, Danger, I know you have absolutely no reason to trust me. Before tonight you'd never even heard of me. But you know Acheron. Have you ever seen him hurt a Dark-Hunter? Think about it. If Ash really were a Daimon, why would he be helping and protecting the Dark-Hunters?"

"Because he uses us to fight his own kind so that his mother doesn't kill him."

Alexion went cold at that. Where the hell had these lies come from?

Acheron would lose his mind if he heard those words. More to the point, there would be no salvation for any Dark-Hunter here. Acheron would destroy them all without blinking. When it came to the existence of his mother, Acheron didn't take chances.

And he showed no mercy.

"What do you know of his supposed mother?" he asked, and hoped that Acheron didn't choose this particular moment to spy on him.

"That she cast him out of the Daimon realm and now he uses us to get back at her and his people."

He snorted in derision. "Now that has to be the most ridiculous thing I've ever heard, and believe me, I've heard a lot of bullshit in my existence. Trust me, it's a complete lie."

She duplicated his snort. "The problem is, I don't trust *you*. *At all*."

"But do you trust Kyros?"

He saw the answer in her dark eyes. No, she didn't. But it spoke a lot for her that she hadn't turned on her Dark-Hunter brother. She was still protecting Kyros. He could admire her for that.

"Look, Danger. Open your heart and listen with your feelings. What does your gut tell you to do?"

"Run for the hills with my Squire and let you guys duke it out for yourselves."

He laughed darkly at that.

Danger only wished she could laugh about it too, but it wasn't funny in the least to her. "However, I can't do that, can I?

So I don't know who to believe and I'm woman enough to admit it. There are great gaping holes in both your stories. So the question I have to answer is, who is leaving out the 'I serve evil' part."

Alexion was amused. "Then let me put it to you this way. There is seldom black and white in our world. Sometimes the things we perceive as good have moments of profound evil, but profound evil will always tell you that it's always good. It never admits that it could, in any way, be evil."

Danger cocked her head. He sounded just like Father Anthony, her priest when she was a young woman in Paris. "So if I were to ask you if you are on the good side?"

"I am. But I won't hesitate to do whatever is necessary to protect the humans and Acheron. I'm here to save those of you who can be saved."

"And the rest?"

He looked away from her.

"You will kill us." It was a statement of fact.

His gaze met hers and this time his eyes were glowing a deep, vibrant green. They were unearthly, chilling, and in no way appeared human. "No. You damn yourselves by your own stupidity. I admit that I could not care less who lives or dies—that really isn't my concern. I'm here to do what must be done to protect the order of things."

"The order of what things?"

"Our existence. Our universe. Call it whatever you want, but in the end, those who turn on Acheron and who prey on humanity will die and yes, it will be by my hand."

This was unbelievable. He was admitting that he was, indeed, the one who would kill them all. "So you are our judge?"

His face was grim, sincere. "Judge, jury, and executioner."

Those words set fire to her temper as she moved to stand toe to toe with him. "What makes you so wise that you can blithely decide who lives and who dies? How do you know what's right?"

He scoffed. "All of you know what's right. You don't need me for that. On the night you became Dark-Hunters you pledged your eternal oath to serve Artemis and to combat the Daimons for her. Every one of you was given wealth, privilege, and servants. All you have to do in return for it is to protect the humans and stay alive. So long as you keep your mandate, you're left alone to find whatever happiness you can. You all know the rules. I'm just here to enforce them whenever one of your kind thinks that he or she is immune to them."

That did it. She didn't want anyone or anything this callous in her home. He truly didn't care who he killed. The Dark-Hunters were nothing to him. But her brethren were everything to her.

He would kill or die to protect Acheron and she would kill or die to protect her Dark-Hunter family.

It was that simple and that complicated.

"Then you can get out of my house."

He shook his head. "That's not how this works. When Acheron sends me in, he places me with a Dark-Hunter he would like to see saved. Unfortunately, it doesn't always work out that way, but in theory, if you cooperate, you should survive this latest uprising. I use you as a friendly, trustworthy face to introduce me to the traitors so that I can decide who among them is worth saving."

"And if I refuse?"

"You die." There was no more emotion in his tone than there was in his face. He really didn't care if he killed her or not.

Danger glared at him as her heart pounded in rage. "Then I hope you come with an army because it's going to take more than you to kill me."

She lunged at him only to run into what appeared to be an invisible wall that surrounded him. She struck out at it, but it didn't budge.

"I can't die, Danger," he said ominously as he watched her from behind his force field. "But you can, and believe me when I say that dying as a Dark-Hunter seriously sucks."

She slammed her hand against the invisible wall, curling her lip at him. "You're asking me to betray my brethren for personal salvation? Forget it. Fuck you and Acheron."

"No," he said in a sincere tone as he shook his head. "I'm asking you to save them. If we can convince them to trust you and believe me, and accept that Kyros is lying, then they can go home and all of this will be nothing more than a bad dream."

"And if we don't?"

"They're history."

Disgusted with him, she pulled back. "You know, you could show a little more compassion when you say that. Don't we mean anything to you? To Acheron?"

She felt a slight shift in the air, as if the wall were gone now. Alexion stared at her with those eerie green eyes.

"Acheron most definitely cares. If he didn't, I wouldn't be here now, and all of you would be dead already. He doesn't need *me* to kill them. He can do it without breaking a sweat. Believe me, I gain no personal pleasure in the killing either. Likewise, I'm ambivalent as to who survives and who doesn't. This isn't a game to me. Nor is it the end of the world."

She swallowed against the painful lump in her throat that had appeared at the thought of her friends dying. "They are all worth saving. *All* of them. You have no idea how hard it is to be one of us. We are created and then abandoned. Some of us go decades, even longer, without a single word from Acheron. None of us ever see Artemis again—"

He snorted evilly, interrupting her. "Count your blessings there."

She paused at his rancor as Stryker's words about Artemis's death came back to her. "Artemis is still alive?"

"Oh, yeah. Believe me, she's alive and well and in Acheron's face daily."

For some reason, that made her feel better—provided Alexion wasn't lying. "Then she does care about us."

"No," he said bitterly. "She cares about Acheron. The rest of you are here so that she can control him. It's why she continues to create new Dark-Hunters to replace those who go free. The day Acheron stops caring about the lot of you is the day Artemis will turn her back on you and most likely you'll all drop. So don't ever tell me that Acheron doesn't give a damn about you, when I see the toll the lot of you take on him every day."

His words hung in her mind. Could it be true?

Knowing Ash, it seemed a lot more plausible than him being a Daimon.

Well, sort of. But then again the Daimon theory was remarkably sound too.

If only she knew who to trust.

Alexion moved to stand just before her, so close that she could feel his breath falling against her cheek. "You have a decision to make, Danger. Are you going to help me save a few Dark-Hunters or do I kill them all now and go home?"

6

Stryker sat in the dark library of his home in Kalosis—the Atlantean hell realm—with his second-in-command standing before his immaculate ebony desk, watching him. The surface of the desk was so shiny that it reflected the candlelight with an eerie glow that danced around them.

Sadness settled heavily in his heart as he remembered a time when it would have been his son, Urian, who was plotting with him this night.

Urian. The mere thought of his once beloved son was enough

to cripple him. Urian's loss still ate away inside him like a festering disease that nothing could cure.

And it was all because of Acheron that he had killed his beloved son. His heir. His heart. There was nothing left inside him now except hatred and a need for vengeance so profound that it made a mockery of the betrayals that caused humans to become Dark-Hunters.

He wanted Urian back. Nothing could appease the emptiness that his son's death had left. Nothing could quell the vivid memory of the hurt and betrayed look in Urian's eyes the instant Stryker had cut his throat.

Stryker ground his teeth as grief tore through him anew. How he wished he could take back that moment.

But it was done and he couldn't live until he had made sure that Acheron knew this pain firsthand. That Acheron suffered out his eternity in bitter anguish. Something that was made more difficult by his need to make it all happen beneath Apollymi's radar.

When you served a goddess, it was difficult to find time for personal revenge that she'd probably disapprove of. But Stryker would be unstoppable until everyone Acheron held dear lay permanently dead in their graves. Already he had caused the death of Nick Gautier and his mother, Cherise.

There were only three others who meant anything to the Atlantean prince. The Charonte demon, Simi, who would be virtually impossible to kill—but then, where there was a will, there was always a way. The human child, Marissa Hunter, and Alexion.

He'd almost succeeded in capturing Marissa a few months back in New Orleans. Unfortunately, his attempt had failed, and for the time being Acheron's guard was up where the child was concerned. Yet there would come a time when his guard would relax.

Then the child would be vulnerable again.

But when it came to Alexion . . .

Acheron thought his right hand could take care of himself. That pomposity was what would be both their undoing.

"Acheron a Daimon." Trates laughed as he picked up the sfora that Stryker used so that he could watch those in the human realm.

The blond man before him, like all Daimons, was well over six feet tall, incredibly good-looking, and in the height of his youth. It was the curse of their ancient Apollite race that no one could live past their twenty-seventh birthday.

At the hour that marked their birth, they began to slowly, painfully disintegrate into dust. The only way to avoid that fate was to begin feeding on human souls. Whenever an Apollite decided to feed on souls rather than to die, he was termed a Daimon and cast out of the Apollite mainstream. Most Apollites feared Daimons as much as humans did, though he'd never understood why.

Very few Daimons ever preyed on their own.

It was after the conversion to Daimon status that the Dark-Hunters were sent in by Acheron to kill them and free the stolen souls before they died.

Pitiful wretch, he sided with the humans and not the Daimons. If Acheron were smart, he would have been on their side. But for some reason Stryker had never understood, Acheron sided with a race that would try to destroy him if they ever learned who and what he was.

What an idiot.

Trates rolled the sfora in a small circle over the polished desk. "I have to say, *akri,* that was a good one. The Dark-Hunters are truly too stupid to live."

Stryker leaned back in his black leather chair as the corners of his lips lifted in memory of his lies. "I wish I could take credit for that one, but alas it was a Dark-Hunter who inspired that rumor somewhere around five or six hundred years ago."

"Yes, but you were the one who invented the whole war between him and his supposed mother. I think Apollymi would be highly offended to learn that you dared to say she had birthed one of Artemis's servants."

The smile froze on Stryker's face. Little did Trates know, that was exactly what he suspected. Although Apollymi refused to admit it, he had begun thinking she was Acheron's mother the night Urian had died. Why else would Apollymi forbid him from killing Artemis's servant?

Artemis held Acheron's soul. Acheron was sworn to her service and spent all of his time fighting the very beings who served Apollymi. Given the Destroyer's profound hatred of Artemis, it would seem only natural that they would be sent out to kill Artemis's favorite boy toy.

And yet the only time one of Stryker's Daimons had hurt Acheron, Apollymi had viciously gone after all of those responsible. Even now his people lived in fear of reawakening her wrath. Not that he blamed them. Apollymi, much like him, lived for brutality.

Of course, he had no real proof of his suspicion where Acheron was concerned. Not yet. But if he was right and Acheron was Apollymi's lost son, then Stryker would have the power to finally destroy the ancient Atlantean goddess. With her gone, he would rule Kalosis and all the Daimons who made this realm their home.

He would have unrivaled power. There would be no one to stop him from enslaving the humans.

The world of man would be his . . .

He could already taste the sweetness of victory.

"Apollymi isn't to learn of this," Stryker said sternly to Trates. "I will tell her about the Dark-Hunter insurrection after they are all dead."

Trates frowned. "Why wouldn't you tell her now?"

He feigned nonchalance. "She has her mind on other matters. I think this should be a surprise for her, don't you?"

His minion paled at the thought. "The goddess doesn't like surprises. She was rather upset with us over the 'surprise' destruction in New Orleans."

That was true enough. Stryker had sent in his Spathi Daimons and they had wrought terror for a few weeks, only to have Acheron save the pitiful humans in the end. Damn him. He'd cost Stryker many a good Daimon that night, including Desiderius. But it wasn't the destruction that had made Apollymi angry, it'd been Desiderius's attack on Acheron she reacted to.

But Trates didn't know that. Only Stryker knew the real source of Apollymi's anger.

"Yes, but she's calmed down and is now quite content again."

Trates looked less than convinced as he returned the sfora to its gilded stand. "So what are your orders?"

"For now, we continue to play nice with the Dark-Hunters. Let them see our good side."

"We have good sides?"

Stryker laughed. "No, but as you said, the Dark-Hunters are too stupid to see otherwise. They will believe our lies for now and allow some of our newer members to hone their skills."

Trates nodded, then took a step back as if to leave.

"There is a new priority though."

Trates paused to look back at him. "And that is?"

"Kill the Alexion."

Trates looked startled by the order, but he quickly recovered himself. "How?"

A slow smile spread across Stryker's face. "There are two ways. We can either make him kill himself or we let the Charontes do it."

Neither method would be easy. And he could tell by Trates's expression that his second-in-command was weighing both courses of action with equal trepidation.

"How do we get the Charontes to kill him?" Trates asked.

"That's the tricky part, isn't it?"

Stryker considered his options. Unless he could get Apollymi to cooperate with him by allowing one or two of her pets to leave the Atlantean hell realm that made up their home, there was no way to get them to the Alexion. That would be damn near impossible. The Destroyer seldom allowed her Charontes out of Kalosis.

Then again, there were some of the Charontes who held no love whatsoever for the goddess who controlled them. Some who might be willing to do his bidding for a chance to be free. . . .

Trates didn't even acknowledge that option. "How can you make someone kill himself?"

Stryker gave a short laugh at that. "Normally, you would

have to destroy their will to live. Or give them a damn good reason to die."

Trates looked even more confused. "What could make an Alexion want to die?"

"*Kyriay ypochrosi,*" Stryker said, using the Atlantean term for "noble obligation." "He is as soulless as the Dark-Hunters he protects. If you inject a strong soul into a Dark-Hunter, it will take him over, but if you inject a weak one . . ."

"He will hear it begging for mercy."

Stryker nodded. That was the hardest part about turning Daimon and it was one of the reasons why they avoided weak souls. The constant whining for compassion was enough to drive even the strongest of them to madness.

But his people had a slight cushion; they still possessed their own souls that could silence the whine. Alexion and the Dark-Hunters didn't. They had nothing inside to overcome and quell the invading soul.

Nothing to absorb the new life force.

The pathetic cries would incapacitate the Alexion, who would have no choice except to either kill himself to free the soul or condemn that soul to die.

If nothing else, it would be an interesting experiment.

Would the Alexion stand by and let the soul die or would he end his own life to save an innocent?

7

Danger stood in the hallway of her house, watching Alexion who was in her kitchen. She'd excused herself to go to the bathroom—not that she had to go so much as she just needed a break from the intensity of his presence. And to be alone while she sorted through all the information he'd dumped on her.

She didn't know what to believe and she hated that feeling of insecurity. All her life, she'd prided herself on being able to strip back the bull to see the truth.

But when it came to this . . .

She didn't know who or what was right. From what she'd

seen of Alexion, she didn't doubt that he could kill her if he wanted to; that he could kill all of them. So far, he'd refrained from doing either, which added some credibility to his story that he was there to protect them.

Maybe.

Damn, I really hate indecision.

Should I run to warn the others or stay and keep an eye on him?

There was no easy answer.

Rubbing her hand across her face, she paused as Alexion picked up the large Hershey chocolate bar from her counter and sniffed it. He ran his hand over the edge of the brown wrapper as if he'd never seen one before. Then he traced the edges of the chocolate through the wrapper as if he enjoyed the tactile sensation of it.

Danger cocked her head, puzzled by his actions. She loved chocolate as much as the next person, but she'd never before molested a bar of it. Something about his caress reminded her of a lover's touch and it made him seem strangely vulnerable.

Yeah . . . she was losing it.

"Should I leave the two of you alone?"

He looked up as if startled by her question, but made no comment about her sarcasm. "What does chocolate taste like?"

Her frown deepened at his unexpected question. "Open it and see for yourself."

He sighed heavily before he set it aside. "It wouldn't do me any good."

"Why not?"

"I can't taste anything."

That surprised her. She couldn't imagine going without her taste buds. God knows, she certainly got a great deal of pleasure from eating Hershey's and other things that would most likely harden every artery in her body if she were still human. "Absolutely nothing?"

He shook his head as he looked back at the Hershey's bar. "I know Simi likes to eat chocolate. She talks about it all the time, but she's never brought any home for me to see. She only eats barbecue and popcorn around me, which she says is very tasty and really salty."

"Simi?"

If she didn't know better, she'd swear he became instantly uncomfortable, as if he'd slipped up by mentioning the name. Without answering her, he picked up her coffee can and smelled it too. She could tell that was about as productive to him as eating the chocolate he couldn't taste.

Which made her wonder about something really important. "So if you can't taste food, what do you live on? Blood? Souls?"

He gave her a bored look as he pushed the can back into place. "I told you, I'm not a Daimon."

"Yeah, but when I stabbed you, you poofed like a Daimon. You're blond and you don't eat food—"

"I'm not a Daimon," he repeated.

"Uh-huh, ever heard the saying that if it walks like a duck and quacks like a duck—"

"It's not a Daimon."

Well, he was quick with that one. She had to give him credit there. "Then what do you eat?"

He gave her an intense, hot once-over. "Woman al dente."

Danger's jaw dropped at his unexpected vulgarity. She made a disgusted face at him. "That was uncalled for."

"Then stop asking me questions."

Charm was most definitely not his forte. But then he didn't really need it. There was such a deep sadness in his eyes that it actually made her ache for him in spite of her common sense, which said she should stake him again . . . just for good measure.

She moved closer to him so that she could study the handsome lines of his face.

His features were perfect. Manly. The dark blond brows were arched perfectly over those eerie eyes of his. His cheekbones were high and dusted with a hint of stubble. It was the kind of stubble that made a woman want to stand up on her tiptoes and nibble it until her lips were raw from it.

It was then that she realized something. . . .

Alexion, unlike her and the rest of the Dark-Hunters, didn't have fangs.

How could that be?

But at least it marked the Daimon question firmly off the list. No full-blooded Daimon could live without feeding.

"What are you?" she asked. "Really?"

He looked at her as if the question bored him "We've already had this discussion."

Yeah, but they'd never finished it. "You have asked me to trust you. Fine. I'm willing to give it a go. But if I do, then I deserve the same amount of respect in return." She gave him a meaningful stare. "Trust me with the truth of you."

She saw the debate flashing across his green eyes before he finally responded. "Let us just say that I am 'other.' I'm truly unique in this world. I'm not a human. I'm not a Dark-Hunter and I'm not a Daimon or Apollite. I'm just me. Plain and simple."

She fought the urge to laugh at that last statement. There was nothing plain or simple about this man.

His gaze narrowed on her and a deep-seated hunger sparked in his eyes. He moved his hand toward her face.

Danger instinctively moved her head away.

His eyes continued to burn her with the intensity of his powerful stare. "Would you let me touch your cheek, Danger?"

She would have said no had it not been for the peculiar note in his voice. If she didn't know better, she'd swear it was one born of needful longing. "Why do you want to?"

He dropped his hand and looked away as if trying to banish a nightmare. "Because I live in a place where there is no human to touch. I miss the warmth of a woman's skin. The softness." He closed his eyes and drew in a deep breath. "The heady, feminine scent that is unique to all women. You've no idea what it's like to crave human contact to the point that it permeates your entire being with a need so strong that at times it makes you wonder if you've gone mad and that your whole life is nothing but a fucked-up delusion brought on by the insanity."

Now that was a scary, intense thought. So much so that she had to force herself not to back away from a man who made Norman Bates seem normal. All he needed was Mother in the rocker.

Good thing she wasn't blond and preferred a bath to a shower. . . .

You're rambling, Danger.

You think? I got a lunatic in my house sent to me by Ash. Thank you, Ash. Any other loons you want to offload on me? And

I thought my aunt Morganette was insane. At least she only thought her cat was Uncle Etienne who she kept dressed in breeches and knee coat. That was almost cute, but this . . .

Oh, yeah, send me the straitjacket, Ash. You owe it to me.

Yet even in the midst of her mental rant, something he'd said struck her and calmed her down a degree. "What do you mean that you live someplace where there aren't any humans?"

His eyes were an almost normal shade of hazel. "In a realm far away from here."

"Is that like in *Star Wars*? A long time ago, in a galaxy far, far away? Want to tell me where *your* Tatooine is located? Is it anywhere in this universe? Near Toledo maybe? The one in Ohio or Spain? I'm not picky. Can I MapQuest it?"

Alexion laughed bitterly. "You know the biggest difference between men and women? Whenever I was sent to a male Dark-Hunter, he never asked me any questions. I simply told him that I'd been sent by Acheron and he either accepted it or tried to kill me. If he accepted it, then he went about his life as if I weren't there, but you . . . you want to know every little detail of my life and being."

She gave him a miffed stare. "Gee, you think? Here's an interesting tidbit about me. I don't let strangers into my house. Ever. So if you expect to sleep here, then you owe me some answers about who and what you are. Now let's get back to this realm thing where you live. What is it?"

Honestly, she didn't expect an explanation, but to her amazement, he gave her one after a brief pause. "It's like heaven or hell. In a weird way, it's a combination of both. It exists in a place that most humans would call another dimension. Sort of." She could tell he was struggling to explain so that it would make sense to her. "Let's just say that there is no MapQuest for it. It leaves Hammond completely stumped."

Well, at least that was a beginning. And it did go a long way in almost soothing her. *Yeah, right. You still don't know anything about him.* No, but at least he'd tried to explain it to her. That was a big leap forward for Mr. Spooky.

He lifted his hand toward her cheek again and froze before he touched her. "May I?"

You really ought to run out of this room and lock your door, Danger. That's what a smart woman would do. The urge to comply with that was strong, but she didn't listen. It had never been in her nature to run from anything.

Taking a deep breath, she took his hand into hers and pressed it to her face. His touch was cold. Icy. There was absolutely no warmth whatsoever to his skin.

But the look on his face was one of pure pleasure and it made her stomach flutter. No one had ever taken such joy from touching her. At least not this platonically.

"You are beautiful," he said in a breathless tone. His eyes filled with wonder and lust, he cupped her cheek in his palm as he searched her gaze with his. "How long has it been since you last made love to someone?"

She was stunned by his question. "I beg your pardon?"

A wicked light danced in his eyes. "I know, none of my damn business." His face turned somber, then he let his hand fall away. "But I, too, have moments of profound curiosity."

"Yeah well, that particular curiosity is likely to get you cold-cocked."

His features softened as if the thought amused him. "I suppose even painful contact with that area is better than none at all."

Her jaw dropped in disbelief. "What?"

He gave her a wicked grin to let her know that he was teasing her again. "You have to forgive me if my social skills are a bit rusty. I don't interact with others much."

"No?"

"No."

She considered all of his disclosures. He didn't seem like the kind of guy who confided in others easily and that made her wonder how she got to be so lucky. "So you don't eat. You don't interact. What do you do?"

Once again, he didn't answer—an action that reminded her much of Acheron and his vagueness whenever someone asked him a personal question.

Instead, Alexion walked away from her.

Danger wasn't willing to let this go. She followed him down the hallway.

Halfway down, he stopped. He had his eyes closed and his head tilted as if he were listening to something. It was a very Ash-like pose.

"Is something wrong?" she asked.

"Do you hear that?"

She listened for a few seconds, but all she could hear was her own heart beating. "Hear what?"

He didn't respond. "Someone's watching us."

Danger went cold with dread as she turned around slowly, searching every corner of her house with her gaze. "Who? Where?"

"I don't know. But I can feel it."

He could feel it. Well, that just explained it all, didn't it?

Danger let out a tired breath. "Maybe you're just over-worked."

"Acheron?" he called out loud.

Danger frowned, half expecting Acheron to make one of his surprising appearances in her house.

He didn't.

It was just the two of them, standing there in her hallway, looking for ghosts in the shadows. Oh yeah, this was so comforting. Like a porcupine in a condom factory. She fully expected something to jump out of the walls at them.

Alexion swore under his breath before he walked away from her, into her living room. He stood in the center and looked around.

"Artemis," he growled, "I summon you to human form."

Part of her waited expectantly to see if Artemis would really show. After a few minutes and no miraculous goddess appearance, she realized he was full of crap. "Artemis can't come here. Remember? I have no soul and the gods won't come near us because of that."

"No," he said from between clenched teeth. "The Greek gods can be around you if they want to, they just don't because most of them are assholes. As for Artemis, she won't come because she's getting back at me by not responding."

"Back at you for what?"

"Oh, there's a multitude of reasons for why she hates me." He glowered up at the ceiling. "I swear, Artemis, this isn't the way to endear yourself to me." He shook his head in disgust. "Simi's right, you really are a heifer-goddess."

"Who is Simi?" she asked again.

He finally looked at her. "Like me, she's 'other.' "

"Ahh, that explains so much. I truly appreciate your trusting me with the honest truth. It just warms me through and through."

A tic started in his jaw as he moved toward the stairs. "Whether you want to believe it or not, there's someone in this house with us."

He was right, she didn't want to believe it. In fact, she knew better. "No there isn't. Believe me, Alcatraz had less security than this house."

"And they had how many people escape?"

He was seriously starting to irritate her.

Danger followed him up the stairs as apprehension ran rampant through her system. Did he really sense something that she couldn't? It wasn't likely that someone could be in here, but then most people would say that her dead existence in the world of the living wasn't possible either. Maybe he did know something she didn't.

He crept down her hallway like a large panther on the prowl. Room by room, he went in and searched. By the time they reached the last bedroom she was tired of it.

"I told you, no one is here."

He cocked his head. "Simi?" he called out. "If that's you, stop playing with me and go buy something."

Danger rubbed her temples. "Do you always talk to your imaginary friends?"

"Simi's not an imaginary friend."

"Oh, then she must be your invisible friend. Would Ms. Simi like her own room while you stay here?"

She could tell by the look on his face that she was working him into apoplexy.

"I don't understand why you can't accept that there are things that exist beyond your knowledge and understanding. To humans the idea of a Dark-Hunter is preposterous. They have no idea that your world, or that of the Daimons, exists. The world that I know is just as real as this one and it is even more carefully guarded— just because you've never heard of it doesn't mean I'm making it up. You've never met the Squires' Ruling Council either, but you know they're all alive and well."

He did have a point. Still. "Yeah, and children the world over believe in Santa Claus and the tooth fairy, which are all figments of their imagination."

Alexion ignored her. He clamped his temper down as he tried to reach out with his senses. There was a hum and an airy sensation that came whenever someone used a sfora to spy on events. He'd learned that aeons ago, once Simi discovered she could use a sfora to watch him while she was home in Katoteros.

But if it wasn't Simi . . .

That would leave someone from the other side. To his knowledge, Apollymi didn't need a sfora. She used a pool in her garden to spy on others. Which begged the question of who else would be interested in his presence here?

Why were they watching him?

Danger sighed. "Look, I don't want to stand here and watch you commune with 'other.' It's been a long night, my brain is fried and my emotions shot. You can stay here and do your hocus-pocus cat prowl, looking for your invisible friends all you want. I'm going to head off to my media room and veg."

Alexion nodded. If she left, then whoever was watching them would have to choose who to follow. That would tell him who their target was. "If you need me, call."

She rolled her eyes at him. "Yeah, I'll just do that when I need the great big, hulking he-man to charge in and save my weak, girly butt."

Alexion wasn't sure if he should be appalled or amused by her. Strangely, he was both.

She left him, and the feeling of being watched didn't cease. He let out a relieved breath. He was the target. Good. So long as it or they was after him, he could handle it. Convincing the Dark-Huntress that something was after her might prove more difficult.

She seemed very stubborn in her beliefs and extremely resistant to listening to him.

"You picked a great time to waylay Acheron, Artemis," he said under his breath. "Do us all a favor and let him go." But he knew that was impossible. Artemis would never willingly allow Acheron to leave her. She spent every waking minute contriving ways to tie him to her even more.

But at least Acheron did have a choice in the matter. If he really wanted to, he could be a callous bastard and walk away from the Dark-Hunters. There had been times in the last few decades when Alexion wouldn't have been surprised to see Acheron do it.

He, on the other hand, had no way out. He couldn't survive in the human world for long. Life outside of Katoteros was only something he could have in his dreams.

For him there would never be love. Children. Wife.

Life was always a trade-off. No one could have it all. Every-thing came down to what sacrifice you were willing to make for your dreams. He had a good life in Katoteros. Simi loved him, and in a weird way, he suspected Acheron did too.

His every wish was reality . . .

Except one.

He wasn't able to have a consort. Acheron refused to open his house to anyone else; not that he blamed him. He more than understood Acheron's need for privacy and his fear of having to explain his past.

Alexion was only grateful that Acheron had been willing to let him in. Had he not . . .

Well, he'd been living in a most painful, pathetic hell that was unimaginable to most people. If not for Acheron, he would still be there. So from where he stood, his current situation wasn't so bad.

At least it wouldn't be if he could find out who was watching him.

But in the deepest corner of his mind, he knew who it had to be. Stryker. There was no one else. Which left him with just one question.

Why?

8

Danger headed to her room to put on a pair of old gray flannel pajamas. They were two sizes too big, just like she liked them, and thick and ratty enough to discourage any romantic notions Alexion might have.

If only they could protect her from such perilous thoughts. She'd gone way too long without sex herself so it was hard to have him here and not have illicit thoughts about that ripped body of his. Holy moley, did he have to look so damned good?

Get a grip.

"I should throw him out of here, consequences be damned,"

she said quietly as she exchanged her black shirt for the pajama top.

If only she could toss him out. With his powers, he'd most likely just poof himself right back into her house, say something snotty, then prowl around searching for his invisible friends. Ugh!

She jerked her top into place, then reached for her cell phone. She pressed the autodial for Acheron.

It rang for several minutes without an answer.

How weird. Acheron always answered on the first ring. She'd never had him not pick up the phone whenever she called.

"Great," she said at the phone. "You know, you could at least use voice mail."

Sighing, she shut it off and finished dressing. Where could Acheron be?

Could he really be a Daimon?

Or should she trust Alexion?

A woman could lose her mind trying to sort this out. Not to mention that the last time she put her faith in a man, it not only killed her, but killed everyone she held dear in her heart.

Trust was for the stupid.

"I just need a break."

A little time to think.

Grabbing a pillow, she headed down the hall to the stairway that led upstairs to her media room. There was no sign of Alexion anywhere.

Maybe that was a good thing.

Pausing by her wet bar, she opened the drawer and pulled out a jar of popcorn. She filled her air machine, then placed a bowl under it and switched it on. While it cooked, she grabbed a Coke from the fridge and went to start her current favorite movie, *Troy*.

Yeah, that was what she needed. Barely dressed men, romance gone bad . . .

It was right up her alley. She might not gain any great insight into what she should do with Alexion, but at least for a little while she would be distracted from a situation that seemed pretty hopeless.

Alexion let out an aggravated breath. There was still no communication to be had with Acheron, Artemis, or Simi. And he continued to have the sensation that someone was watching him.

"You know," he said out loud for their benefit. "It's time you cut the shit. Either show yourself or knock it off."

The sensation stopped.

Alexion frowned. Hmm, that had been easy enough. He should have tried that in the beginning. "It better not be you screwing with me, Sim. If it is, I'm seriously unamused by it, and the next time you accidentally glue something to your wings, you can fix it yourself."

Feeling somewhat better, he decided to find the Dark-Huntress and make sure she was okay. For all he knew, the sfora was now trained on her.

He used his senses to locate her upstairs. Closing his eyes, he flashed himself to the outside of the door. There was no need to scare her any more with his powers. He should act as normal as possible around her.

With that thought in mind, he opened the door to her media room to find her curled up on the padded dark green couch, watching the television. He cocked his head as he saw two ancient Greek armies on the large-screen plasma TV.

Danger felt the air stirring behind her. Turning her head, she saw Alexion watching her TV. There was a strange look on his handsome face. It was an odd mixture of pain, remorse, and longing. If she didn't know better, she might think he was homesick or something.

"You through prowling the house?" she asked him.

The familiar stony expression returned to his face. "Yes. They're gone now." He moved a little closer to the couch while he continued to watch the screen curiously. "What is this?"

"Troy."

He frowned as if that didn't make sense to him. Then sudden recognition lightened his face. "Oh," he said in a low tone. "Ilion."

Now there was a term she hadn't heard since her days of studying classical Greek history as a girl in a convent school. It was then she realized something about her "guest." "You're an ancient Greek, aren't you?"

He looked briefly startled by her question, but he quickly recovered himself. And true to form, he avoided answering her question. "Why are you watching this?"

She pointed to the scene where Brad Pitt as Achilles was lying naked on a pallet with two equally naked women. "That right there," she said with an appreciative note in her voice. "That is truly the finest butt on the planet."

He scoffed. "That's not the finest butt on the planet. Trust me."

She arched a brow at that. "So you're an expert on male butts, huh?"

His jaw dropped as he gave her an offended glare. "Hardly."

Danger couldn't resist teasing him more . . . "Yeah, you're an ancient Greek all right."

"What's that supposed to mean?"

She shrugged. "Well, we all know about you ancient Greeks. You were a friendly bunch with each other. Wrestling naked, groping each other's heinies."

"We were not!" he snapped angrily.

Finally, she got some real emotion out of him. She was actually proud of herself.

And to be honest, she had to admit that she thoroughly enjoyed being on the teasing end for once. "Please, it's all over the history books. You guys were always shacking up with each other. Even Achilles was shacked up with Patroclus. Of course not in this movie, but in Homer's *Iliad* they were more than just friends."

His green eyes flared in outrage. "Those were later Greeks. Not us. They gave all the rest of the city-states a bad name."

"Then you admit you're Greek."

His gaze narrowed as he realized she had tricked him into a confession.

"Oh, don't pop an aneurysm," she said playfully. "I won't tell anyone that you were once a Greek. Although why you would hide it, I can't imagine, since Greek Dark-Hunters are 'the thing' in our world." She indicated the other end of her couch. "Have a seat, Mr. Cranky."

He moved to perch uncomfortably on the arm of her couch as he went back to watching the movie.

Danger was more fascinated by him and the sadness that seemed to engulf him while he was transfixed by Hollywood's interpretation of his world. For the first time, there was something about him that almost seemed human. "Were you a soldier?"

He gave a subtle nod.

She glanced to the screen, then back at Alexion as she tried to imagine him in Greek armor. Most likely, he would have been a fine-looking warrior. He was lean and absolutely ripped . . . that kind of ripped that made a woman want to spend hours tasting his abs and pecs. And she realized that his shoulder-length blond hair would have been really sexy peeking out from the back of his helm.

It made her wonder how his butt would compare to Brad's . . .

His scowl returned. "Why, if they're supposed to be Greek, are all of them speaking with an English accent?"

She laughed. "Didn't you know that British is, like, the universal 'foreign' language in Hollywood? They use it in any movie where they want to have a foreign feel to it, regardless of where it's set."

"But they're Greek. They should at least sound it."

"I know, just go with it."

He quieted down until they showed Brad confronting Brian Cox, who was playing King Agamemnon, the leader of the Greeks. "That's not Agamemnon," he said, making a face. "He wasn't that old. Clytemnestra killed him off long before he had a chance to go gray."

Not wanting to encourage him to interrupt any more, she hid her laughter. "Would you just watch the movie?"

"But that didn't happen. They're making all this up."

She tossed a pillow at him. "Look, Chatty Cathy, I'm not interested in historical accuracy. If I was, I'd be reading the *Iliad*—"

"That wasn't accurate either."

Danger paused as he gave her a clue to his real age. "Just how old are you?"

He scoffed. "Older than Ilion, obviously."

"So did you teach Ash how to be vague or did he teach it to you?"

He tossed the pillow back at her, then returned his attention to the TV where Helen was entering the scene. "They never get Helen right, do they? Man, she was truly beautiful. You should have seen her. She had a laugh that sounded like angels singing. And her body . . . Well, it was no wonder they had to get all her suitors to swear that they wouldn't kill her husband out of sheer jealousy."

Danger didn't comment. Scoping out other women wasn't her forte. Not to mention, she was turning a little green over his appreciation for a woman that had been dead for thousands of years.

"We can't all be Helen, now can we?"

She saw the "uh-oh" descend on his face as he realized what he'd just said. "You're beautiful too."

"Yeah," she said sarcastically. "Save it, bud. Too little, too late."

For once he was quiet.

At least until they got to the scene with Paris and Helen

naked in Helen's bedroom. Alexion looked back at Danger. "So his butt has no appeal for you?"

Danger choked on her popcorn. Good Lord, the man had no couth. He'd ask her anything. She was never sure what might come flying out of his mouth next.

Coughing, she looked at him in disbelief.

"Not really," she answered once she could catch her breath again. "I'm not a big Orlando Bloom fan, unless he's playing Legolas in *Lord of the Rings*. Now Legolas is one elf I wouldn't toss out of my bed for eating crackers. I have to give the casting director credit. Whoever looked at him and thought, 'gorgeous blond elf,' definitely deserves an award of some kind."

He indicated Eric Bana, who was playing Hector. "What about him?"

"He's okay, but not my taste. I'm not that attracted to brunets. I like blonds better, which is why I adore Orlando as Legolas and not Paris."

There was no missing the spark of interest in his eyes. "That's good to know."

Danger had no idea why she liked teasing a man she really should hate, and yet she couldn't seem to help herself. "Well, that information does you no good."

"Why not? I'm blond."

"Yes, but you're not human." She looked back at the screen where Brad Pitt, as Achilles, was fighting with his cousin. "Then again neither is he," she said with a breathless sigh. "I swear, that man is a god."

Alexion snorted. "He's not a god and that wasn't Achilles's

cousin in real life. Not unless you make him a 'kissing' cousin if you catch my drift."

"Drift? That was more like a typhoon, Mr. Suave, and you're not telling me anything I didn't know except for the Brad being a god part. There you're most definitely wrong. Just look at that body."

"It does nothing for me."

"Well, it should."

He made a sound of disagreement. "I've seen better."

She gave him an arch stare.

"Not like that," he snapped indignantly. "I mean . . . I never—"

"Give it up, Greek man. You've already drifted out to sea and are drowning fast."

Alexion should have been angry and appalled by this turn in their conversation, but he strangely wasn't. It had been countless centuries since anyone had teased him like this. He had to give her credit, she was swift and intelligent.

He watched her as she ate the popcorn. "Why is that white?"

"How many questions are you going to ask me?"

"I was only curious. And given how many questions you've asked me, it's only fair that I return the favor."

"Yeah, well, you don't have to do it in the middle of my movie." She sighed as she raked her hand through the popcorn. "It's always white unless you put stuff on it." She held the bowl out to him. "Want some?"

"There's no need. I can't taste it," he reminded her.

"It's air popped without butter or salt. There's not much to taste, but you can feel the texture of it, right?"

He supposed. Reaching out, he took a small handful and ate it. True to her prediction, it did feel odd in his mouth. It was crunchy and light. "Why do you eat this if it has no taste?"

"I like it. It's good for you."

"You're immortal. Nothing foodwise is bad for you."

She gave him a menacing glare. "Would you just watch the movie?"

Danger was a bit stunned when he shifted so that he could sit beside her on the couch. He also continued to eat her popcorn. It was really odd to have someone here with her. Not even Keller shared her late-night/early-morning movie. It was something she'd always done alone to unwind after her duties. There wasn't a great deal of Daimon activity in Tupelo. Most Dark-Hunters got rather testy when they weren't busy, but she kind of liked it.

So she spent many nights at home alone with her DVD collection or on the phone talking to other female Dark-Hunters. Her favorite ones to talk to were Ephani, who was a local Huntress and Zoe, who had just been moved to New York City. Both of them ancient Amazons, they had some interesting takes on how to treat men.

Most of which involved whips, chains, and handcuffs.

Alexion's hand collided with hers as they both reached into the bowl. She was still surprised by the coldness of it. No wonder he kept his coat on.

"Why are you so icy?" she asked.

"I'm cold?"

"Like a corpse."

"Oh," he said, as if he really weren't aware of the fact that his body temperature would rival an ice cube's. "Well, I am dead."

"So am I, but I have a pulse and some warmth." Which gave her a strange idea. Taking his wrist into her hand, she realized that he didn't have a pulse.

She swallowed as he watched her. "Why don't you have a pulse?"

No sooner had the question left her lips than a heartbeat started. His skin actually warmed while she held on to it.

Dropping his hand, she shot to her feet. "That ain't right. What the hell is wrong with you?"

"I didn't mean to offend you," he said honestly. "The only one who touches me is Simi and she's cold too. I didn't think about what my skin would feel like to you or I would have warmed it up first."

She was completely confounded by his words. He could control his heartbeat and body temperature? That was unheard of. "How do you do that?"

"I think it and it happens."

Danger sat back down and reached out to touch his face. It felt like any other man's face. Granted, his skin was warmer than before, but it still wasn't quite the temperature of a normal human.

His dark whiskers were rough against her palm, prickly, and it sent a foreign ache through her.

He closed his eyes as if savoring the feel of her hand on his skin. He turned his face ever so slightly in a gentle caress. When he opened his eyes, the deep-seated hunger in his gaze almost frightened her.

Before she realized what he was doing, he dipped his head and captured her lips.

Her first inclination was to pull back and slug him, but there was another part of her that sparked to his gentle kiss. And it was gentle. Tender. It was a lover's kiss and it set her blood on fire.

She could only barely remember the last time she'd slept with a man. One-night stands had never appealed to her. Well, that wasn't exactly true. For a brief time, when she had first become a Dark-Hunter and learned of her freedom from disease and pregnancy, she had explored her sexuality.

But that hadn't lasted long. Since Dark-Hunters were forbidden to develop romantic relationships, it left her with nothing but sex. And sex without some kind of mutual caring wasn't fulfilling to her.

She pulled back. "I'm not an easy lay, Alexion."

He actually smiled a real smile at her. It was charming and unexpected. "I am."

Shaking her head, she laughed at him. "Most men are."

Alexion didn't respond to her comment. How could he while his body and lips were still burning from the sensation of her mouth on his? That woman had a tongue that set every fantasy in his mind alive. It made him wonder what else she did well along those lines . . .

"If you change your mind, Danger . . ."

"I won't."

Damn. It was one of the reasons why he wished Acheron had sent him to a male Dark-Hunter. By now a man would have been on the prowl for a woman of his own which would have allowed Alexion ample time to find a bedmate for himself.

He somehow doubted Danger would be open to taking him out to get laid.

"I understand," he said to her.

Yeah, right. He might mentally understand, but his body wasn't listening. It wanted a taste of her so badly that it was all he could do to remain seated.

His celibacy was hard enough on him in Katoteros. On earth, it was unbearable. To be so close to a woman and not have her . . .

He actually whimpered.

"Are you all right?"

"Fine," he said, wishing a cold shower would work. But he was long past that. He'd been so long without a woman's touch that nothing except release would help him.

"So do you have any cheap friends?" he asked.

She gave him a disgusted glare. "You are a pig!"

"You go two hundred years without sex and see how you feel," he said defensively. "It's easy for you to sit there sanctimoniously while you condemn me, but you can have sex anytime you feel like it. All I have are the next few days. After that, I have to pray for a Dark-Hunter uprising to have another shot at a woman. Have you any idea how often those happen?"

"So you look forward to killing us?"

"No, but after a couple of hundred years, you do start having some radical thoughts."

Danger stared at him in disbelief.

"And it would help if you had chosen a movie where people kept their clothes on. You know, Disney makes a damn good movie too."

He was unbelievable! "I can't believe you're Ash's chosen whatever and all you can do is think of getting laid. You are such a man-slut! You don't even care who you sleep with."

"That's not exactly true. I do have some standards. Granted, not many, but still . . ." He sucked his breath in sharply. "I'm so hard it's painful and when you consider the fact I don't really feel pain like a human does, that says a lot." He actually pouted and that succeeded in making her feel sorry for him. But only a little.

"You're just having a really bad night, aren't you?"

"You have no idea." He expelled a heavy sigh before he got up and headed for her hallway.

"Where are you going?"

"I'm going to walk around your house and try to think cold, disgusting thoughts."

Danger didn't laugh until he'd left the room. Part of her really did feel for him. Then again, it'd been nearly that long since she'd last slept with someone. She just didn't like getting naked with a stranger. Like many other female Dark-Hunters, she wanted the one thing she could never have again—a relationship. That was the hardest part about their immortality. With the exception of the Amazons, who were born to never have a relationship with a man, the rest of the female hunters missed what they'd had as humans.

It actually bothered her some nights how much she missed her husband. Up until the moment he'd betrayed her, she had loved him more than anything else in the world. Michel had had that debonair charm that won over everyone he met. Unlike Alexion, her husband had never once placed his foot in his mouth.

But then, Alexion, according to his words, hadn't been around many people.

"Oh, don't do it, Danger."

But it was too late. She was already getting up to go check on him.

She found him downstairs, holding one of her DVDs as if it were a foreign object.

"You okay?" she asked.

He nodded even though he was scowling. "What is this?"

"It's a DVD. That's what we were watching upstairs."

"DVD?"

He didn't know what a DVD was? Was that even possible? "Yeah, isn't that how you watch movies at home?"

"No. They just play."

She scowled at that. "What do you mean, they just play?"

He acted as if there were nothing unusual about his declaration. "Whenever Simi or Ash want to watch something, it just comes on."

"Without a video?"

"Yes."

Such a thing wasn't possible. "You mean you have streaming movies?"

"We have anything we want whenever we want it. At least I do if Simi's not there. She tends to be a movie hog when she's home."

There was that name again. "Who is this Simi person you keep talking about?"

Alexion stood up. At first he wasn't going to answer, but there really wasn't any reason to keep it from her. It wasn't as though the information would cost him anything. "She's a cross between an adopted daughter and an annoying little sister."

"And she lives with you and Acheron in his house that no one knows exists?"

"Yes."

Danger was actually surprised she was getting something personal out of him. Hoping for more, she asked, "No one else ever comes to visit?"

"Only Artemis and Urian."

Artemis she knew. "Urian?" Before he could respond, she answered for herself. "Wait. Let me guess. He's 'other.' "

"Yes."

"Is Ash the only non 'other' there?"

His features immediately went blank, as if he were hiding something.

Danger caught herself before she gaped. "Are you telling me Ash is 'other' too?"

"I'm not saying anything about him."

He didn't have to. His omission said it all. She wanted to ask more about what Ash and Simi were, but it had been futile enough tonight. She was rather tired of banging her head against the proverbial wall.

Sighing in defeat, she looked over at her plasma TV, which had had a miraculous recovery while she'd been upstairs. "Did you fix my TV?"

"It only seemed right since I was the one who broke it."

She walked over to it to inspect it. Everything looked normal. As soon as she was in front of it, it came on.

Danger jumped, especially since its remote was lying on the bookshelf in front of her. "How did you do that?"

"Same way I always do it." The television shut off.

She quickly moved away. Just how much power did this guy wield?

He moved to stand behind her. His presence there was disturbing to her well-being. She was more aware of him than she had ever been of any man before. There was something about him that was electrifying and magnetic.

"Don't be afraid of me, Danger," he whispered near her ear. Chills shot through her body. "Unless you threaten Acheron, I will never harm you."

"No, you just intend to harm my friends."

She felt him pick her braid up and hold it close to his face so that he could inhale her scent. "I really wish you wouldn't do that."

"I know." He set her hair down and moved even closer. His presence was overwhelming. Powerful. She could feel his desire to hold her.

Yet he refrained.

Alexion ground his teeth as he imagined what it would be like to pull her flush to his body. To reach around her and cup her breasts in his hands. It would be so easy to slide his hand underneath the waistband of her flannel pajamas. . . . To brush his fingers through the triangle of hair between her legs so that he could stroke her. Touch her. Hear her moaning in his ear as her breath tickled his flesh.

He could already feel the slickness of her.

His mouth watered hungrily for a small taste. Carnal pleasure was the only thing that he could still experience as an immortal with the same degree that he had known as a human. It was why he craved it so much. There for a few minutes, he could forget his icy, lonely existence and feel truly human again.

He could feel connected, almost wanted.

But she didn't want him.

His bitter loneliness tore through him, shredding his heart. It was ever his destiny to want and not have. In many ways, he was Tantalus. He could see what he wanted, but every time he'd ever dared to reach for it, something came along and took it away just as he grasped it.

Damn.

Grinding his teeth, he stepped away from her. He sensed her instant relief and that saddened him even more.

"So, do all the male Dark-Hunters pimp for you?"

He shook his head. "No. They just tend to frequent places where . . . shall we say . . . loose women congregate." And normally those women threw themselves at him. It was a pity Danger didn't follow their actions.

"I'll bet they do."

He ignored her dripping sarcasm. She had no idea how important such contact was to him. She interacted with other people nightly. He didn't. His only contact with the world was through the monitors and the sfora in Katoteros. It was cold and sterile.

Like me.

That was true enough. Every century seemed to get a little harder for him. Like Acheron, he lost more and more of his humanity. That was one of the reasons why it was so important for him to try and save Kyros. This was the first time in centuries that something had truly gotten to him.

He really did want to save his old friend.

But that would have to wait for now. He could already sense that dawn was about to break.

Danger looked to the window as if she sensed it as well. "It's getting late. I think I'll turn in."

He nodded as she left him alone.

No sooner had she vanished from his sight, than he felt the prickly sensation of being watched again.

Alexion rubbed the back of his neck uneasily. "I swear, Simi, if that is you messing with me, I won't lock up your credit cards next time. I'll shred them."

9

Danger spent a fitful day in her bed, trying to sleep and finding it almost impossible. It was barely six in the evening when she woke up, her heart racing, her mind whirling from horrible images.

Wicked dreams of Alexion had mixed with nightmares of him trying to kill her. No matter how hot the dream started out, it always ended the same way—Alexion locking her into a cramped, dark room that held other Dark-Hunters. Ragged and ill-kempt, barely more than human skeletons, they begged for mercy until they were led outside, one by one, to the Place de Grève where the guillotine in its red-painted frame waited to behead them.

The haunting swoosh of the eighty-eight-pound blade falling down rang in her ears, along with the sound of the crowd of humans and Daimons cheering their deaths.

But the weirdest, most disturbing part of her dream was the image of Alexion sitting to the side of the crowd, à la Madame DeFarge, knitting a list of all their names so that the executioner (Acheron) would know who next to murder.

Damn you, Charles Dickens, for that image! Her own memories of the Revolution were bad enough. The last thing she needed was for someone to add to them.

Danger lay in bed, clutching at her throat. The horrifying screams of the past rang in her ears. Over and over, she saw the faces of the innocents who had been killed by a hungry mob bent on vengeance against an entire social class of people. It had been decades since she'd last recalled her human life.

Her death.

But now it tore through her with stunning clarity and acidity. Even worse, she remembered the time not long after the Revolution when it had been fashionable for Parisians to hold Victim's Balls where the only people who were allowed to attend were those who had family slain by the Committee. The attendees all wore red ribbons tied around their throats in remembrance of Madame La Guillotine's handiwork. It had been gruesomely morbid and had sent her fleeing her homeland, never to return.

She hated these memories. She hated everything about them. It'd been so unfair to lose everything because of one man's greed. A man she, herself, had brought into the family. But for her, her father and his wife and her brother and sister wouldn't have died.

Why had she ever believed Michel's lies? Why?

The guilt and shame of that was still raw inside her.

She had killed her own family because she had fallen in love with a lying, beguiling asshole. Tears gathered in her eyes as her throat closed so tight that she could barely breathe.

"Papa," she sobbed, aching anew for the loss of her father. He had been a good man who had taken care of the people who worked for him. Never once had he neglected either her or her mother. In fact, he had wanted to give up his noble titles so that he could marry her mother when she'd become unexpectedly pregnant.

Had he done so, his life would have been spared. . . . But her mother had refused his suit. Self-reliant and bold, her mother had never wanted a husband to tell her what to do. She was one of the most renowned actresses of her day, and her mother had feared that her father would insist she give up the stage for home and family.

Even after her rejection, her father had pursued her mother, begging her to marry him while he made sure that both of them had everything they needed. It was only after Danger had reached maturity that he had given up hope of her mother ever changing her mind.

It was then he'd found himself a lady to wed.

Even then, both he and his lady-wife had always been kind to her. Her stepmother had welcomed her into their home with open arms. Maman Esmée had swathed her in love and devotion.

Not much older than Danger, the lady had never looked down on her illegitimate status. She'd quickly become one of her dearest friends and confidantes.

Even now she could see their faces as they lovingly teased

each other. See Esmée's face as she took her shopping for hats— Esmée's one great weakness in life. Never could she pass by a shop without dashing in to see what they had. She would spend hours in the haberdashery trying on every bonnet and hat they had while her father watched her and laughed.

Danger had loved them both so much. . . .

And then in the dreaded heat of summer, the Revolution had swept through France worse than a plague. Thousands had died in a matter of weeks.

Her brother, Edmonde, had only been four, her sister, Jacqueline, less than a year old, and her countrymen had brutally slaughtered them. None of her family had deserved the deaths they had been granted.

None of them.

Except for her husband. He had earned every wound she had given him for his cruel betrayal. And all because he had coveted her father's home and wanted it for his own. He'd gotten it, all right, and she had seen to it that he hadn't lived long enough to enjoy it.

Shaking with anger and grief, she pushed back her red and gold covers, then parted her gold curtains so that she could leave her antique tester bed.

Alexion could rot in hell before she ever helped him go after the Dark-Hunters or anyone else. She would never be part of such a witch hunt. If Acheron wanted them dead, then he could do it on his own.

She wasn't about to help Alexion judge anyone. She'd seen enough of that in her human lifetime.

With her conviction set, she quickly washed her face, dressed, and went to find him to give him a piece of her mind.

But those thoughts fled when, after a brief search of her house, she found him sitting on the couch in her media room. Perfectly coiffed, he seemed strangely at home. There was a stack of DVDs in front of him. He looked just as he had when she'd left him the night before. If she didn't know better, she'd swear that he hadn't slept.

She paused in the doorway as he literally used his finger to fast-forward the machine to a new scene selection.

How did he do that?

"Where's the remote?"

He turned his head toward her. "Remote?"

"Yeah, you know, the thing you turn the television off and on with?"

He looked at his finger.

Bemused, Danger went to the DVD shelf beside her television and picked up the remote. "How do you control the player with-out this?"

He waved his hand and the TV turned off.

Completely baffled, she returned the remote to the shelf. "You're a total freak."

He arched a brow at her, but said nothing.

Danger crossed the small space to stand before him. She took his hand into hers, grateful that for once it was warm. It looked like any other hand . . . well, except it was rather large and well manicured.

It was a man's hand, callused, strong. She pointed it at the television.

Nothing happened.

"Are you sitting on a universal remote?" she asked suspiciously.

He just stared innocently at her.

"Get up," she said, pulling him to his feet so that she could see the cushions.

No, there was no remote.

Frustrated, she glared at him. "How did you fast-forward and turn it off?"

He shrugged. "I wanted it off and off it went."

"Wow," she said, "that's amazing. I guess this makes me the luckiest woman in the world."

"How so?"

"I've found the only man alive who won't ever shout out, 'honey, where's the remote?' then tear my house apart in pursuit of it."

He gave her a puzzled look that most likely matched the one she was giving him. "You know, I don't understand you. You are an immortal creature of the night with fangs and psychic abilities. Why is it that you're having such a hard time accepting me for what I am and for what I can do?"

"Because it flies in the face of every belief I've had up until now. See, we"—she motioned to herself—"Dark-Hunters are supposed to be the baddest things after the sun goes down. Then, in steps you and now I find out that our powers are nothing in comparison to what you can do. It really messes with my head."

She could tell her words baffled him. "Why does that disturb you? You've always known that Acheron was the most powerful being in your world."

"Yeah, but he's one of us."

His face did that blank thing it did every time she said or did something he didn't agree with.

"What?" she asked. "Are you going to tell me now that Ash isn't a Dark-Hunter?"

"He is unique in your world."

"Yeah, I noticed. We all have. It's been the topic of many late-night discussions on the Dark-Hunter bulletin boards."

An evil, mischievous glint darkened his eyes. "I know. I spend many an hour logged on under a pseudonym, leading all of you down murky paths just so that I can watch your minds work out the speculation. I have to say all of you are highly entertaining as you grapple with the puzzle of who and what he is."

The idea of him doing such a thing both amused and irritated her. "You're a sick man."

He shrugged nonchalantly. "I have to do something to alleviate my boredom."

Maybe that was true and it was a rather harmless way to break monotony. Still, she didn't like to be toyed with.

But that was neither here nor there. At the moment she had a much more pressing issue to discuss with Monsieur Oddball. "You know, I've done some thinking."

"And?"

"And I've decided that if you and Ash want to play this . . . whatever, game-scenario thing that you seem to run every few centuries where you kill some of us off, then you can do it without my help. I don't want any part of judging someone else. I've already seen firsthand where that leads and it's not pretty. I never want to wash innocent blood off my hands."

He took a deep breath as if he were digesting what she said. His gaze was dark and sincere. "We're not the Committee."

She was amazed that he understood what had prompted her decision, but it made no difference. "No, you're judge, jury, and executioner. In my book, that makes you worse. If you want to kill me, then kill me. I'd rather be a Shade than betray one of my friends or even enemies to that end. Believe me, having been betrayed myself, it's not something I would ever do to anyone else."

His eyes turned their eerie glowing green color. "It's easy to be brave when you have no real understanding of what being a Shade means."

"Yeah, I do know. You're hungry and thirsty all the time with no way to sate it. No one can see you, hear you, yada yada yada. It's a fate worse than death because there is no eternal reward, no reincarnation. It's true hell. I got it."

"No, Danger," he said his voice filled with pain. "You don't."

Before she realized what he was doing, he placed his hand on her shoulder. His touch seared her with pain and images. She saw a man she didn't know. He stood in the middle of a crowded New York street, screaming for someone to see him. To hear him.

He tried to reach out to people, but they all walked straight through his body. As they did so, the sensation of their souls brushing through him pierced his phantom body like shards of poisoned glass. It stung and burned so raw that it was an indescribable pain.

She could feel the rancid hunger that gnawed so deep inside of him that it, too, defied description. The thirst that burned his parched mouth and lips like some unquenchable fire that refused to be sated. He was overwhelmed by the unrelenting physical agony, by the mental loneliness that ached for one second of conversation.

Some inner, silent part of him was screaming out, begging for death.

Begging for forgiveness.

Alexion released her. He dipped his head down to speak angrily in her ear. "That is what being a Shade feels like, Danger. Is that really what you want?"

She struggled to breathe through the emotions that choked her. It was beyond even her worst nightmare. She'd never imagined such a hell could exist. Even now the image of that man was still branded in her mind. It hurt her in a way that surprised her. "Who is he?" she asked, her voice trembling.

"His name is Erius and for more than two thousand years he has lived that horrific existence."

Alexion's tone was deep and resonant. He stood so close to her that as he spoke, his hot breath tickled her skin. "At one time, he thought he could be a god. He thought all he had to do was kill humans and suck out their souls like a Daimon. Just like Kyros is trying to do, he gathered together a group of Dark-Hunters to revolt against Acheron and Artemis. He told them that he could lead them to freedom. That all of them had the ability to be gods too. All they had to do was listen to him and follow his example."

Swallowing against the sudden lump in her throat, she looked up at him, searching for the truth that was finally coming to light. "Are you the one who killed him?"

"No," he said, his tone and gaze gentling. "Acheron did. He went to him and tried to explain everything, but Erius refused to listen. He had it in his mind that Acheron had discovered the secret of the Daimons' powers and that Acheron was hoarding the secret from the rest of them. All Acheron's presence did was anger him more, and in the end that was what caused Erius to damn himself. It was the last time Acheron went to a Dark-Hunter to try and save him."

His gaze turned dull, haunted. "After that I took over. I go to them and pretend to be a Dark-Hunter too. I try to explain to them that Acheron hoards nothing and that they are all wrong with their assumptions about the origins of his powers. Usually a majority of them listen to me and go home."

It made sense for Alexion to go in. No doubt if Acheron showed up around Kyros, Kyros would attack him and fight. Ancient men weren't usually known for reasoning their way out of conflict. "They're much more likely to listen to one of their own."

He nodded. "By their very natures, Dark-Hunters are vengeful people. They were wronged in life and to many of them it's easy to believe they were wronged in death. They look for someone to hate."

"Acheron is an easy target."

"Yes. He's more powerful, and all of you know that he hides things from you. So once the kernel of the lie is planted, it takes root and grows into hatred and revolution."

She took a step away from him so that she could think clearly without his presence distracting her, then turned so that she could watch his face. "Then why doesn't Acheron tell the truth? Why does he hide his past from us?"

He shrugged. "When I asked you to have sex with me last night, you rejected me by saying you didn't want to sleep with a stranger. Yet for the first fifty years of your life as a Dark-Huntress, you burned through lovers like—"

She covered his mouth with her hand to silence that sentence. "How do you know that?"

He nipped at her hand with his teeth, causing her to jerk it away. His smile was wicked and warm. "I know many things about all of you. Just as Acheron does."

She didn't like the thought of that. "Did you spy on me?"

"No, but I know you. I have many of the same powers that Acheron has. Just as he can see into your heart and past, I can as well."

Danger tilted her head as she considered that. She wasn't sure she liked being transparent to anyone. Everyone needed to be able to hide parts of themselves. "Then do you know about Acheron's past?"

She saw the shame in his gaze before he moved away from her. "Answer me, Alexion."

He let out a long, tired breath as he returned the DVD boxes to her shelf. "Yes. I discovered his past by accident."

The haunted look on his face told her that he wished he'd never learned it. "It was in the early days when I was first learning to use my powers." He paused shelving the boxes to face her. "I didn't know how to control looking into the past and I stumbled upon his. When he came home, he found the sfora—the scrying orb—in my room. He looked at me and I knew he knew I had seen it."

She'd never known Acheron to be angry, but given the stead-fast way he guarded his past, he must have been furious. "What did he do?"

Alexion's gaze dropped to the floor as if he could see that day clearly in his mind. "He came forward and picked the sfora up, then said, 'I guess I should show you how to use this correctly.'"

She blinked in disbelief. "That's it?"

He nodded before returning to put her DVDs up. "I've never spoken of it and neither has he."

"Then what did you s—"

"Ask me nothing about his past," he said, interrupting her before she could ask him that very thing. "Believe me, it's not something you want to know. There are some things that are best left alone."

"But—"

"No buts, Danger. He has good reason for not speaking of his human life. There's no information there that could benefit anyone. But it would hurt him a great deal personally. It's why he doesn't speak of it. He's not hiding some great secret of the Dark-Hunter world. Except for the fact that Artemis doesn't care about any of you. But what good would that do any of you? You're better off with the lie than the truth."

Perhaps that was true. Personally, she could have lived quite happily not knowing Artemis could care less what happened to them. "Then why were we created?"

"Honestly?"

"Please."

He sighed as he put away the last movie. "I already told you. Artemis wanted a hold over Acheron. The only way to get it was to play on his guilt. So she used his own powers against him to create the first Dark-Hunters. She knew Acheron would never turn his back on the innocents who wouldn't have been offered Artemis's bargain had it not been for him."

Alexion pinned her with a menacing glare. "His guilt is what made Acheron go out of his way to make sure that all of you had servants and pay for your work. The Dark-Hunters owe that man everything, and I do mean everything. He pays in blood every time one of you wants to go free, and he suffers every day so that you can all live your cushy little lives of wealth and privilege."

His eyes literally snapped green fire at her. "And I have to say that every time one of you turns on him, it seriously pisses me off. Acheron asks nothing from any of you and that's exactly what he receives. When was the last time one of you even said thank you for his help?"

A twinge of guilt went through her.

He was right. She'd never thanked Acheron for her training or anything else. She didn't think to. If anyone was given thanks for their lives, it was Artemis.

"Why doesn't Acheron tell us the truth?" she asked.

"It's not his way. His ego doesn't require worship or even acknowledgment. All he asks is that you do your jobs and that you don't die."

A tic started in his jaw. "And now to know that Kyros, one of the first who was created, has turned on him. . . . It angers me on a level you can't even begin to comprehend. Of all the Dark-Hunters, he and Callabrax should know that Acheron would never use any of you in his own personal war."

Danger nodded. If Alexion was telling the truth, and to be honest, she was starting to believe him, then it must hurt Acheron to know that Kyros had turned on him. "Kyros and Brax are legendary."

"Yes, and that is why I have to stop Kyros. More Dark-Hunters will listen to him than anyone else because he's been around for so long."

He made a compelling argument, but she still wanted him to leave her out of it. As she opened her mouth to speak, he got that odd, faraway look again.

"They're back," he said between clenched teeth.

Danger let out a weary breath. "Okay, Carol Anne, enough with the *Poltergeist* interpretation. If we can't contact them and they're not bothering us, I don't want to know they're watching us, okay?"

He ignored her. "Simi," he growled. "I have serious matters here. I don't need you annoying me. I owe Kyros too much to watch him die, but I can't save him if you distract me."

Danger frowned as two thoughts hit her simultaneously. "You sound like you've been talking to Simi all day."

"I have been. It must be her. She watches for a bit, then goes away only to come back again."

That sounded positively freaky to her, but whatever. "Did you not sleep?"

Again he didn't answer, which played right into her second thought. "You said you owe Kyros. What do you owe him?"

He hesitated before he answered. "I owe him a chance to live."

Yeah, she believed that one . . . not. It didn't even make sense. The sudden absence of emotion in his face told her he was hiding something.

And in that moment, she knew what it was. "You knew him."

Still the emotionless, blank stare. "I know all the Dark-Hunters."

Maybe, but she sensed more than that in him. "No. It's personal between you two. I can feel it."

He moved away from her.

She followed after him. "Talk to me, Alexion. If you really want my help, give me an honest answer."

"I've been honest with you from the very beginning." He headed for the door.

Danger stopped and waited until he was almost out of the room.

She had a sneaking suspicion of who he might be and it was time to play her hunch. "Ias?"

He stopped to look back at her. "What?" He responded to the name automatically.

Her jaw went slack. She'd been right, and he realized it two seconds later.

His face turned to stone.

"*Mon Dieu,*" she breathed as every weirdness about him suddenly made sense. That's why he couldn't taste food. Why he didn't feel real emotions.

How it was that he knew what it was like to be a Shade. . . .

"It's true," she breathed. "You were the third Dark-Hunter created after Acheron. The first one who died."

"No I wasn't, and Ias is a Shade."

She still didn't believe him. Not about this. "And if I were to take you to Kyros right now, what would he say? What name would he call you?"

Alexion ground his teeth in aggravation at her ability to see through him.

There really was no point in hiding the truth from her. It wasn't like she wouldn't find out the minute Kyros laid eyes on him.

Damn.

"He would call me Ias. But I wasn't the first Dark-Hunter to die," he added, wanting her to know that he was telling her the truth. "There were two before me who were killed by the Daimons before Acheron learned of us."

He sensed that something inside her changed in that instant. For one thing, her face softened. She crossed the room to stand just before him. Her gaze searched his as she reached a hand up to touch his cheek.

That simple touch wrecked him. How could he have such emotions? For centuries he had felt nothing for anyone except Ash and Simi.

To feel such raw emotion now . . .

It was incredible.

Her dark eyes showed him her heart. "Shades aren't supposed to have human form."

"They don't."

She caressed his cheek. "But you feel real enough to me."

Her touch aroused him to a painful level. In the past his encounters with women had always been brief. They'd lasted long enough for him to sate his lust and then the woman had vanished, never to be seen again. There had never been a tender touch like this one. A touch meant to comfort. It eased him and it burned through him like lava. "I'm different from the others."

"How?"

He pulled her hand away from his face, unable to bear the unfamiliar tenderness any longer. All it did was make him ache for things he could never have. He was beyond human relationships.

Beyond human feeling.

"Acheron held himself responsible for my death," he explained quietly. "Had he not made a fatal mistake in judgment, I wouldn't have become a Shade. For that reason, he gave me form and took me in to live with him and Simi."

"That is why you defend him?"

He nodded. "I assure you, living as a Shade is not something to take lightly. My short time as a true Shade taught me well that there is nothing on this earth or beyond worse. I'm grateful every day for Acheron's mercy."

She could respect his loyalty to the man who had saved him, and yet it added a most macabre twist that he would damn other people to the fate that he'd escaped. "How many others have you and Acheron damned to Shadedom?"

"I assure you, it's not something either of us does lightly. Those who died because they were preying on helpless humans are left to wander. The ones who die in the line of duty are given a paradise of sorts to spend eternity in. They don't suffer. Acheron won't allow it."

Danger frowned at his disclosure. That was something that no one had ever told them before. They were all left believing that if they died in the line of duty, they suffered the same as all the other Shades.

There wasn't supposed to be any way back from Shadedom.

"Why doesn't Ash tell us this?"

"Because a Shade, unlike a Dark-Hunter, can't go back to being human. Any hope of a future incarnation is gone. They have no hope for ever having a normal life again."

That didn't make sense to her. He was real. He had flesh and form. "But you—"

"I'm not in a human body, Danger." He looked down at himself with an anguished grimace. "This form that you see, that you touch, has an expiration date on it. In a few days, I have to return to my realm or perish completely. Acheron is afraid that if the Dark-Hunters ever learned that they could be spared the torment, they would become more reckless and not fear death. But believe me when I say there are things out there far worse than dying."

"Such as?"

The misery in his eyes singed her, and when he spoke, she knew it was from personal experience. "Living out eternity alone with no hope of release. You have no idea how lucky you Dark-Hunters are that in the back of your mind is always the knowledge that one day you might go free again. You still have your hope."

Danger's throat drew tight at his words. He had been one of them once. He was the whole reason they had an out clause at all. If not for him, Artemis would never have made provisions for the rest of them. How awful to know that you had given such an incredible gift to others that was now forbidden to you. "I'm sorry for the way I treated you."

He looked confused by her apology.

"You should have told me you were a former Dark-Hunter."

"Why does it matter?"

"It matters," she said, lightly stroking his arm. "If you're telling me the truth and I'm sure that you are, then I know Stryker was lying."

His face went pale at the mention of the Daimon's name. "Stryker? The Daimon?"

"You know him?"

Alexion cursed. He looked up at the ceiling. "Acheron! If you can hear me at all, get your ass here right now, boss. We've got a serious problem."

When nothing happened, he cursed again. "Acheron!"

"What is going on?" Danger asked.

Alexion looked ill. "I don't even know where to begin explaining to you how fucked we are if Stryker is here and Acheron isn't."

"He's just a Daimon."

"No," he said, in a deep warning tone, "he's a god, a very vicious one who hates Acheron with an unreasoning mind."

Now that didn't sound promising at all. Fear swelled inside her. If someone as powerful as Alexion was afraid of this guy, then there was definitely something to fear. "Are you serious?"

"Do I look like I'm kidding?"

No, he looked all too earnest and that left her cursing too.

Alexion shook his head like someone trying to shake off an annoying insect. "Simi," he snapped. "Stop watching me and go get *akri*. I need him."

Barely five seconds later, Danger heard a voice that made her sigh in relief.

"Danger? Alexion?" Acheron said from her hallway.

"Thank goodness," she said, moving toward the door.

"No!" Alexion snapped as she reached for the knob. He ran at her and knocked her back at the same time the door splintered. Pieces of it rained all over the room.

Danger's eyes widened in numbed terror as she saw what appeared to be a demon of some sort entering the room. Completely bare except for a small black loincloth, it had deep, dark green skin marbled with black. Probably no taller than four feet, it flew into the room with a pair of large black, oily-looking wings. It held glowing yellow eyes that stared at them with open hatred. The dual set of fangs flashed as it hissed at Alexion.

Danger gulped. "Please tell me that's the Simi person you've been calling."

The creature arced toward the ceiling as if it were preparing to swoop down and attack them.

Alexion's green gaze mirrored the horror she felt. When he spoke, the words went through her like hot shrapnel. "It's definitely not Simi."

10

Alexion stared in complete stupefaction of the Charonte demon as it flew at them. Where the hell had it come from? Simi was supposed to be the last of her kind, and yet there was no denying that this demon was a Charonte. Nothing else on this earth or beyond looked like *that*.

"What is it?"

He didn't respond to Danger's question as he moved away from her to keep the demon's attention on him. *"Qui'esta rah-pah?"* he asked the demon, wanting to know where it had come from.

Pausing momentarily, the demon showed its own surprise that Alexion spoke its native language. But that didn't stop him from attacking.

Before Alexion could move, it dove down, seized him by his throat, and slung him to the floor. He hit the ground so hard that had he been human, every bone in his body would have shattered.

The demon tore at him with its claws. Alexion brought his leg up to kick the demon off.

It didn't work.

He flashed away from it, but somehow the demon anticipated the action, and when he reappeared, it grabbed him again. This time it slammed him facedown on the floor. His teeth rattled as the demon seized him by the hair.

From the corner of his eye, he saw Danger grab a sword that she had hidden beneath her sofa.

"Stay back!" he shouted an instant too late. The demon caught her with his tail and knocked her off her feet. There was no way to win a fight with a Charonte. Not unless you were a god; and though Alexion could call upon Acheron's powers, they weren't really his.

That left him with one serious disadvantage.

The demon rolled with him. Alexion flashed out again only to have the demon seize him while he was invisible.

Give it up, Lex. The damned thing can obviously see you transmutate. Damn.

He punched at the demon, who didn't feel his blows at all. But Alexion did. His hand throbbed as if it were broken. The demon laughed at him as it grabbed him up, dropped him to the ground, and slammed his head painfully against the floor. It felt as if his brains really did rattle in his skull. He could taste the blood in his mouth, feel it running from his nose.

If he didn't get the demon off him soon, it would kill him. And this time, Acheron wouldn't be able to bring him back.

Alexion tried to call up the force field to block his blows. It was less effective than a flyswatter against a rhino. No wonder the Greek gods lived in fear of this species. They were horrifyingly powerful. The only real question was, how did the Atlantean gods ever subjugate them?

"Get off me, you lard-ass, halitosis, flea-infested horror-movie reject," he snarled in Charonte.

That succeeded in another head slam to the floor. The Charonte pulled back and wrapped itself around him like a boa constrictor. And much like the snake, he knew this was its final move before it tore him apart and ended his existence.

Alexion tried to pull its arms away.

Yeah, that's going to work. Why not spit at him while you're at it?

What he needed was Simi.

But in lieu of that . . .

He was pretty much screwed.

Danger was terrified as she watched the demon maul Alexion while Alexion was helpless against it. Until this moment, she hadn't even known he could bleed. It was frightening to see something do that much damage to someone she'd foolishly assumed was invincible.

She reached for her sword.

The demon let go of Alexion to lunge at her. She grabbed the sword and plunged it deep into the demon at the same time Alexion shouted, "No!"

She quickly figured out why he would say that when the demon snatched the sword out of her hands, removed it from his body, then went after her with it.

She braced herself to fight and die, but just as the demon reached her, Alexion rushed it and knocked it back. The two of them spun away from her.

"*Protula akri gonatizum, vlaza!*"

She had no idea what those words meant, but the demon immediately released him. To her utter shock, it actually dropped down to one knee, crossed its arms over its chest, and bowed its head reverently.

"Whoa," she breathed, in awe of what had just quelled the unstoppable. "What did you say?"

He didn't answer as he gently took her arm and led her toward the door. He wiped his hand against his split lip and bloodied nose, and hurried her through the house.

"What are we doing?" she asked.

"Getting the hell out of here while we're able," he whispered.

"But it stopped."

"Yeah, I stunned him with a command I'm sure he doesn't hear much. The thing is, I'm not the one who actually has the power to make him obey me, and I'm not sure how long it will take him to realize that. Therefore I vote we blow Dodge before that demon breaks us into pieces."

Fleeing sounded good to her. She looked back over her shoulder to make sure it wasn't following them through her house. "What was that thing?"

"It's a Charonte demon."

"A what?"

He led her to the garage and opened the door to her merlot-red BMW Z4. "Get in."

She stiffened at his commanding tone. No one told her what to do.

No one.

"Don't order me around."

He gave her a bland stare. "Fine. Then stay and fight him on your own. I'm out of here."

She glared her irritation at Alexion before she complied with his order. Yeah, if the demon could do that to him . . . Well, if she wanted her face rearranged, she'd call a surgeon.

At least then she'd be unconscious for the worst of it.

It wasn't until he joined her in the car that a thought occurred to her. "Do you know how to drive?"

He answered her by starting her car without keys and backing it out. Her garage door opened in record time. Alexion did an impeccable J-turn in her driveway, then raced them down the street.

"I guess you do," she said quietly. He handled the car like a pro. "So, Magellan, where are we going?"

"Away. I'm open to any location, so long as it doesn't involve returning to your house while Wart-Head is there."

She couldn't agree more. "How long do you think the demon will wait before it comes after us?"

"I have no idea. It could depend on who's pulling his chain or what his orders were. Let us hope that time has no meaning to him and he stays there a few centuries."

"I don't know about that. It is my house, you know? I'd like to return to it in a day or two. You don't really think he'll still be there for days, or God forbid, longer, do you?"

Alexion expelled a tired breath. "I don't know. I really don't."

Great. She now had an image of her house looking like Mrs. Haversham's from Dickens's *Great Expectations*—complete with cobwebs and running mice—once she returned to it. She shivered. "Will you at least tell me what you said to him to make him stop attacking you?"

He gave her a wry grin that was strangely becoming on him. "Basically, I said, 'Bow down before your lord and master, slime-ball.'"

She laughed. Only Alexion would try that one. "What language did you use? I've never heard anything like that before."

"Atlantean."

That didn't make sense. He'd admitted to being an ancient Greek, not an Atlantean. "How do you speak the language of a country that was long gone before you were born?"

He gave a low laugh. "I live with Acheron. It's about all he speaks when he's at home."

"Really?"

He nodded.

Wow. She'd love to hear a conversation in Atlantean. The words were odd, but there was a wonderful lyrical quality to the language that was extremely musical.

But she had much more important things to think about than a long-dead language. Such as evicting the demon from her house. She just hoped he didn't have any friends who wanted to come and party in her living room while using her and Alexion as pogo sticks. "Do you think there are any more of them?"

"I don't know. I thought Simi was the last of them. It's what Acheron was told and it's what he told me. Apparently someone lied."

"Simi? The imaginary friend you've been talking to is one of those scaly, nasty things?"

"No," he said in an offended tone. "Simi's precious. She's beautiful . . ." He paused before adding, "In a very demon kind of way."

"Yeah," she said, her voice laden with incredulity. "Does she slam your head against the floor too?"

"Not intentionally . . . much. She just forgets how strong she is sometimes."

"Uh-huh. I think she damaged your brain one of the times she slammed your head."

He glared menacingly at her, and when he spoke, his tone was defensive and angry. "Simi is like a daughter to me, so I expect you to show some respect when you talk about her."

She held her hands up in mock surrender. "Fine, if you want to claim a scaly demon as a daughter, that's your business. In the meantime, any idea on how to kill one of those?"

He shook his head. "The only way I know to kill one is to use an Atlantean dagger."

"Where do we find one of those?"

His grip tightened on the wheel as he drove. "We don't. Acheron destroyed them all to make sure no one could hurt Simi."

"Well, that was mighty insightful of him, Yorick. What about the other demons who want to play basketball with your skull? Didn't he ever think he should keep a dagger handy, just in case?"

"It wasn't worth the risk to him of someone hurting Simi. Besides, Acheron can kill them without a dagger."

Well, that would be helpful if Acheron were here, but as it stood . . . "Lucille certainly picked a fine time to leave us, didn't he? I just wish our only problem was four hungry children and a crop in the field."

Alexion slowed the car as he turned his head to grimace at her. "You know, your sarcasm isn't helping any more than your bizarre and scattered references to literature and bad country songs."

"Not true, it's helping me maintain a calm façade that I most definitely do not feel."

"Well, it's starting to piss me off."

"Ooo," she breathed, "you almost scare me when you say that."

He growled at her as he whipped the car onto the highway that led toward Aberdeen.

"Where have you decided to take us?"

"I'm here to see Kyros so I figure there's no time like the present."

She supposed, but there was one important fact he was over-looking. "Kyros is most likely going to freak."

"Probably. I'm hoping to shock some sense into him." He glanced over at her. "You were telling me about Stryker before our rude demon interruption. Care to finish that discussion?"

Danger opened her glove box to pull out her pack of travel

tissues. She grabbed two, then gently used them to blot the blood that was still around Alexion's nose.

He gave her an odd frown before he took the tissue himself to wipe his face clean. There was something almost boyishly charming about the way he moved. It amazed her that he'd taken such a beating and sucked it up without a single complaint.

No matter what he said, it had to hurt badly.

Feeling for him, she ran her hand through his hair, brushing it back from his cheek. He didn't say anything, but the look on his face showed that he was touched by her tenderness.

Awkwardness consumed her. She dropped her hand away and returned to their conversation. "There's not much to tell," she said as she closed the glove box. "He showed up claiming to be Acheron's brother."

Alexion burst out laughing.

"Don't laugh," she said, offended that he was kind of laughing at her since she had briefly bought into the idea of them being related. "He's got the same black hair and swirling silver eyes like Ash does. Damned if he doesn't favor Acheron. A lot."

"No he doesn't. Trust me."

"Then why do they have the same eyes?"

"They don't. Their eyes are very different. Acheron was born with his. Stryker was given his after he scorned his father, Apollo."

She scowled. "How do you know that?"

He shrugged. "I live with a sfora, an orb that can tell me anything that happens here in the human realm. Not to mention, Simi is a font of information about what happens in Kalosis—the realm where—"

"Stryker is from. He mentioned that to me. So you're telling me that Ash isn't his brother?"

"Hell, no. Only in Stryker's dreams. Trust me." Alexion grew silent as he considered her words. He slid the tissue into his pocket as he continued to drive them down the dark highway. "So why is Stryker lying to Kyros? For that matter, what the hell is he even doing here? It's not like him to bother with something like this. He normally takes on Acheron directly."

She hoped that was rhetorical. "I don't know. But he has Kyros sold completely on the idea. For a time, he had me too."

Alexion let out a disgusted breath. "You didn't know better, but Kyros should." A muscle worked in his jaw while he kept his gaze focused on the road. "Well, whatever Stryker's up to, it's not good. And if he's the one unleashing and commanding that Charonte back there, we're in real trouble."

"You think?"

He shook his head. "Sarcasm aside, you have no idea how much power Stryker wields. You think I'm here to kill you? At least I take no joy in it. Stryker lives to torture people. Last time he was out of his hole, he had a Spathi Daimon possess a Dark-Hunter and they wreaked havoc all over New Orleans."

"What's a Spathi?" she asked. That was one term she'd never heard before.

"They're the ancient warrior class of Daimons who have been around for hundreds, if not thousands, of years. And in that time, they've learned to be seriously pissed off. Unlike the younger Daimons you're used to fighting, these guys don't run away. They run toward you."

"Oh, goodie. It just gets better and better. A ticked-off demigod, a demon, and now warrior Daimons out to possess and kill us. Anything else you need to warn me about?"

"Yeah. Can the sarcasm before I decide I don't need a guide after all."

Stryker glared at the Charonte who stood before him. He and Trates had been in the great hall of Kalosis, drinking Apollite blood from their goblets as they celebrated the demise of the Alexion.

At least until the demon had returned with news Stryker didn't want to hear. Trates had stepped back in expectation of Stryker's wrath, which was already simmering to a boil as he came to his feet to confront the demon.

"What do you mean, you let him go?"

Caradoc's pupils spiraled as they narrowed on Stryker. "Watch your tone with me, Daimon," he said in that strange singsongy accent that his kind held. "You are not fit for me to blow my nose on your weak tissue. I only agreed to this because you said you could liberate me from the goddess. You did not tell me that you were sending me after another of her kind."

Stryker went cold with those words. "What do you mean, another of *her* kind?"

"That was no man you sent me to, but rather something else. He spoke my language and he speaks Atlantean. He knew the command the Atlantean gods gave to mine to control us. No human knows those words. Only the gods do."

He scoffed at the demon. "The Alexion is not a god. Like you, he's only a servant."

"He did not speak as a servant," Caradoc argued. "Nor did he shatter as a human should have. I dealt him death blows and still he fought."

Stryker snarled at him, then stepped back as the demon moved toward him. Like it or not, he knew that if it came down to a fight, the Charonte would win.

"You didn't have to obey him. I promise you. He is not a god and is incapable of harming you."

Caradoc tilted his head as if digesting that. Finally, he shook his head. "I will not go for him again. The risk far outweighs the possible benefit. The goddess would kill me if I harmed one of her family. Even from here, she would hunt me down and assassinate my entire existence. Find another fool for your errand."

The demon tucked his wings around his body and walked arrogantly from the room.

Stryker cursed. He truly hated those things. They disgusted him even more than the humans did.

One day, he would destroy both races.

"What do we do now?" Trates asked.

"Fetch Xirena."

Trates laughed nervously at the command. "Xirena? Why? She's the fiercest of the Charontes. She barely takes direction from Apollymi, never mind one of us. I don't think anyone can control her."

Stryker smiled slowly. "I know. That's why I want her. She won't be afraid of a mere servant. She'll come back with his heart for me and she won't care what Apollymi thinks."

11

Well, the trip to Kyros's house was a complete wash. He wasn't home and his Squire didn't want to let them in until Kyros returned. Danger sighed as they stood on the wraparound porch of Kyros's blue and white antebellum mansion.

Aberdeen was quiet tonight, with a little breeze whispering around them through the large oaks that flanked the white wooden steps. The old Mississippi town had a very special charm to it that was indicative of a town lost in a time warp. Even the downtown area, where the sidewalks were covered with a metal awning, harkened back several decades.

Danger was particularly fond of the small Catholic church, which had a distinctly old world feel to it. She really loved this town. It was a hidden historical jewel that most people didn't even know existed.

Alexion looked strangely out of place with his urban-chic of a black turtleneck—which was no longer torn from the dagger toss—his black wool slacks, and white cashmere coat. He honestly looked as if he'd just stepped off a runway in Milan. He was so incredibly masculine . . . so much so that he was downright edible.

What was it about him? If he could bottle that sexual attraction, he'd be richer than Bill Gates.

You've got much more important things to think about than what he'd look like naked.

True, but there was something about him that just made her want to take a bite out of him and it was starting to really irritate her. She wanted herself focused and detached—her normal state of functionality.

"What do we do now?" she asked, trying to distract herself. "Wait here for him?"

"No, it could be hours before he returns. I think we should patrol. If the Daimons are in league with Kyros, then they'll be hunting and feeding tonight. Where's the closest population center for them to draw from?"

Danger thought about it for a minute. Tupelo was really spread out, and though there were a few clubs that the Daimons would occasionally stalk, there really wasn't much Daimon activity in her neck of the woods. Not like there was in other areas of Mississippi, such as the coast, Tunica, and various college towns—

which was why there were six Dark-Hunters in the Golden Tri-angle area of Mississippi where Kyros was stationed.

"There are two colleges they hit a lot. The W, which is the Mississippi University for Women in Columbus, and MSU in Starkville."

"How far away are they?"

"Not very. Columbus is about half an hour. Starkville an-other fifteen, twenty minutes from there."

He nodded as if he were considering the information. "Which school is larger?"

She gave him a teasing look. "I thought you had a mystical orb that could tell you these things?"

He narrowed his eyes at her, letting her know he didn't find her ribbing humorous.

"Lighten up," she said with a smile. "Starkville. It has over fifteen thousand students in residence. The Daimons love to party there with the co-eds. Kyros, Squid, and Rafael are assigned to it. Tyrell, Marco, and Ephani are in Columbus."

Alexion indicated the car with a tilt of his head. "Then that's probably where we should start. With any luck, Kyros might be there tonight." He headed down the steps.

Danger followed him, trying not to notice the fact that he had a killer walk. In more ways than one. It was predatorial and deadly. The kind of walk that women would stop to stare at and admire.

When he went to the passenger side of the car to get in, she gave him a puzzled stare. "What, no hocus-pocus this time? You're not going to get in and start driving away?"

"I don't know the way."

She was rather stunned he admitted that. It made him seem

almost human. He'd been so larger than life up until now that she assumed he could do just about anything. "You knew how to get here without my help."

"I cheated. There were signs along the road, and once we were in Aberdeen, it wasn't hard to find this house since it's right off the main stretch. I recognized the outside of it from the sfora. But I didn't see any road signs for Columbus or Starkville."

Danger laughed. She liked a man who was honest . . . and relatively normal. "Okay. OnStar is here and you're covered. Get in."

She got into the driver's seat and belted herself in while he joined her. She went to start the car, only to realize that in their haste to leave the Charonte, she'd forgotten her keys. "Um, a little help here, please?"

He frowned, then smiled. "Sure."

The car started.

She shook her head as she put it in gear. "You know, as handy as that power is, it could also get you arrested."

The smile he gave her warmed her all the way to her toes. Not to mention she loved the way he smelled . . . like fresh soap and all man.

"Then I'll be careful of whose motor I start," he said in a devilish tone, indicating that he meant the double entendre she inferred.

"I wish," she whispered under her breath as she backed out of the driveway. She really wished he wasn't starting hers all the time. It was hard to stay on track when her libido was literally drooling in his presence.

At least in the driver's seat she had more to focus on than how much she'd like to take him out of those clothes for a test-drive.

Jeez, Danger, stop with the bad car analogies and clichés. You're acting like a slut-puppy, panting after him.

It was true, but she couldn't seem to help herself. He was compelling.

Clearing her throat, she forced her thoughts back to business. "Is there any magical way you can pinpoint where Kyros is right now?"

"I wish, but no. Not without the sfora."

"Why didn't you bring it with you?"

He sighed before he answered. "It's forbidden. It could be very destructive for something that powerful to fall into the wrong hands."

"You think?"

Alexion shook his head and forced himself not to laugh. The last thing he wanted was to encourage her. She had to be the most sarcastic human to ever live. But he found her strangely entertaining.

More than that, he found her invigorating. She was such a welcome change from the monotony that made up his regular life. His world was without color or emotion. It was cold and lonely. She, on the other hand, was vibrant and warm. He wished he could have a part of her to take back to Katoteros with him.

But it could never be.

All too soon, he would return to what he'd been.

And she wouldn't even know that she'd ever met him. He wouldn't even be a faint memory of a dream. All knowledge of the time they were together would be removed from her mind.

But he would remember, and he would miss her always. Strange how that had never happened before. He thought of the Dark-

Hunter men he'd spent time with in the past while he judged the others, but there was no regret in not keeping in touch with them.

He'd only just met Danger and already he knew he'd miss her. How peculiar.

He watched as she handled the car with total precision. For the first time ever, he found himself completely curious about her.

What did she like? What did she hate?

Normally, he asked no personal questions of anyone. After living so long with Acheron, he knew the futility of it. Not to mention, he didn't like getting to know someone he'd have to leave and never see again.

Don't get personal. It would be a mistake of grand proportions.

Still he couldn't listen. "Do you like being a Dark-Hunter?" he asked her before he could stop himself.

Her answer was automatic. "Most days."

"And on the others?" *Stop it.* But that was easier thought than done. He really did want to know what she thought about everything.

She gave him a winsome smile that made his groin jerk in reaction. She was truly lovely and it wasn't just her looks. There was something infectious about her. It drew him in, making him want something he knew he couldn't have.

"Like with any life," she said, "some days are wonderful and some stink. It gets really lonely late at night when there's really no one around. Sometimes you wonder if you made the right choice. If maybe you reacted in anger too soon and made a pact you shouldn't have. I don't know. I wasn't completely dead long enough to remember it or to know if death would be preferable to this life, so maybe I did choose rightly."

She glanced at him. "So, Mr. All-Knowledge, you want to clue me in on what the alternative is like? Do you remember being dead?"

He thought it over. "Yeah, I do. When you're not a Shade, it's peaceful. I always thought as a mortal man that I'd spend eternity in the Elysian Fields with my family gathered around me."

"So what made you go with Artemis instead?"

The old pain lanced through him. It was weird that after so many centuries it would still hurt to remember the wife he'd once loved so much and the callous way she'd allowed him to die. But as Acheron so often said, there were some wounds that not even time could heal. Humans learned from their pain. It was a necessary evil for growth.

Yeah, right. He sometimes wondered if Acheron was a sadist or masochist. But he knew better. Acheron understood pain in a way very few did. Like Alexion, he lived with it constantly and if he could he'd banish it forever.

He looked at Danger, and watched as the streetlights illuminated her fragile face. With the exception of Kyros, Brax, and Acheron, no one knew much more about him than his name. He was a vague legend who was held up as the first of their crew to become a Shade.

He was essentially their bogeyman. An example of what happened if the wrong person tried to restore their soul back into their body. But that was the extent of what they'd been told.

They knew nothing about the shame of his trust in his wife, or the fact she'd had a lover. They knew nothing about the fact that he'd been a blind, trusting fool.

Kyros and Brax had held their silence on the matter all these centuries. It was one of the reasons why Alexion had wanted to come back and save Kyros if he could.

Even in death, the man had been his friend.

Alexion took a deep breath before he spoke. "The first time I died, I was murdered," he said simply. "Like you, betrayed by someone I trusted."

Her brow wrinkled in sympathetic pain. "Who killed you?"

"My wife's lover."

She grimaced. "Ouch."

"Yeah."

"And then your wife dropped the medallion instead of freeing your soul," she said, her voice filled with anger. "I can't believe she'd do that to you."

Alexion appreciated her rage on his behalf. "Hell of a way to find out that the children you thought were yours weren't."

To his amazement, she reached over and placed her hand soothingly against his. The unexpected kindness of that single action sent chills over him. It meant a lot to him that she treated him like a normal man when they both knew he wasn't. "I'm really sorry."

He covered her hand with his other one and gave a light squeeze. The delicate bones under her skin belied the strength he knew she carried within her.

"Thanks. I'm sorry your husband was a dirtbag."

Danger laughed at his unexpected use of that slang word. Against her will, she felt her guard softening toward him. It'd been too long since she'd spent time with a man chatting like this. Most of the people she talked to were other female Dark-Hunters, and all of them she'd known for decades. This was a nice change of pace. "Did you go back and kill your wife?"

"No." He gave a short, bitter laugh. "I have to say, it was truly one of the finer moments of my life . . . or death. I felt like a complete and utter asshole, lying there, looking at her as she watched me die. There wasn't even pity or the smallest amount of regret in her eyes. If anything, she was glad to see me go."

Poor guy. She knew firsthand that it was not only painful but humiliating to have misjudged someone so badly. "So what happened to her?"

One corner of his mouth quirked up in wry humor. "Acheron turned her to stone. She's now a statue that stands in the hallway outside my room."

Danger widened her eyes. "Are you serious?"

"Absolutely. I blow her a sarcastic kiss every morning when I walk past her."

"Man," she said, shaking her head, "that's cold."

"You think so?"

"Honestly? Not at all. I'd have been much crueler."

Alexion was curious as to what would be a worse punishment than the one he had meted out for her. "How so?"

"I'd have put her in a park somewhere so the birds could crap all over her."

He laughed. Okay, that really would be much worse. "Remind me to stay on your good side."

"Yeah, well, my mother used to have a saying, 'hell hath no fury as a woman angered.'"

"I thought it was 'as a woman scorned.'"

"Angered, scorned, either one. I come from a long line of vengeful women. My grandmother would have given Madame Defarge a run for her money any day."

He nodded. "Then I'll make sure I don't tweak that portion of your personality. The gods know I've had my fill of vengeful women."

Danger sighed at his light tone about a matter she was sure he didn't find amusing. In fact, his words made her heart catch. "I guess you have."

She squeezed his hand. "So what happened to the kids after Ash turned their mother into stone?"

"Acheron found them a good home. He's not the type of person who would leave a child to suffer over something he did."

"Yeah, I've noticed that about him."

Neither of them spoke again while they rode the rest of the way to the MSU campus. It was an overcast night without much moonlight. But what little light there was reflected against the trees, forming eerie, monsterlike shadows.

Danger had always liked to drive at night. There was something very peaceful about it. Well, except for when the occasional deer turned suicidal and decided to play "chicken" with her on the highway. That she could leave behind.

But at least she didn't have to worry about that in Starkville. It'd grown so much over the last few years that until they headed back toward Tupelo, deer dodgers wouldn't be a problem.

Alexion looked out the car window as Danger drove them past the sorority houses toward central campus. It looked as if a party of some sort were going on at one house. He could see cars parked in the lot with kids hanging out of the windows while others leaned up against the frame, talking to the ones inside. Groups of college students were milling about on the porch and in the yard while more could be seen inside, dancing.

"Look at them," he said quietly. "Do you remember being human and that age?"

She glanced over at the partying co-eds. "Yeah, I do. At that time in my life, I thought I was going to be one of the greatest actresses in France, like my mother. I thought Michel and I would retire wealthy, to the countryside, to raise our multitude of children and to watch our grandchildren play." She sighed as if the memory were too painful to dwell on for long. "What about you?"

Alexion let his mind drift back all those countless centuries ago. It wasn't something he did often, for many reasons. But old dreams never really died. They were always there, living as regrets for what might have been.

"I wanted to retire from the army. I never really wanted to join in the first place. But my father insisted on it. When they came to our village for boys, he grabbed my older brother and I, and literally threw us at the recruiters. He wanted us to be more than just simple farmers trying to eke out a living from a stingy soil that would rather see us starved than fed. He thought a soldier's calling would be our chance for a much better life."

"What happened to your brother?"

Alexion paused as he remembered Darius's face. His brother had been full of life and had never wanted anything more than to be a farmer with a good wife by his side. All he'd ever talked about was going home again, seeing the cattle and tending the fields.

His heart ached at what had happened to both of them. "He died about a year before I did. I would have, too, had I not been in a regiment with Kyros. For some reason I never understood, he took me under his wing."

"He was older?"

"By only three years, but at the time it seemed like he was an adult while I was just a terrified kid."

Danger could hear the admiration in his voice. It was obvious he'd once worshiped his friend. No wonder he wanted to save him.

"The other boys didn't think much of me," he confided. "Like Kyros, they came from a long line of soldiers and thought that I should go back to the farm. They didn't want to waste time training or supplying someone they figured would die soon anyway. Better to save the food for someone who could earn his keep."

She didn't need his sfora to see how they'd made their displeasure known. Nine thousand years later, she could still hear the pain in his voice.

"But you hung in there."

"As Nietzsche said, 'that which doesn't kill you—'"

"Will only require brief hospitalization. And if you're a Dark-Hunter, just a good day's sleep."

Alexion laughed at her humor. She definitely had a unique way of looking at things.

He returned his attention to the campus and to the cars that sped past them with stereos thumping and kids screaming and laughing just from the sheer joy of being alive.

How he envied them. With the exception of Danger, who had an incredible knack for poking his sore spots, he normally felt nothing at all. "You have no idea just how amazing this world is. It hasn't really changed all that much since your birth, but mine . . ."

"Yeah, you're from what, the Bronze Age?"

Alexion snorted. "No, I predate even that. We were so primitive, we really should have had dinosaurs to ride."

"Primitive how?"

Inwardly, he cringed at the memories of how his people had lived, what they had been forced to endure just to survive. It had been survival in its purest, rawest form. "Modern" man had no idea how good they had it.

"We had no swords, no real metals, no pottery. Our daggers and spear points were made of stone that we chipped with our own hands until our hands were bloody and bruised from it. Our armor was made of leather from the hides of the animals we killed for food. We boiled and shaped it ourselves. We had no government to speak of, no real laws. If you got screwed over, there was no one to appeal to. You either handled it yourself or you let it go."

He sighed at the harsh memories of his human life. "Hell, there were no judges, police, or politicians. We only two classes of people: the farmers who fed themselves and the soldiers who protected the farmers from those who wanted to steal their food and kill them. That was it."

"You didn't have priests?"

"We had one. He'd been a farmer who'd lost the use of his right hand in a fire. Since he couldn't support himself, he interpreted signs and the farmers fed him for it."

Danger frowned as she tried to imagine the world he described. And she had thought her life without a proper toilet was primitive. Suddenly her eighteenth-century world looked very high tech indeed.

"My people never dreamed of a world like this," Alexion continued. "Of having so much without backbreaking, debilitating work. And yet for all the physical improvements, people are still people. They're killing each other to get more or to prove a point only the killer understands. Still brutalizing and torturing each other over things that in another hundred years won't even matter."

Danger's eyes teared as his words struck a particular chord in her own heart. "Tell me about it. Despite all the changes in the twenty-first century, it seems that the rich are still rich and the poor are still poor. There are still countless people in the world who starve every day, and it's not because they're anorexic or fasting. It's because they can't afford food while the rich waste money all the time on trivial things. Every time I hear about famine, I ask myself if we've learned nothing from the past—from the revolutions, all the wars. All they did was ruin thousands of lives."

"*Chronia apostraph, anthrice mi achi.*"

She frowned. "What is that?"

"It's Atlantean. Something Acheron says a lot. Roughly translated, it means 'time moves on, people do not.'"

Danger thought about that. It was very true and very Ash-like. "Can you imagine the world he must have known? As backward as yours—"

"His world was extremely advanced," he said, interrupting her. "The Atlanteans most definitely weren't in the stone age."

"What do you mean?"

"The world he was born into was amazingly high tech. They had carriages of sorts, medicine, metalworking, you name it. The Greece and Atlantis he knew were several millennia ahead of their time."

"Then what happened that it was all lost?"

"Succinctly put, the wrath of a goddess. Atlantis was swept into the sea, not by natural means, but by the anger of a woman who wanted vengeance on all of them. She ravished her own continent and people, then moved across Greece, throwing them all back into the dinosaur age."

"Why?"

He let out a tired breath. "They took something from her that she wanted back."

Danger nodded as she suddenly understood. "They took her child."

He looked stunned that she had jumped to that conclusion. "How did you know that?"

"I'm a woman and that is pretty much the only thing that would cause a woman to destroy her own people."

He didn't comment. In fact, he seemed to be extremely uncomfortable about the turn their conversation was taking. If she didn't know better, she would think he was hiding something from her.

Suddenly, Alexion went rigid in the seat beside her.

"What's wrong?" she asked.

"Turn right."

His tone told her it was urgent. Deciding not to argue, Danger turned off Creelman Street to the small road that ran in front of McCarthy Gym. At the end of the road was a series of parking lots.

"Stop the car."

As soon as she did, the car's engine turned off on its own and Alexion was out of the passenger side, headed toward the Holmes building. Danger immediately ran after him.

She caught up to him just behind the gym. As she slowed down, her heart hammered at what she saw there.

Deep in the shadows, Kyros was coming to his feet over the body of what appeared to have been Marco, a Dark-Hunter who was from the Basque region of France.

"What happened, Kyros?" she asked, her tone breathless from her sprint.

She knew Kyros hadn't killed Marco. No Dark-Hunter could harm another. Whatever blow or wound one Dark-Hunter gave to another, the one who gave it felt the pain ten times greater than the one who received it.

Had Kyros killed Marco, he would be dead too.

Kyros turned slowly to face her. He looked pale and shaken. "Don't mess with me, Danger. Not tonight."

"Kyros?"

His head snapped toward Alexion. If she thought he'd been pale before, it was nothing compared to what he looked like now. He stared at Alexion as if he were seeing a ghost . . . and that's exactly what he was doing.

"Ias?"

Alexion walked toward him slowly. "I have to talk to you, brother."

She saw Kyros's gaze narrow as he took in Alexion's white coat.

"You?" he asked, his voice disgusted and yet she heard a note of hurt beneath it. "You're Acheron's right hand? You're the one who delivers his ultimatum?" He shook his head in disbelief. It's not possible. You're dead. You've been dead."

"No," Alexion said calmly, moving another step toward him. "I'm alive."

Kyros stepped back. "You're a Shade."

Alexion held his hand out to him. "I'm real. Take my hand, brother, and see for yourself."

Danger held her breath. Given his hostility, she half expected Kyros to attack Alexion.

But he didn't.

He reached his hand out methodically until he could shake Alexion's. But the instant he touched Alexion's hand, he let go and stumbled back.

She could tell that Kyros still didn't want to accept what was right before him.

"It's okay," Alexion said, as he moved another step closer to the angry, terrified Greek.

"Don't touch me!"

Alexion drew up short. She could see the pain in his eyes that Kyros's harsh words caused.

Kyros continued shaking his head as if he couldn't believe it. "It can't be you. You can't be Acheron's destroyer. You can't."

"I'm not his destroyer. I'm here to help you avoid making a fatal mistake. Whatever you do, you can't trust Stryker. He's lying to you. Believe me, Kyros. We were brothers once. You trusted me then."

Kyros's eyes snapped fire at his former friend. "That was nine thousand years ago. We were human."

Alexion searched his mind for the words it would take to make his friend believe him. But he could tell it wasn't working. There was too much anger and mistrust. It was as if Kyros were looking for a reason to hate him.

"C'mon, Kyros. Trust me."

"Fuck you."

"Then trust me," Danger said, moving nearer to Kyros. "You've known me for five years. You trusted me enough to introduce me to Stryker and let him spiel his bullshit about Acheron." She looked over at Alexion who stood with an anguished glint in his eyes. He wanted to save his friend and she wanted to help him. "I believe Alexion, Kyros. Completely. Stryker is lying to us. He wants you to die."

Kyros glared at Alexion. "I made myself sick over your death. Why didn't you ever tell me that you were alive and well? Why didn't Acheron?"

"Because I can't live in this world," Alexion explained in that same rational tone. "What would have been the point of telling you?"

Kyros returned the words with even more rage. "The point was that we were brothers. You owed it to me to let me know you were all right."

"Maybe I was wrong then, but I came here now to save you."

"Bullshit. This is just a game to you, isn't it?" Kyros looked up at the sky as if searching for something. "Are you watching this, Acheron? Fuck you, you lying bastard. How could you not have told me?"

Kyros started away from them.

Alexion grabbed his arm. "What happened to Marco?"

He shoved Alexion away from him. "What do you care? You were sent here to kill him anyway."

It was true. Because he'd killed the college student the night before, Marco was destined to die. "He'd crossed over to the point there was no way back for him, no reprieve. But you . . . there's still time. I can save you, Kyros. If you'll let me. Don't be stupid, *adelfos*."

Kyros curled his lip at him. "I don't want your damned help. I don't want anything from you."

Alexion fought his own temper down. He had to remain calm and rational to get through this. But really, what he wanted to do was shake Kyros for being so blind and stupid. "Acheron isn't a Daimon."

"Then what is he?"

Alexion looked away, unable to answer. Yet he was torn. Part of him wanted to betray Acheron and tell his friend the truth that he needed to hear to save his life.

But if he did that . . .

No, he owed Acheron too much to betray his trust.

"He is one of you," Alexion said with a calmness he didn't feel.

"Yeah, right," Kyros said sarcastically. "Then why can't *I* walk in daylight?"

He had to give him that. "Okay, so Acheron is a little different."

"A little? And what are you?"

"I'm a lot of different."

"And I'm a lot of pissed off." Kyros pushed past him and headed toward the parking lot.

Alexion closed his eyes as he debated what to do. What to say.

What would make Kyros listen to him?

Then suddenly he thought of something. "It wasn't your fault Liora killed me."

That succeeded in stopping Kyros's retreat. He froze in place.

"I should have told you she was a whore," he said without turn-ing around.

Alexion was grateful that he was at least talking to him in an almost civil tone. "I wouldn't have believed you. Ever. I would have hated you for trying to save me. Please, don't make my mistake, Kyros."

He turned to face him. "Don't worry," he said as his black gaze burned Alexion with its intensity. "I won't. Your mistake was that you wouldn't have believed your friend had he told you the truth. My mistake would be listening to my 'friend' now. . . . Then again, you're not my friend, are you? My friend died nine thou-sand years ago, and had he lived, he would have told me and not left me to live centuries with guilt over his death."

Kyros turned around and renewed his angry stride toward the parking lot.

"Kyros—"

"*Dialegomaiana o echeri*," Kyros said without even look-ing back.

"What language is that?" Danger asked.

"It's our native tongue."

"And what did he say?"

Alexion let out a disgusted breath. "Briefly put, 'talk to the hand.' "

She looked as deflated as he felt. "Should we follow him?"

"To do what? I can't beat sense into him, much as I would like to. The choice has to be his."

Damn fate for that. He hated free will at times. No wonder Acheron cursed it constantly. His boss was right, free will sucked.

His gaze went to Marco. The poor, hapless Dark-Hunter still had a dagger protruding from his chest, where someone, probably a Daimon, had stabbed him. Shaking his head in regret at the man's foolishness, Alexion went to the fallen Dark-Hunter and pulled the dagger free. Of course it wasn't the dagger that had killed him. His decapitated head lay a few feet away.

Danger moved to stand just behind him as she examined the body too. He could sense her revulsion, but like a trouper she kept herself calm and professional. "You don't think Kyros did that, do you?"

"He couldn't have."

"Then who?"

The voice that answered her question wasn't his and it came from the other side of the shadows. "Just your friendly neighborhood Daimon patrol."

Alexion leaned back ever so slightly so that he could see behind Danger.

There in the shadows was a group of six Daimons . . .

12

Danger's gaze narrowed angrily at the sound of the Daimons' taunting. How rare for the Daimons not to try and run away. Could they be the Spathis Alexion had mentioned?

Then again if they really had killed one Dark-Hunter already, they were probably drunk on their own power and looking to kill more.

"Oh, I so don't like you people," she growled.

"The feeling's entirely mutual," the lead Daimon said.

The Daimon glanced over to Marco's body. "We do nice work, don't we?"

She shrugged, unwilling to give them any sort of reward or praise for their barbarism, which brought back one too many nightmares from her human life. "Looks like he committed suicide to me. He probably took one look at your ugly face and went blind, so he decided it was better to be dead than have your heinous form be the last thing he'd seen."

Alexion actually laughed out loud at that.

The Daimon glowered at her. "I assure you he died screaming like a girl."

She looked over at Alexion and shook her head in disgust. "Oh, I am so offended by that. What is the deal with that sexist statement? I'm a female and I don't scream. But I've killed many a male Daimon who did."

Alexion didn't comment.

Danger turned back toward the Daimons, who were still eyeing her as if she were a main course. She was definitely going to beat the life out of them, but before she did, she had one question. "So why did you kill him?"

The Daimon shrugged. "He had a victim he didn't want to share. Seems he thought he could take the soul into his own body like we do. We thought turnabout was fair play so we staked him to free it. You know, Dark-Hunters don't burst apart when a soul is freed. Why is that?"

"We're not scum?"

Alexion laughed again.

She looked at him over her shoulder. "You're enjoying this whole thing way too much." She gestured toward the Daimons. "Keller said you could make them poof?"

"Normal Daimons, yes."

"And let me guess, these are Abby Normal kind of Daimons?"

He shook his head. "You watch way too many DVDs, and yes, they're Abby Normal." She was amazed he understood her reference to the movie *Young Frankenstein*.

"Oh, goodie," she said, wrinkling her nose in distaste. "And here I am without my favorite stake and why is that? Because the ugly winged demon from hell—literally—came after us." She looked back at the Daimons and sighed heavily. "Now we got these guys to fight. Well, at least they're not scaly."

"And they are blond," Alexion added. Danger found it amusing that he was adopting her light tone. "You like blonds."

"True, but after looking at them, I think my tastes just changed. I think I'd rather do the demon than one of them." Danger spun, grabbed the dagger out of Alexion's hands, then rushed the Daimons with it.

Alexion watched in awe as she took the Spathis on. She was an incredible fighter with more daring than skill. Not that she lacked skill by any means. She didn't. It was just that her daring outdistanced it by a long shot.

She cut one Daimon across the chest as she ducked a second one. Her smaller size gave her a distinct advantage over the much larger Daimons.

She stabbed one.

He burst into dust.

It was then she turned to face Alexion with a scowl. "You just gonna stand there and look impressed or are you actually going to help me with this little situation?"

He shrugged nonchalantly. "You seem to have it under control."

She glared at him as she jumped away from another attacking Daimon. She kicked him back. "I really hate men most nights," she mumbled.

It wasn't until one of the Daimons went for her back that Alexion rushed forward. He caught the Daimon with a fist to his jaw.

Danger twisted around like she was about to stab him. Alexion caught her hand, kissed her clenched fist, then pulled the dagger from her grip.

"I'll give this right back," he said, an instant before he plunged it into the Daimon. Golden powder shot all over him before it drifted to the ground.

He turned and then tossed the dagger into the chest of another Daimon who was about to attack Danger.

The Daimon froze mid-motion, mouthed the word "damn," then burst apart.

The last remaining Daimon ran.

Danger grabbed the dagger from the ground, then launched it at his back. It caught him dead between his shoulders. Like the others before him, he shattered into dust.

Alexion held his hand out for the dagger to return to him. It flew through the air until he had it firmly in his grasp.

Danger gave him a peeved stare. "You know, those parlor tricks would be much more impressive if they had actually helped me."

With a wry twist to his lips, he handed her the dagger. "I wanted to see what you had in you."

"Piss and vinegar. Next time you don't help me, I'll unleash it fully against you."

He had to admit that he loved seeing the fire in her eyes whenever she was angry. The passion pinkened her cheeks and made him wonder what she would look like naked beneath him. She would definitely be a wildcat and that made him smile even against his will.

What he wouldn't give for a taste of Danger.

"I don't find it funny," she said testily.

"Believe me, I don't find the idea of you getting hurt funny either."

"Then why are you smiling?"

"I'm smiling because you are absolutely beautiful."

Danger couldn't have been more stunned had he told her to take a flying jump off the Eiffel Tower. It'd been a long time since a man, especially one as handsome as Alexion, had complimented her. She'd almost forgotten the weird fluttering such a thing caused in the stomach. The little bit of embarrassment that was counterbalanced by a slice of pride and gratitude. "Thank you."

"You're welcome."

The weirdest part was, in that moment, she wanted to kiss him. Badly.

But that was nuts and she knew it.

He's not even human.

Neither are you.

Well, her mind had a point, but still . . . This was neither the time nor the place.

Alexion glanced at Marco, then off into the direction Kyros had fled. The familiar look of torment came back into his hazel-green eyes, as if he wanted to go after his friend. It was followed by a look of reservation that said he knew how futile that action would be.

"Give him time to think it over," she said gently, feeling for him. "He'll come around."

"And if he doesn't?"

He'd be dead, most likely by Alexion's hand. And as distasteful as she found that, she could only imagine how much more so he did. Therefore, it would only be cruel to point it out, and she had a feeling that Alexion had had enough cruelty in his life.

"Can't Ash tell you the outcome? I know he can see the future."

"Yes and no. Neither he nor I can see the future when it relates to us or to anyone close to us."

That didn't seem fair to her. What would be the point of seeing the future if you couldn't help the people closest to you? "It must stink to know everyone's future but your own."

He let out a tired breath. "You've no idea. It's actually cruel in my opinion. But then maybe it doesn't matter after all since futures can and do change. Something as simple as you're supposed to turn right down a street one day . . . in your bones you know it, and yet for reasons no one understands, you decide to debunk fate and go left. Now instead of meeting the spouse of your dreams and having a house full of kids, you get flattened by an ice-cream truck and spend the next five years in physical therapy recovering from the injuries; or worse, you die from it. And all because you exercised free will and turned the opposite way on a whim."

That was something to give her nightmares. It really didn't bear thinking on since it made her wonder where she had gone so tragically wrong with her own life. Was it fate or free will that had screwed her over?

"Now that's really morbid, Doc Sunshine. Thank you for that one."

He made a small face, as if he realized just how doom-and-gloom he'd been. "It can work in reverse too."

"Yeah, but I notice you didn't think of the positive one first. Freud would have a blast with you, wouldn't he?"

"Probably so," he said flippantly. "I'll have to ask him when I get back."

She paused at his words and what they signified. "You know Sigmund Freud?"

The grin he gave her was absolutely dazzling in its charm and beauty. "No, but I had you going there for a minute, didn't I?"

Danger shook her head. There was something so oddly infectious about him. She hated the thought that she could be charmed so easily, and yet he was doing it little by little.

"So what should we do with Marco?" she asked, returning to the matter at hand.

Alexion looked at the body. "There's not much to be done now."

Danger did a double take as she realized the body had already decomposed. She stared at the blank spot where he'd been lying just a few minutes ago. The only thing left to mark where he'd been was his clothes.

"*Mon Dieu,*" she breathed. "Do we all do that?"

Alexion's tone was emotionless. "All humans do eventually."

"Yeah," she said, her voice carrying the weight of anger that was building inside her at the thought of just evaporating like that. "But it usually takes more than five minutes."

"Not for a Dark-Hunter."

Danger continued to stare at the spot. It was highly disturbing. She wasn't even sure why. Only that it seemed a body as strong as theirs, which was immune to so much, shouldn't just crumble away in a matter of minutes.

The finality of the death hit her hard.

Alexion pulled her into his arms. Her first instinct was to push him away, but honestly, she needed his touch right now. She needed something to ground her and to keep her from panicking over a reality that had never hit her before.

Ultimate death.

No Artemis to bring them back. No heaven. Just total annihilation and desolate pain. She could be like that man Alexion had showed her earlier. Without hope. Without anything at all.

"It's all right, Danger," he said softly against the top of her head as he cradled her. "I don't know if it'll make you feel better, but he had started killing humans."

In a way it did, in a way it didn't. "I don't want to die like that, Alexion."

And then she realized something. . . .

He had. He'd died alone with the woman he'd loved dropping his soul and refusing to help him.

How could his wife have done such a thing? It was so cold. So callous.

Danger pulled back ever so slightly to look up at him. "Is that what happened to your body?"

He nodded. "It's why I don't have one now."

But he felt so real, so solid. "Then how can you be here to hold me?"

There was a tenderness in his eyes that fired her blood. He

might be a destroyer but he understood compassion, and she truly appreciated his showing it to her now when she needed it most.

"Acheron has a lot of powers and luckily reincarnation is one of them. This temporary body is identical to yours, except it really is indestructible. Cut my head off and I can still poof right back here."

That didn't make sense to her. "I don't understand. Then why were you afraid of the Charonte?"

He gave a nervous laugh. "The Charontes don't just destroy the body. They destroy the *ousia*."

"The what?"

He smoothed the hair back from her face as he explained it. "It's the part of us that exists beyond the body or the soul. The soul is our spiritual part. The *ousia* is what gives us our personality. It is our essence, our life force if you will. Without it, there's nothing left of us. It is the ultimate death, from which there is no return of any kind. A Charonte is one of the few things that can easily end what little existence I have left. And though my existence might suck a lot, I'll take it with all its drawbacks over total destruction any day."

She still didn't understand. "But if Acheron is so powerful that he can grant you a temporary body, why can't he give you a permanent one?"

Alexion grew quiet and took a step back.

His face had turned to stone again, letting her know that she had touched on a very sensitive subject. "C'mon, Alexion, spill it. There's something even weirder about you, isn't there? Something that scares you."

She could see it in his eyes.

He moved away from her, back toward the car. She went after him, not really expecting an answer.

But after a few seconds he said, "Acheron was young when he brought me back. At that time, he didn't have a full understanding of his powers, and the gods know Artemis wasn't forthcoming with instructions. If she'd had her way, he wouldn't have learned anything."

A bad feeling went through her. "So basically what you're saying is he screwed up with you."

He nodded without looking at her. "If I'd died even a hundred years later, it would have been a different story for me. But what was done to me is irreversible even for Acheron. I can never again be human or live as a man. There's nothing to be done for me. Ever."

He took that with remarkable dignity, but then he'd had a long time to get used to the idea. She, herself, would still be pissed off that Acheron had screwed her up. "I'm really sorry, Alexion."

"It's okay. At least he cared enough to save me. If he hadn't . . ." He glanced over to where Marco had been.

Crap. She didn't like the thought of him dying like that at all. She supposed he was right. What he had now was much better than the alternative.

Danger tilted her head to indicate the direction of the car. "Why don't we go get something to eat? I'm really hungry."

"Sure."

The car unlocked by itself the instant they drew near it. Danger shook her head at his powers. He was every bit as scary at times as Acheron.

She got into the car on the driver's side while he entered on the passenger's side.

"So what name would you rather I call you?" she asked as she headed out of the parking lot. "Ias or Alexion?"

He gave her a devilish grin that set fire to her hormones. "I would rather you call me 'lover.'" He wagged his brows playfully at her.

Danger rolled her eyes. Like all men with a one-track mind, he was incorrigible.

"Don't blame me," Alexion said in an almost offended tone. "I can't help it. You should see the way you fight. It really turned me on."

"Could you tell me how to turn you off?"

He snorted. "Go two hundred years without sex and then ask that question. There's not a shower cold enough." His gaze trailed over to the tennis courts they were passing where a handful of college students were playing. "Aren't co-eds supposed to be women of loose—"

She made a sound of disgust in the back of her throat. "Don't you even go there."

"Well, if you don't want me . . ."

She cut him a mischievous look of her own. "I never said *that,* now did I?"

13

Kyros entered his house, his hands still shaking. He couldn't believe what he'd seen tonight. What he'd heard. Marco had been
slain.

And Ias was alive.

Ias had been alive for all these centuries.

Rage and grief battled relief and happiness. He was so confused by his emotions that he didn't know what to feel or think.
Part of him wanted to embrace his old friend.

As men, they had been closer than mere brothers. There was
a special bond that came from entrusting your life to another

man's hands, a bond that came from him entrusting you with his. It was communal and unbreakable. They had shared that.

How many times had they fought together? Starved on the long marches to and from battle? When one had fallen from wounds, the other had stood over him and battled the attackers off until the fight ended. Then the one standing had rendered medical aid to the other.

Back to back, they had fought countless times, keeping one another safe.

He owed Ias more than could ever be repaid by coin or by deed. It was that part of himself that was ecstatic that Ias was alive.

But the other part of him was so betrayed, so hurt. How could Ias have survived and not told him?

How?

Why hadn't Acheron ever mentioned it? He more than any other knew just how much Ias's death had torn him apart. In the beginning, the loss of Ias had been more than he could bear. He'd felt so responsible. If he had told Ias about his wife, then his friend wouldn't have made the tragic mistake of thinking she loved him. But he'd known that knowledge would have destroyed Ias, who loved Liora more than anything else.

Even his own life had been forfeit because he'd kept silent. He'd died protecting Ias from Lycantes, who'd been Liora's lover, the first time Lycantes had gone for Ias.

Why didn't I ever tell him?

For centuries he had carried that guilt and second-guessing on his shoulders like Atlas. There had been very few nights over the last nine thousand years when remorse hadn't gnawed at him.

Every time a Dark-Hunter had talked about the possibility of going free, of having a lover drop the medallion that contained their soul before it was returned to them, he'd remembered his friend.

More than that, Ias had been the one who had given all the Dark-Hunters their out clause. Without Ias, Artemis, or Acheron or whoever had come up with it wouldn't have permitted them to regain their souls or go free. Ever.

But in spite of it all, Kyros knew one thing, Ias wouldn't lie to him. It wasn't in his friend to do such a thing. His friend had never been anything but honorable.

But was this Ias the same one who had been mortal?

"What are you doing?"

Kyros looked to see Stryker standing just inside the doorway of his office where he was headed. With a nonchalance he didn't feel, Kyros pushed past him and sat behind his carved mahogany desk in a burgundy leather chair. "I'm contemplating."

"Contemplating what?"

He pinned the Daimon with a murderous glare. "Did you know the destroyer was once my best friend?"

Stryker paused as those words hit him like cast stones. Now there was something he hadn't seen coming. He'd always wondered where the Alexion had come from.

But let's face it, Acheron wasn't really into sharing any kind of information with him, especially nothing Stryker might be able to use against him. That was the shame about enemies. They were ever tight-lipped.

But his mind whirled with this newfound knowledge. So the Alexion had once been human . . . and he had known Kyros. . . .

Good. He could work with this.

"You must be feeling very betrayed right now," Stryker said in a calculatedly sympathetic voice. "Did he say anything to you?"

"He said he came to save me from following *you*."

Stryker kept his face blank. He had to play this carefully if he were going to pull it back from the fire that was waiting to engulf it and ruin all his plans.

"Interesting."

So, the Alexion wanted to save Stryker's pawn from death. This could be extremely beneficial. The Alexion would think twice before he damned his friend to Shadedom and it would give Stryker a pawn to use against him. Surely the Alexion wouldn't kill the very man he'd come to save.

Oh, yeah, this was very good news indeed. "You do know he's lying to you, correct?"

Kyros shook his head as he leaned back in his chair. "I don't think so."

"Don't you?" Stryker asked as he moved forward to push aside the black leather pencil cup. He sat on a corner of the desk. "Use your head, Kyros. He claims to be your friend, but where has he been all these centuries?"

"He said he couldn't make contact."

"Couldn't or *wouldn't*?"

Kyros's eyes narrowed on him. "Just say what you're going to say, Stryker. I'm in no mood for your bullshit right now."

"Fine," he said, leaning forward to meet Kyros's gaze levelly. "What I have to say is this. If he really is your friend, where has he been all this time while you've been languishing in the backwoods of hell? How many times have you requested Acheron move you from Mississippi into an urban area where there is something going on other than a keg party? And how many times has your request gone unanswered?"

Kyros looked away from him. "Ash had his reasons."

The poor pathetic little fool. He had no idea what he was dealing with when it came to either Acheron or himself.

"Did he?" Stryker asked. "Or was it your *friend* who refused your request? Think about it, Kyros. Acheron is a busy man who doesn't have time to oversee all the thousands of Dark-Hunters out there that he has created to destroy us. Who would he defer to in such matters? Hmm?"

Stryker didn't give him time to answer. He didn't want Kyros to formulate a logical argument before he planted doubts in his mind. "His right hand, that's who. The one he trusts above all others to carry out his orders."

He tsked. "Hell, the Alexion even has the ability to command part of my brother's powers. There are some of us who believe that your friend, the Alexion, even shares the blood of Acheron. So you know it's your so-called friend who has been responsible for your assignments. He was the one who didn't think you deserved to be around more people. And even if he wasn't the one making the decision, surely such a *friend* would have the ability to sway Acheron's mind and intervene to *save* you long before now. Wouldn't he?"

He saw the uncertainty in Kyros's eyes and forced himself not to smile in victory.

"They're both playing you, Kyros. Think about it. This is just another mind fuck. They're off laughing at you right now. This instant. Both of them. The Alexion is here to kill you all, not save you. If he'd really wanted to save you, he would have given you a decent assignment in a thriving city long ago. But he didn't, did he?"

Stryker tried to look sympathetic. "Trust me, there won't be a single Dark-Hunter left alive in this area once he returns to Acheron unless you kill the Alexion first."

Stryker slid off the desk, moving closer to him. "Already you've seen his work. Wasn't Marco where I told you he would be?"

"Yes."

Good, his Daimons had done what they were supposed to. "Was he not killed how I told you?"

"Yes."

"And was the Alexion not there?"

Kyros nodded. "Everything you've told me has come to pass."

"Then who is lying to you?"

His answer was automatic. "They are."

"Yes," Stryker said, finally smiling. "They're lying and so what are we going to do about it?"

Kyros gave him a hard, sinister glare. "Kill him."

Danger watched Alexion as he sat at the small round table looking completely defeated. For a man who claimed to have no emotions whatsoever, he was definitely showing them now.

At his insistence that they not return to her house where they could be found again by the demon (or for all they knew, the demon might still be waiting for them), they'd rented a hotel room.

To be honest, Danger was a little nervous about staying here.

She didn't like feeling this exposed. If the maid were to open the door during the day and let sunlight in . . .

Alexion, according to his own admission, wouldn't explode into dust, but she would. And no offense, being roasted wasn't something she wanted to experience unless it involved one of her friends telling embarrassing stories about her.

But Alexion had assured her that he wouldn't let any harm befall her.

I suppose this is the test then.

If she survived the day, he was honest. If she didn't . . . she would be seriously pissed.

And dead.

In the meantime, it was just the two of them in the small hotel room. And to be honest, Alexion looked weary and beat by what had happened with Kyros. The poor man had been so upset that he hadn't even touched his dinner.

"He'll come around," she said as she pulled her boots and socks off.

He looked up at her. "I wish I had your faith."

"Then have faith in Acheron. That's what you keep telling me to do. Would he have sent you here to fail?"

"Yes," he said, his voice tired and yet strangely determined.

His answer surprised her. "No he wouldn't. That would be cruel."

"Yes," he insisted. "He would have. As Acheron would say, sometimes you have to fail in order to succeed. Whether we want it or not, there is an order in the universe. It's hard to understand and many, many times it's hard to swallow, but it's there and our choices are our own. Failure is part of life and no one can succeed every time they try something."

She huffed at that. "Well, that sucks."

He nodded in agreement. "But failure is the price of having free will."

"Maybe we would be better off without it then."

He gave a short laugh. "That's what Acheron thinks most of the time. He really hates free will, but he will never interfere with it."

"How could he?"

Alexion grew quiet again.

She could sense his restlessness and yet he sat there perfectly still. She'd eaten twice during the night. He hadn't. He'd only said that he wasn't hungry. But then given the fact that he couldn't really taste food, she could understand that.

"Are you going to come to bed?"

He let out a long breath before he answered. "I'll sleep later."

"Alexion . . ."

"I'm fine, Danger. Really."

No he wasn't. She didn't need a sfora to see that.

Feeling for him, she went to stand beside his chair. "You're not really fine."

He looked up at her. Those green eyes of his were haunting in their beauty and pain. "No, I'm not."

His confession caught her off guard.

"You know," he said quietly, "I'm the one who monitors Acheron's e-mail account. I'm there in Katoteros when his cell phone starts ringing off the hook from all of you wanting to talk to him, day and night. There are times when it makes him completely insane. But I envy him the chaos. The 'human' contact. I think it's why he never verbally complains about it around me. He knows how much I would kill for it."

Her heart ached for him and for the lost sadness she saw in the depths of those glowing green eyes.

"My life is so endless," he said, his voice carrying the full weight of his misery. "The only contact I have outside of Acheron and Simi is with other Shades. The ones who are damned scream at me to help them because they know I'm one of the few beings who can hear them. The ones who live on the Isle of Padesios aren't interested in making friends with me. They avoid me every time I go near them."

"The Isle of what?"

He sighed. "It's a region in Katoteros where Acheron allows the Shades a facsimile of paradise. Their existence, like mine, is limited, but they don't suffer. Not like the others do. Although I think the knowledge that they can never again be human is punishment enough. I think that's why they hate me so. I at least have some semblance of a corporeal form. They don't and they never will again."

"Why doesn't Ash give it to them?"

"Same reason he doesn't send me to earth unless he has to. It's cruel to be so close to being human and know that you're not. That you'll never be again. It just brings it all home."

The anguish he suffered tore through her. He looked lost, alone. She understood both feelings. She'd felt them a lot over the last two hundred years. She could only imagine how much worse it would be to experience it over nine thousand years.

She laid her hand against his whiskered cheek. The stubble teased her palm, sending a chill up her arm.

He closed his eyes and inhaled deeply as if he were savoring the scent of her skin. The feel of her touch.

His loneliness touched an inner, foreign part of her. It touched the part of her that was like him. Eternally alone.

Her heart pounding, she tilted her head down to taste his lips.

Alexion was stunned by her kiss. He wished that he could really taste her. Really know the full sensation of her breath mingling with his as her tongue spiked through his mouth.

His body roared to life, wanting to feel her naked against him. He deepened his kiss a moment before he pulled back to look up at her. "Don't do this to me, Danger. It's cruel when you know how long I've been without a woman."

Her staccato breaths fell against his cheek a moment before she pulled her shirt off over her head.

His heart stilled at the sight of her black lace bra that left very little of her breasts covered. Her pink nipples were taut, just begging for his mouth.

It was the most beautiful thing he'd ever seen.

Danger knew she shouldn't be doing this and yet she couldn't stop herself. Like him, it had been too long since she'd last had sex. But more than that, she felt an odd connection with him. Right or wrong, she wanted this moment. In a weird way, she needed it as much as he did.

Taking his hand into hers, she led it to her breast.

He sucked his breath in sharply before he dipped his fingers beneath the lace to touch her. His skin was rough, but his touch was gentle as he lightly kneaded her breast.

She rose up ever so slightly to kiss him feverishly as she began frantically unbuttoning his shirt. Every inch of flesh she exposed was perfect. There wasn't a scar or blemish anywhere on his ruggedly masculine body. The only mark he bore was a strange tattoo on his left shoulder of a yellow sun that was pierced by three white lightning bolts. She touched it lightly, wondering at what appeared to be a series of letters in the middle. It was an alphabet she'd never seen before.

"What is this?" she asked as she traced it.

"Just a tattoo," he said, his voice ragged. "It was on me when I woke up in this form."

Dismissing it, she untucked his shirt, then pushed it and his coat off his shoulders.

He pulled his hand away from her breast to let her undress him.

Alexion actually shivered at her harried speed. It had been far too long since he'd last tasted desire like this. Danger literally crawled into his lap as she returned to hungrily kiss his lips.

He growled at the ferocity of that kiss, at the way his body hardened, wanting a taste of her. Her breath mingled with his as she ran her warm hands over his naked back. He reached around her to unfasten her bra. The black lace fell free, allowing her small breasts to tease his bare chest.

His head spun at the sensation of her hard nipples against his flesh. He'd never wanted any woman more than he wanted her right then.

She left his lips to trail her mouth over to his ear. He swore he saw stars as her tongue stroked the sensitive flesh there. Unable to stand it, he stood up, cupping her to him.

She wrapped her legs around his waist as he carried her

toward the bed. He needed this woman more than he needed to live. He didn't know why it was so important that he have her. But it was, and if anyone had tried to stop them right then, he'd have hurt them badly.

He hurriedly jerked the covers off before laying her down on the sheets. His heart hammering, he unzipped her pants, wanting to see the full, unadorned beauty of her body.

Danger groaned as Alexion sank his hand beneath her panties to touch her where she was on fire for him. Hissing, she arched her back and spread her legs so that he could ease the bittersweet ache that craved his touch. While his hand pleasured her, he pulled back slightly to look down at her face.

His eyes were dark from his passion and filled with wonderment. They flared a strange shade of green an instant before he pulled her pants and panties free of her body and tossed them to the floor. Before she could move, he returned to place himself between her spread thighs. His hot breath scorched her upper leg as his hand returned to torment her.

She couldn't think straight as he pulled his hand away and replaced it with his mouth. Danger cried out in ecstasy. She sank her hand deep into the golden strands of his hair. He took his time pleasing her. No man had ever made her feel so desired, so needed as he did and she didn't understand it.

Thoughts and feelings swirled through her mind as his tongue pleasured her with deep, probing licks. And when she came, she swore she saw stars.

Alexion closed his eyes as he felt her shuddering. There was nothing he'd ever enjoyed more than teasing a woman's body, watching her enjoy the feel of him. And Danger was the sweetest woman he'd ever known. He laid his head against her thigh while his body still throbbed from the want of her.

But he didn't want this to end. For some reason, he wanted to take his time just feeling her skin against his. There was something about her that reached deep inside him and somehow made him live again.

It didn't make sense, but he could feel when he was with her. For the first time in centuries, he did have emotions in a human state. She made him feel even when he didn't want to.

Her black eyes were searing as she sat up slowly, like a hungry lioness. She crouched on the bed in what had to be the sexiest pose he'd ever beheld.

"What are you . . ."

He didn't get a chance to finish his question before she had him flat on his back, pulling at his pants. Alexion didn't argue as she freed him. He almost choked as she cupped him in her hand. It'd been so long since anyone had touched him like this . . .

Danger paused at the look on Alexion's face. She'd never known anyone to be so pleased by something so small as a lover's touch. That alone told her just how truly lonely he was. It was almost a crime to have a man like this locked away by himself.

He cupped her face in his hands and kissed her deeply, lovingly. She could tell just how much this meant to him. How much he needed to feel her.

It did something to her. Made her feel a tenderness for him that she wouldn't have thought possible.

He lifted her up then and set her down on him. Danger bit her lip at his fullness inside her. She leaned forward on her hands, which she had braced against his chest, as she rode him slow and easy.

Alexion arched his back to drive himself even deeper into her warm, wet heat. He took one of her hands into his and kissed the palm. She was so precious to him. The feel of her, the heat of her skin. He placed her open palm to his cheek, reveling in the softness, the scent of her flesh.

He wanted to devour her with a savageness that astounded him. Her lithe body slid sensuously against his, setting fire to every inch of him.

He threw his head back as he came in a fierce wave of pleasure.

Danger's eyes actually teared up at the sight of Alexion's climax. It was as if he were being torn asunder by it. And when his gaze met hers, she melted.

He cupped her face in his hands, then gently pulled her forward for one of the sweetest, tenderest kisses she had ever experienced. He didn't speak, but then he didn't have to. The gratitude and admiration on his face said it all.

Danger smiled at him as she slid slowly down his body. She lay in the bed with the scent of Alexion strong in her head. She loved the intimacy of having his naked body wrapped around hers. Her head was resting on his biceps while his breath tickled her neck.

"Thank you, Danger," he whispered softly.

She rolled over slightly so that she could see him in the early morning light. She hadn't spent a full night with a man since she'd been human. It was so odd to be with one now.

And there was an easy peacefulness to Alexion that hadn't been there before.

"You're welcome," she said, taking his hand in hers and lifting it so that she could lightly nip his fingers. "I have to say you were incredible."

"Yeah, well, they don't let me out much."

She laughed at that as she traced his hard nipple. "I think I'm glad about that."

He kissed her gently, then urged her back down on the mattress. "You should get a good day's sleep."

She wrinkled her nose at that. "It's kind of hard. I haven't slept away from my home in centuries. I'm not sure about that daylight that's starting to spill through the curtains either. It's making me a little nervous."

He wrapped his arms around her and snuggled close. "I won't let it hurt you."

Warmth spread through her. "It's a nice thought, but even with your powers, I somehow think Apollo might win."

The room went pitch-black. There was no sign of a single ray of sunshine now. "Sleep in peace, Danger. I won't let anything hurt you. I promise."

And that was the kindest thing anyone had ever done for her. Her eyes tearing from the strange tenderness that flooded her, she moved her head to kiss his arm, then snuggled down to rest.

She fell asleep with the sensation of his hand gently stroking her hair while he whispered softly to her in a language she didn't understand.

Alexion felt her relax. A slow smile curved his lips as he remembered the way she'd made love to him.

She'd been superb. His lips were still raw from her fanged

kisses and he wouldn't have it any other way. But with that feeling of total satiation came the knowledge that what they had at this moment was so fleeting—it was nothing more than a mere blink.

He would remember her forever and she would forget him completely once he left here.

That was Acheron's mandate. No Dark-Hunter could ever remember they had seen him. Those who were saved always had their memories purged.

Her life would go on without him. That had never bothered him before, but today . . .

Today he wanted more.

Wanting more is the root of all evil. The concept has ruined more lives than it has ever made.

If it wasn't for the fact that he knew it was an echo of Acheron's words, he would almost swear his boss was in his head again.

"Where are you, Ash?" he whispered. "I could really use your guidance right now."

But it was futile. There was nothing Acheron could tell him that he wanted to hear and he knew it. He was without an out clause. He was without a body or a soul. Literally, he had nothing to offer her. Ever.

He had nothing to offer any woman.

Everything has a price. Nothing is ever free. His price for not being damned was eternity spent alone.

At least I have this moment.

For that he was grateful and he would not regret it. He wouldn't.

Alexion tensed as he felt that odd prickling sensation of the sfora again.

"If that's you, Stryker, then do your worst."

If he didn't know better, he'd swear that he heard a voice in his head sneer the words, "I intend to."

14

Danger came awake to something tickling her nose. Shaking her head, she brushed it away, only to have it return again to annoy her.

Aggravated, she opened her eyes to find Alexion kneeling on the floor beside her with a devastatingly gorgeous grin on his face. He laid the rose he'd been tormenting her with down on the mattress in front of her.

"Good evening, beautiful. I was afraid you were going to sleep the night away."

Danger returned his smile as she stretched and yawned. "What time is it?"

"Almost eight."

She froze at his words. "What?"

He leaned his chin on the mattress. There was something very innocent and sweet about that gesture. It was wholly unexpected from a man who was capable of the power this one commanded. "I told you. You were sleeping the night away."

She was completely stunned. She couldn't remember the last time she'd overslept. Come to think of it, she'd never done this before. Six hours a night was her maximum. But this time she'd managed to sleep twelve and she wasn't even in her own bed. How had that happened?

Maybe you need mind-blowing sex more often?

Well, that went without saying.

Yawning, she sat up slowly, clutching the sheet to her to find a nice dinner laid out on the small table by the window. This was just too good to be true—a man who could be terrifyingly powerful and protective, awesome in bed, and still be considerate enough to feed her a decent meal the next day.

No guy was this perfect.

She cringed as that thought went through her. Oh, yeah, he did have one serious drawback. He was rather dead and "other." But for an eternity of this kind of pampering, she just might be willing to overlook that one disturbing flaw. After all, she was no picnic herself.

Alexion turned a lamp on by the table. "I hope you like Chinese."

"As a matter of fact, I do." For some reason that made no sense whatsoever, she had a sudden case of shyness about leaving the bed buck naked while he stood there with that intense stare. She looked about the room awkwardly, wondering how she could dress without him seeing her.

Blind him?

That might be a problem, not to mention . . . rude.

He scratched his chin before he indicated the door with his thumb. "You want a Coke to drink? I can go get you one."

She smiled, relieved that he was a little more intuitive than most men. He really was "other." No mere mortal man would do such a thing. "Yes, please. That would be great."

He nodded, then left her alone.

Picking up the rose to inhale its fragrance, Danger took the time to lie back in the bed and remember the way they had spent the early morning hours.

To be awakened like this was something wonderful indeed.

"A woman could get used to this." She sighed dreamily as a foreign sensation of warmth and happiness rippled through her. "I think I like 'other.'"

"Other" gave her a satisfaction the likes of which she'd never known before. He made her feel things that she had never thought to feel again. She was actually giddy with the idea of spending another night with him.

Giddy? Me?

It was inconceivable that she would feel that. Yet she did. There was no way to deny it.

If only it could last. But she knew better. Their time together was all too limited.

Sighing, she got up and went to take a quick shower.

• • •

Alexion hesitated inside the room as he heard the water running in the bathroom. He had a perfect image in his mind of the water running over Danger's naked body. Of her soaping herself . . . Touching her flesh intimately.

An image of her in there running her hands over her breasts with her legs slightly parted.

His cock hardened immediately.

It was more than he could stand. His mouth dry, he set the drink down and went to push open the door to the bathroom. "Need someone to scrub your back?"

She made a squeak as if he'd startled her. "What are you doing in here?" she snapped.

"Wanting to see you naked in the shower," he said without embarrassment or hesitation.

She opened the curtain to stare at him. Her hair was plastered to her body, but the strands parted over her breasts, leaving the tips of them bare to his hungry gaze. "You need to learn control."

"That I have in spades."

She ran an equally hot look over his clothed body. "I am tempted, but I slept too late. We need to get back out there and see what's up with Kyros and crew."

She was right.

"Fine," he said, hating the fact that he had a job to do that didn't include more naked time with her. "Hormones leashed." He let out a tired breath, then started away.

She caught his hand to stop him. "There's always the dawn, you know?"

He lifted her hand so that he could place a kiss to the back of her knuckles. "Is that a promise?"

She nodded.

He closed his eyes and savored the softness of her skin before he released her and allowed her to finish her bath. But it was hard.

Not as hard as I am.

That was certainly true enough. He was having a difficult time sitting with the erection that wouldn't be denied.

While she finished showering, he distracted himself by preparing her food. Impulsively, he picked up a piece of the chicken to taste it.

His heart clenched as he tasted nothing. It was like the popcorn. There was no difference whatsoever. Only the texture differentiated one from the other.

"I miss eating," he breathed, moving away from the white containers of food. As a man, he had liked nothing better than that long feast at the end of a battle. The roasted lamb and beef that had been marinated in wine and spices. Goblets of rich, red wine and mead.

His mother had made the best honeyed bread he'd ever tasted.

Of all the things he'd lost by being reincarnated, he hated losing the ability to taste the most.

No, that wasn't true, he hated losing his soul, but the food was a close second.

He heard the door open. Turning, he saw Danger leaving the bathroom, fully dressed. She had a white towel wound round her head. "How is it?"

"Still warm." That was all he could tell about it.

"Are you eating?"

"I ate already," he lied. She was suspicious enough about what sustained him. The last thing he needed to do was confide in her how Acheron kept him alive. There were some things she didn't need to know.

Just as she sat down, her cell phone rang. Picking it up, Danger looked at the caller ID. "It's Kyros."

She opened the phone, then answered it.

"Yeah," she said after a brief pause. "We're still in Starkville. Where are you?"

Alexion closed his eyes and concentrated so that he could hear Kyros through the phone.

"Where are you staying?" Kyros asked.

"In a hotel."

"Is Ias with you?"

Danger cleared her throat before she answered. "Why do you want to know?"

"I've been thinking about what he said and I wanted to talk to him again."

"Hang on." She handed the phone to him.

Hoping his friend had come to his senses, Alexion placed it to his ear. "Yes?"

"How close are you to Acheron?"

"Very. Why?"

"Is it true that he has his own demon?"

Alexion decided to play vague. Simi's existence was something Acheron only shared with a few Dark-Hunters, and Kyros wasn't one of the privileged few. "What demon?"

"Be honest with me, Ias," he snarled. "Dammit, you owe me that much."

Alexion ground his teeth. What harm could there be in answering that one question? It wasn't as if Simi couldn't protect herself, especially against a Dark-Hunter. "Yes, he has a demon."

"Then, if I were you, I'd summon it."

"Why?"

No sooner was the question out of his mouth than someone knocked on their door.

Kyros hung up on him.

"That's weird," he said, pushing the button to turn the phone off while Danger got up to open the door.

Before she reached it, a small ball of light came through the wood as if it were nothing tangible. The door itself was left intact while the ball twirled to the center of the room where it grew larger and larger until it was the size and shape of a grown woman.

Two seconds later, a bright burst of light flashed into the room and the shape became that of a tall, fanged female demon.

She had black horns, black lips, red wings, black hair, and yellow eyes. Her skin was marbled with red and black.

But what caught him by surprise was the fact that he knew her face as well as he knew his own.

"Simi?"

She hissed at him, then attacked. She grabbed his arm and slung him into the wall.

Alexion rebounded off it, but caught himself. What the hell was going on here? Simi would never hurt him. Not like this.

She moved to hit him again.

He jumped back, out of her reach. "What is wrong with you, Sim?" he asked in Charonte.

"Do not defile my language, human scum," she snarled angrily.

At least that's what he thought she said. Her words and pronunciation were different from the Charonte that Simi spoke. It was like another dialect.

Danger started for her.

"No!" he snapped. He had to understand this. How could this demon look so much like Acheron's?

"Who are you?" he asked her.

She cocked her head and glared at him with absolute hatred. Her white fangs flashed against her much darker skin tone. "I am death and destruction and I am here to claim your life, worm."

Danger actually growled at him. "Alexion . . ."

"Please, Danger, trust me."

The words were barely out of his mouth before the demon grabbed him by the throat and slung him to the ground.

"Protula akri gonatizum, vlaza!"

The demon curled her lip at him. "You are no god to command me, servant. Xirena bows before no one."

He would have made a comment to that, but the grip on his throat made it impossible to speak. She tore open his shirt as if she were about to rip his heart out.

"I think I need to interfere, Alexion," Danger said, inching closer to them. "From where I'm standing, you're losing big time."

"No!" he choked out, afraid the demon would tear her apart if she tried anything.

The demon pulled a dagger from her waist. Alexion struggled with all his might. It was what he feared most—a dagger from the Destroyer.

That would kill him.

But in spite of his struggling, he couldn't get her to budge off him or her grip to loosen even a tiny bit.

Until her eyes fell to his shoulder where he bore Acheron's mark.

Her eyes flashed red. She let go of his throat to pull the fabric back so that she could study the mark more closely.

Still he couldn't get her off him.

She cocked her head as she studied the tattoo intently. "You serve the one who is cursed?"

"Yes."

She looked even more puzzled by that. "You called me Simi in a child's language. Do you know my Simi?"

Alexion drew deep, ragged breaths in through his bruised esophagus. It burned and ached. He wasn't sure if the pain would ever cease.

"Simi's mother is dead. We were told all the Charontes were gone. Who the hell are you?"

Her gaze narrowed threateningly at him, as if she were offended that he didn't know of her. "I am Xirena, the eldest hatchling of Xiamara and Pistriphe—the supreme guardians of the hall of the gods. I was the protector of my mother's simi . . . her baby. My simi was taken from me by the bitch-goddess Apollymi, after my mother's death, to be a gift for the cursed god. Do you know where my simi is?"

Alexion couldn't think as he stared up at the demon on his chest.

Simi meant "baby" in Charonte?

Sonovabitch. He wondered if Acheron knew that. "*You* are Simi's sister?"

Xirena hissed at him in anger. "She is named Xiamara after our mother."

"She doesn't know that. Believe me."

She pulled back from him ever so slightly. Her face showed her confusion. "You know her?"

"I take care of her."

To his complete shock, bloodred tears filled her eyes. "You care for my sister?"

He nodded. "Always. She's like my daughter."

A single red tear streaked down her cheek. "My simi lives? She thrives?"

"Like a queen on a throne."

She threw her head back and let out an inhuman cry that sounded like a bizarre mixture of anguish and joy. She got off him and squatted by his side. Her wings curled around her body, forming a cloak. "Summon her for me, please."

He met Danger's gaze. She looked as confused as he felt.

Simi wasn't alone in the world? There were two of them? He wasn't sure if that was good news or bad. "I would summon her for you, but that's not exactly something that's done."

"Yes it is," she said in a very Simi-like tone. "You tell her to come and she must obey you."

"Yeah," he said in a tone that was a mixture of nervous humor and doubt. "Simi doesn't obey anyone but Simi."

Xirena shook her head. "She obeys her *akri*. She must."

"Well," Alexion said slowly, still afraid the Charonte might go back into attack mode. "In her case, her *akri* obeys her. And neither one of them is listening to me at present."

She scowled at him. "That is not natural. Once a Charonte is bound, it must obey. I refused the bond and am free, but my simi was bound as a small one to the cursed god. She must obey him. She has no choice."

Yeah, right. Never once had Alexion seen it work that way.

"In the case of Simi, I think it's more Acheron is bound to her, not the other way around."

She didn't seem to understand that. "But you can take me to my simi?"

"Yes."

She threw her arms around him and held him close. It lasted for about two heartbeats, before she pulled back and glared at him again. She grabbed him by the throat. "If you are lying to me, worm, I will rip out your brains and eat them all."

Alexion screwed up his face at the thought. Yeah, she was Simi's sister all right. Some things must run in their family. "That is really disgusting and no, I wouldn't lie to you. Not about this."

She turned to look at Danger. "Is she your female?"

"No."

"I'll kill her anyway if you are lying to Xirena."

"I'm not lying."

Danger didn't understand a single word of what they were saying, other than the name Acheron. She watched apprehensively as the demon got up, then helped Alexion to his feet.

"What's going on?" she asked him.

Alexion still looked a bit nervous and shaken. "It appears we have a new friend. Danger, meet Xirena."

Xirena came over to sniff her. She moved much like a bird, cocking her head at strange angles and with jerking movements.

"You are not human," the demon announced. "You have no soul."

"Thank you for the obvious. Did you know you have horns on your head?"

The sarcasm appeared to be lost on the demon.

"Actually, she brings up a good point. Xirena, can you make yourself appear human?"

The demon snarled as if the very thought disgusted her. "Why would Xirena wish to do that?"

"So as not to cause a panic with the other humans," Alexion explained. "Simi does it all the time."

She looked horrified. "Her *akri* makes her appear as human? That is the worst torture. My poor simi to be so abused!"

"Not really. Simi enjoys it."

She covered her head with her hands as if she were in great pain. "What have you done to my simi?"

Alexion pulled one of her hands away and gave her a meaningful stare. "We have loved her as if she were the most precious thing ever born."

Xirena appeared even more baffled. Two seconds later, she looked like a beautiful blond woman.

Except for one thing.

"Uh," Danger said, pointing to the top of her head, "the horns need to go too."

They vanished immediately.

Xirena moved to the mirror to look at herself. She jumped

back and curled her lip. "I look like the Atlantean bitch-goddess."
She turned her hair black. "Better."

Danger stared at her. "Is it just me or does she look a lot like
Acheron now?"

"Don't ask," Alexion said. "Xirena, I take it you were sent
here to kill me?"

"Yes."

"Who sent you?"

She blew a strange-sounding raspberry. "The moron half-god
Daimon, Strykerius. He said you were a servant, but you do not
bear the mark of a servant on you. You bear the mark of royal
family."

Alexion was surprised by that. Acheron had never explained
the sign to him except to say that he had to bear it in order to
live. "Really?"

"Did you not know?" the demon asked.

He shook his head.

Xirena sighed. "Humans, even those who are no more, are
stupid."

He ignored her very Simi-like words. There was a lot more to
her presence here and he wanted to understand it. "Why does
Stryker want me dead?"

"I do not know. Does the reason matter? Dead is dead. Who
cares why when what matters is avoiding it, yes?"

She had a really good point with that. "Why did you agree to
kill me?"

Xirena drew herself up and gave him a harsh look. "I thought
the cursed god had abused my sister. That he had harmed her or

mistreated her. She was not old enough to be sent out. The bitch-goddess knew this and yet she took her from me, even while I fought her to keep my simi safe. My simi was barely more than an infant and unable to fend for herself. I have hated the goddess ever since for it."

Danger held up her hand to get their attention. "Just out of curiosity, is Acheron the cursed god?"

Alexion cringed.

"Yes," Xirena said before he could stop her.

"And the bitch-goddess?" Danger asked.

"Apollymi."

Alexion told Xirena to stop in Charonte, but she didn't listen.

"The Daimon queen?" Danger asked again.

"Daimon queen?" Xirena made a sound of complete contempt. "No. She is the Destroyer of all things. The bringer of plagues and pestilence. She is the force that will end the world for all time. She is the ultimate in power and destruction. Her will is divine law."

Danger looked thrilled by that. "Oh, goodie. That's just what I wanted to hear."

"Relax," Alexion told her. "Apollymi's contained. She's not going to destroy anything in the near future . . . I hope."

Danger only heard part of that. The rest of her thoughts returned to what Xirena had said a few moments ago. "So Ash is a god and not a Dark-Hunter. Is that what you've been protecting?"

A tic worked in Alexion's jaw.

"You might as well admit it. That's what the demon said, and unless I'm stupid, which I'm not, he is a god."

Alexion gave her a harsh, penetrating stare. "No one can ever know that about him. He'll have a fit of titanic proportions, and trust me, a pissed-off god is not something to relish."

Danger let out a long, exasperated breath. Suddenly everything was clear to her for the first time ever.

"You know, Ash as a Daimon made a lot of sense. But this . . . this explains everything, doesn't it?"

He looked away from her. No wonder he was sworn to secrecy.

But why wouldn't Ash tell them? What was the point of keeping that to himself?

And as her mind grappled with this new tidbit, she thought of what Alexion had told her about Ash and Artemis's relationship. "That's why Artemis needed us, huh? She can't just command another god without some major leverage."

"No, she can't."

She had to say that it sucked to be said leverage. Poor Acheron, to be controlled by them. It was a wonder he didn't hate every one of them. But for them, he would be free. "So we are her pawns while she and Acheron play games with each other."

"No," Alexion said, his sincerity burning into her. "Acheron never uses human life as a pawn. Ever. He doesn't find anything entertaining about playing with people."

He sighed. "But Artemis isn't so kind. She doesn't understand humanity the way Acheron does."

"How is it he's so fortunate?"

"He lived as a human," he said simply. "That's the cursed part Xirena refers to. He was born as a human baby and he died brutally as a human man."

That didn't make sense to her. "But he's a god."

"A *cursed* god."

"Why was he cursed?" Danger asked.

The veil fell over his face. "That is something best left undiscussed. He'll be angry enough over this little bit having escaped. Let's not tweak him any more, shall we?"

Xirena's attention pricked up at that. "Is he an angry god, like the Destroyer?"

"No," Alexion assured her, "he's remarkably calm ninety-nine percent of the time. It's that one percent, though, that's a killer . . . literally."

The demon nodded as she poked at the television. "Your warning is taken."

"So what are we going to do with her?" Danger asked, indicating the demon with a tilt of her head.

"That's a really good question and I have absolutely no answer for it. I'm completely open to suggestions of any sort." Alexion sighed. What could they do with the demon? Simi had spent a lot of time around humans and she was still less than civilized.

Xirena . . .

He paused that thought as she shattered the television.

Xirena stared at it in horror. "Why did that break?"

"You can't slam your fist into the screen," he explained.

"Why not?" she asked in a voice that sounded eerily close to Simi's.

"It breaks," Danger answered.

"But why?"

Danger placed her hand against her temple as if she were beginning to feel a pain there. "Is this normal demon behavior?"

He nodded. "Just wait. This is very mild. It gets a whole lot worse."

"Great. I'm really looking forward to it."

Xirena picked up the remote to place it in her mouth. Alexion grabbed it away from her. "Plastic isn't good for demons."

Xirena glared at him. "How do you know?"

"It gives Simi a bellyache every time. Trust me. It's just not a good Charonte snack."

As Danger watched the demon explore the hotel room, a thought occurred to her. "You know, I think we can return to my house now."

"How so?"

She tilted her head toward Xirena. "We have our own demon now, right?"

Alexion smiled as he understood her meaning. "If the other one is still there, she can wrangle him out."

"Yep. Let's check out of here and go on a demon hunt, shall we?"

The drive back to Tupelo was positively boring, except for when the demon discovered the radio. She almost caused Danger to wreck as she leaned over the front seat, playing with the stations.

With every new song, Xirena tried to sing the words, which she didn't know.

Worse, she couldn't sing on key at all.

Danger glanced over to Alexion who took it all in stride.

"Aren't you going deaf?" she asked him.

He shook his head. "I'm used to it, though to be honest, Simi is at least on key most of the time. She lives to sing."

After a while, the demon shrank in size and then lay down on the seat with her feet up in the air and her head hanging off the cushion, toward the floorboard.

Danger frowned. "What's she doing?"

"Resting. They sleep like that."

"Really?"

He nodded. "Simi props her feet up on the wall most nights. I have no idea why."

"It's comfortable," Xirena said. "You should try it."

And two seconds later, the demon was asleep.

Danger cringed at the horrendous sound of her snoring. "Don't tell me Simi does that as well?"

"No, she's louder."

"And you tolerate her?"

"Considering she is the one thing Acheron loves most in this world, yes. I honestly think he would literally die if anything happened to her."

"What about you?"

"I would kill or die to keep her safe."

Danger smiled at that. "There aren't many men in the world who would die for a demon."

"That's only because they don't have one to love."

Maybe, but it would take a special kind of man to look past the scaly weirdness of such a creature and be able to love it. "You must have been a good father."

Sadness creased his brow an instant before he turned away from her to look out the window.

Danger mentally kicked herself for saying that out loud. "I'm sorry, Alexion, I didn't mean to—"

"It's okay," he said gently. "Simi tells me that all the time—whenever she's not pissed at me for trying to teach her manners." He gave a light laugh. "She says I'm the best 'other' daddy a demon ever had."

Even so, she could tell that it bothered him. But then it bothered her too. She'd wanted children so much as a human that it still ached whenever she thought about it.

That was one of the nice things about being nocturnal—she didn't come across children except in movies and on television. And even that hurt.

But not as much as seeing kids playing in real life, hearing their laugher.

What she wouldn't give to hold her own child in her arms, just once. To be in a delivery room with her husband holding her hand as she cursed him for the pain of the life that was struggling to be born.

It really was all she had ever wanted.

She swallowed against the painful lump in her throat. Some things weren't meant to be.

Love. Family . . .

They were gone from her future. But at least she had some semblance of life. Alexion didn't even have that much. He was denied even more than she was and that made her hurt for him deep down inside her heart.

Danger turned onto her street. She didn't speak as they neared her house, which looked just as it had when they'd fled. She pulled into the garage, but left the door open in case they had to make another hasty exit.

Alexion got out first, then paused. "Xirena?"

The demon snorted, then rolled to her side.

She exchanged an amused look with Alexion before he leaned into the car and gently shook her shoulder. "Xirena?"

"What?" the demon snapped.

"We're here, and if you wish to meet Simi, I need you to come inside to make sure the other demon isn't still here."

She opened her eyes, which were no longer human in appearance. They were again that eerie yellow. "What demon?"

"The one that tried to kill me before you."

She made a strange snorting noise. "He's not here. Why do you think Strykerius sent me? Caradoc is a wuss."

"Caradoc?"

"You know," she said in that singsongy accent. "Big, ugly Charonte who smells bad. He was afraid to kill you because you spoke to him in Charonte. Like Xirena said . . . wuss demon."

He finally understood her. "Ah, okay. Well, at any rate, we need to get you inside for the time being so that we can hide you."

Huffing in aggravation, she got out of the car and followed him inside.

"So what's our game plan?" Danger asked, as Xirena wandered through her living room.

"I want to find Kyros and talk to him."

That didn't make sense to her. Kyros had made his position more than clear. She shook her head at his suggestion.

Alexion was a serious glutton for punishment.

"Why?"

"I want to know why he called to warn me about Xirena. If he'd really wanted me dead, he wouldn't have bothered."

She saw the hopeful look in his face that said he believed Kyros had somehow been won over. She wasn't so sure about that. "We could just call him back."

"No. I want to see his face. I think he's still salvageable."

For his sake, she hoped so. "All right. What do we do with Xirena in the meantime?"

"Leave her here."

She didn't like the idea of that at all. "But what if another demon comes after you while we're gone? She can't help if she's here."

He took a deep breath as if he were considering it. "I don't think they'd bother. Two have already failed. Why send another?"

"Persistence?"

He laughed at that.

Danger jumped as one of her expensive vases fell to the floor and shattered.

"Uh-oh," Xirena said in a tone that reminded her of a child. "That was breakable too."

"We can't leave her here unattended," she said to Alexion. "She'll destroy my whole house."

Suddenly, her vase reassembled itself and returned to her mantel.

Danger frowned at him.

He offered her a lopsided grin. "Xirena," he said to the demon. "Do you know how to write?"

"Of course I do. I'm not one of them illiterate demons. What kind of Charonte do you think I am?"

"Good." He said, ignoring her tirade. He looked back at Danger. "Could you get me a pad and pen or pencil?"

"Why?" Danger asked.

"Trust me."

Not sure if she should, she went to comply while Alexion turned on her television without touching it.

She came back into the room to find the TV on QVC. The demon was parked in front of the set as if she'd found the Holy Grail. Her beautiful face reflected pure joy. Danger had never seen anything like it.

"What is Diamonique?" Xirena asked Alexion in an awed tone.

"Something I am sure you will love. And according to Simi, it's really good and crunchy, and it'll sharpen your fangs." He took the pad from Danger and handed it to the demon. "Here. Write down anything you see that you want and—"

He broke off as a caller spoke on the television show.

"Hello!" the chipper singsongy voice said.

"Hi, Miss Simi," the announcer said to the caller. "We're so glad to have you back."

"Oh, thank you," Simi said. "I just love them spark-lies. I gots to get me lots of them. How many you got this time? Tell them other people they can go buy something else, 'cause the Simi wants all the Diamonique you got. I gots a whole new plastic card just waiting to be used."

Xirena's head came up as pure happiness lightened her face. "My simi? Is that my simi?"

Alexion looked absolutely ill. *"Akri,"* he said under his breath. "I hope you're there to get her off that phone."

But apparently he wasn't.

"I'll take me seven dozen of them rings," Simi said. "Oh, and them necklaces, too, that you had up a little while ago. I needs to have lots of sparklies in my room. They are really nice whenever them dragons come in to play. But that little one, he keeps eating my Diamonique. I tell him no. It's for me to eat. But does he listen? No. That's the problem with dragons, they—"

"Well, Miss Simi," the operator said, cutting her off, "thank you for calling. We'll transfer you over to an operator and let you place your order."

Xirena was in front of the television now, with her cheek pressed up against the screen and her hand spread out beside her face. She looked as if she were trying to peer into the set. "Where is my simi?" The sadness and pain in her voice brought an ache to Danger's chest.

"She's in Katoteros," Alexion told her.

"The gods are all dead there," Xirena said in a ragged tone. "She'd be alone in Katoteros."

"Not all of them are dead."

"Simi!"

Danger cringed at the cry, which was so shrill and loud she was amazed it didn't shatter her windows or her eardrums. It was a cry of pain and of happiness.

Alexion moved forward to take Xirena into his arms as she sobbed and continued to scream out for her sister's return. Her longing was so sad that it brought tears to Danger's eyes.

"Shhh," he said, rocking her in his arms. "It's okay, Xirena. Simi is well and happy and shopping like a demon. Literally. She has never known a moment of pain in her life."

Xirena pulled back. "Never?"

"Almost never and I assure you that the ones who hurt her paid dearly for it."

"How do I know you're not lying to me?"

Alexion took her hand into his.

Danger frowned as she watched him close his eyes and rock the demon. They stayed there on the floor for several minutes before the demon opened her eyes and looked up at Alexion. There was admiration and love in that odd yellow gaze.

"You are good people," the demon announced. "I won't doubt you anymore."

Alexion inclined his head to her before he released her and rose.

The demon sniffed loudly, then brushed her tears away.

Danger cocked her head as he neared her. "What did you just do?"

"I showed her part of my memories with Simi so that she would understand the way her sister is treated."

"Could you share memories with me?"

He didn't answer as he started back toward her garage door. "We need to find Kyros."

"Answer me, Alexion."

He paused in her hallway. "Yes," he said, without looking back.

A shiver went through her at his power. "You are spooky."

He turned to face her. One corner of his mouth was lifted into an almost taunting smile. "You have no idea."

Maybe, but she had a bad feeling that before all this was over, Kyros would get a taste of those powers firsthand. She only hoped she didn't end up on the receiving end of them too.

15

Danger paused as she left her car. They were at Kyros's house and they weren't alone. There was a red Ferrari parked on the street, along with a motorcycle. She knew that flashy Italian car well.

"What's Rafael doing here?" she asked.

Alexion shut his door. "Kyros is most likely trying to sway him to his cause, just as he attempted to do with you."

Surely her friend wasn't that foolish. She liked Rafael a great deal and the last thing she wanted was to see him hurt by this. "It'll never work, will it?"

Almost as if in answer to her question, the front door opened.

A tall, good-looking African-American male came out of the house. His hair was shaved, leaving his head bald so as to show off the intricate scrollwork that was tattooed up the back of his neck to the crown of his head. Rafael Santiago wore his signature long black leather coat, black pleated pants, and a skin-tight black knit shirt that showed off every tiny detail of his ripped eight-pack.

Gorgeous and deadly, the man was the epitome of the word "tough." As a human, he'd been known to cut the throat of anyone dumb enough to look at him too long. He let no one get away with anything. His only motto in life was, Do unto others before they do it to you.

But for all his bluster and razor-quick quips, she knew him for a sweetheart. Those he considered his friends, he would kill to protect, and he was loyal to a fault.

He wore a pair of dark sunglasses that completely obscured most of his face, but Danger knew the former pirate captain well. He'd been living happily over in Columbus for the last sixty-six years.

"Rafael," she said in greeting as he drew near them.

He inclined his head to her as he stopped by her side. He turned to look at Alexion. Even with the sunglasses on, she could feel the intense curiosity of his stare. "Who's your friend?"

"His name is Al," she said, not wanting to say "Alexion" in the event Kyros had already dropped that bombshell. She would have used Ias, but there was only one Ias, and the last thing she wanted was for Rafael to question him about that. "He's an ancient Greek."

Rafael offered his hand to Alexion. "New Hunters are always welcome."

"Thanks," Alexion said as he shook his proffered hand.

"What are you doing here?" Danger asked.

Rafael took his sunglasses off and rolled his eyes. "There were five of us here originally, but the others left a little while ago. Kyros kept me and Ephani longer because, unlike the other jack-offs, we don't believe his bullshit."

"What bullshit?" Alexion asked.

Rafael let out a tired sigh as he rubbed his hand over his muscled jaw. "He has some demented notion that Acheron is a Daimon. I'm sure that's why he called you two. He wants to try and convince you too. The man's an idiot. I'm going to patrol before I hit the asshole and do myself some damage."

Danger laughed. "Are the others buying it?"

"Like it's a cheap whore on the dock after a long trip at sea."

"What makes you so sure he's not right?" Alexion asked.

"You ever met Acheron?"

Danger hid her amusement as she admired the way Alexion kept his composure. Not to mention, she was proud of Rafael for not being stupid.

Alexion's face was completely emotionless. "I've met the man a time or two."

"Then how can you doubt him?" Rafael asked. "Damn, you people are stupid. I got to go before it rubs off."

Alexion stiffened. "You know, I take offense to that."

Rafael gave him a menacing glare. "Take offense all you want to, it doesn't change the facts." He looked at Danger. "C'mon, Little French Flower, restore my faith and tell me you don't believe it."

"No, I don't."

"Good girl," he said with a charming wink, "I knew I could depend on you."

Alexion shook his head and laughed.

Rafael leaned down to give Danger a quick peck on her cheek. "Later, Frenchie."

"*Au revoir,*" she said as he headed off for his car.

Turning back to Alexion, who was watching her in a way that made her a bit nervous, she indicated the house with a tilt of her head. "Shall we?"

"*Après toi, ma petite.*"

"Are you okay?" she asked.

"Fine, why?"

"I don't know. I'm getting a weird vibe from you. You're not jealous of Rafe, are you?"

Suddenly, he looked extremely uncomfortable. "We should go inside."

Stunned, Danger pulled him to a stop. "You're jealous?"

Alexion ground his teeth at her question. He knew how stupid his reaction was, but as Acheron would say, emotions didn't have brains. And he shouldn't have them at all. He hadn't had any feelings for a woman since the day his wife had let him die on the floor of their cottage.

Yet there was no denying what he felt at this moment. And what really bothered him the most was the knowledge that when he was gone, Rafael could still see Danger, talk to her, while the best he could hope for would be glimpses of her in the sfora.

It just wasn't right. And it made him angry that he had to leave the something special he'd found with her last night. It might be selfish and greedy, but he wanted more than to just leave her in a few days.

This is stupid and you know it.

He raked his hand through his hair. "Yeah, okay, so I was jealous for a minute. I didn't like the way he was looking at you."

"We're just friends."

It didn't stop it from tweaking a part of him that was unfamiliar to him, a part of him that wanted to keep her to himself. "I know."

Danger stood up on her tiptoes and cupped the back of his neck before she pulled him down for a hug. "You have nothing to fear, Ias."

He treasured those words . . . the fact that she used his name. It'd been far too long since anyone had talked to him like that. It made him feel human again.

He clenched his fist against her back as his heart pounded and tenderness flooded him. Closing his eyes, he wished he could stay right here in this moment with her forever.

Oh, to have that power. To make this one instant last for eternity.

But all too soon, she released him, and headed for Kyros's house. Alexion ground his teeth as he fought against the urge to call her back and hold her for just a little while longer.

It was stupid. They had a job to do.

He had to save Kyros.

As they neared the steps, Ephani came out the door, across the porch, and down the stairs to meet them. The Amazon was a full twelve inches taller than Danger. Lean and beautiful, she was as hard-boiled and surly as any man could hope to be. Her flaming red hair fell down her back from a silver barrette she had at the crown of her head.

"Take my word for it, Danger," she said in her thick Greek accent, as she joined them. "Go home and stay out of this mess."

He could tell by Danger's face that she was relieved to hear the Amazon say that. "So you don't believe it either?"

Ephani let out a profane curse. "Let's just say, I don't want to believe it."

"But?"

The Amazon shrugged. "I don't trust Acheron. I never have."

Danger laughed. "You don't trust any man."

Ephani's gaze went meaningfully to Alexion. "And neither should you, little sister. Take a bit of Amazon advice. Ride him into the ground all night long, then slide a blade between his ribs come morning."

Alexion arched a brow at that unexpected comment. "That's harsh."

"So is life." Ephani cocked her head as if she had suddenly realized what he was wearing. "You've got on a white coat."

"Awesome cognitive powers you have there."

She looked less than pleased by his dry tone. "Are you the destroyer?"

"No," he said without hesitation. "That title actually belongs to a woman. You can't miss her. She's tall, blond, and looks really pissed off ninety-five percent of the time."

That went over well. . . . Ephani looked as if she could kill him.

"He's here to help us," Danger said before Ephani could do him any harm.

When Alexion didn't speak up, Danger turned toward him. "Aren't you, hon?"

He shrugged. "Ephani knows the truth. There's no real doubt in her mind. She'll choose wisely in the end."

Danger sighed in relief. She'd always liked the Amazon warrior and didn't want to see her hurt any more than she'd wanted Rafael killed.

Ephani's gaze narrowed dangerously. "Are you doing that Acheron mind-meld bullshit?"

"Yes," he said with a taunting grin, "and it's okay that you can't stand me. I'm not here to make friends."

She looked back at Danger. "Ditch him, little sister. Your man is a freak, and I need to go while I still have some powers left. I was here with Kyros and the others way too long." She pulled her sunglasses out of her pocket and put them on. "Take care, Danger."

"You too."

Ephani inclined her head before she left them.

Danger turned toward Alexion. "So how are you going to save anyone if you're antagonizing them?"

"I was only antagonizing Ephani who, as I said, isn't in any danger of being misled. It's the other ones who need me."

She only hoped he was right. Ephani's mistrust of Acheron, or any man for that matter, wasn't to be taken lightly. Her friend had been known to bite her nose off to spite her face on many occasions. She only hoped this wasn't one of them.

She sprinted up the stairs with Alexion right behind her.

Danger knocked on the door while Alexion stood back. It took a couple of minutes for Kyros to answer the door.

His gaze narrowed ominously as he saw them. "What are you doing here?"

"I want to talk to you," Alexion said.

"I've already said my piece."

"Yeah, but I haven't had mine with you. Why did you call and warn me about the Charonte?"

Kyros shrugged. "I was feeling sentimental. But the feeling has passed. I gave you one warning, there won't be another."

"Kyros—"

"Don't," he growled.

He started to close the door, but Alexion stopped him.

"Let me in the house, Kyros."

Kyros's face turned to stone. "You need to go home." He spoke each word slowly, with careful enunciation.

"I *need* to talk to you."

A tic started in Kyros's jaw. "You never did listen, farmboy." He shoved Alexion back with a curse. "Leave."

He slammed the door shut.

Before Danger realized what was happening, Alexion had kicked the door open. It rattled as it was flung back against the wall and torn free of the top hinges.

Kyros looked disgusted by the damage done to his house. "Don't make me kick your ass, Ias."

Out of nowhere, a maelstrom of power seemed to coalesce around Alexion. An invisible wind whipped at his coat and hair. It swirled around him, making the very air around him crackle with energy. Danger forced herself to stay calm in the midst of the chaos as she joined the men in the foyer.

The door slammed shut behind her and was instantly repaired.

Alexion's eyes glowed an eerie, supernatural green. "The days of your kicking my ass are long gone, Kyros. I'm the one who wields the power now."

"Actually, that's not entirely true, is it?"

Danger hissed as she heard Stryker's voice. The Daimon sauntered out of the parlor to join them. He stood beside Kyros and eyed the two of them with hatred.

The Daimon tsked. "It seems my Charonte idea was a complete waste of time. Tell me, what command did you use to quell Xirena?"

The air calmed as if Alexion were pulling the power back inside himself. "I didn't. Xirena likes me."

Stryker laughed even though he didn't look particularly amused. "I will give you credit, you are a resourceful bastard. But even resourceful bastards can die."

Alexion laughed at him. "I'm sure you would know."

Stryker turned toward Kyros. "Your friend is very arrogant for a man wielding borrowed powers. But you know the thing about that is when they're not your own they are limited."

Alexion snorted. "Even limited, they're greater than yours."

"Are they?"

A bad feeling went through Danger. Had all this been a setup? It was starting to feel like one. Maybe that was why Kyros had called to warn them. He'd probably known that if the Charonte failed, then Alexion would come seek him out for an explanation.

Stryker moved to stand just before Alexion. There wasn't even the smallest amount of fear in his eyes. He raked an amused glare over him. "It is a wonderful thing to stand at the right hand of power, isn't it?"

Alexion shrugged nonchalantly. "I'm not complaining."

"No, but perhaps you should."

Before anyone realized what Stryker had planned, he plunged a dagger straight into Alexion's chest.

Alexion burst apart instantly.

Kyros cursed. "What the hell did you do to Ias?"

Danger rolled her eyes. "That was a waste of time."

True to her words, Alexion rematerialized before them. But just as he was coming into form, Stryker shoved his hand, which held a strange-looking plaster rock, into Alexion's chest. Stryker squeezed the rock, shattering it instantly, then jerked his hand out again.

Alexion gave him a droll stare as he came back into being. "You knew better than—"

She watched as a look of horror descended on his face. His breathing became ragged, labored.

"Alexion?" she asked, taking a step toward him.

He stumbled back as pain darkened his eyes.

He gave Stryker a disbelieving stare. "What did you do to me?" he gasped in an agonized tone.

16

Stryker smiled snidely. "I thought you might be missing your soul, Alexion. Of course, I don't have your original one. However, after a little search I did find you a substitute." His pitying tone was belied by the gleam of satisfaction in his swirling silver eyes. "Poor thing. She's a bit whiny and you'll find her extremely weak and helpless. She'll probably last no more than a day or two before she dies completely."

Stryker held the dagger out to Alexion that he'd used to stab him originally. "You know the rules. You're the only one other than a Charonte who can end your life. So be the good guy you claim you are. Give up the ghost. If you don't kill yourself to save her soul, you'll have to stand by and listen to her die. Imagine the poor little human, gone forever from this world. Her soul forever lost. Surely you're not that callous, are you?"

Danger saw the horror she felt mirrored on Kyros's face. But it didn't last long before he recovered his stoicism.

How could they do such a thing to him? Alexion didn't deserve this. Damn both of them for it!

Rage clouded her sight an instant before she ran at Stryker. "*Vous enculé!*"

He lashed out to hit her. Danger ducked the blow, then spun low to swipe his feet out from under him. She launched herself on top of him, pulling out her dagger as she went.

Just as she would have buried it in his chest, Kyros pulled her back.

She sank her fangs into Kyros's arm and couldn't suppress a hiss at the answering intense pain in her own arm. He let go, cursing. Immediately, she went for Stryker who vanished.

"You coward!" she screamed. "Come back here and get the ass-kicking you deserve!"

But he didn't return.

The three of them were alone now.

She turned on Kyros with a snarl. "Why did you stop me?"

"You can't kill him, Danger. No Dark-Hunter can."

"Bullshit. If he bleeds, he can die."

"He doesn't bleed, Danger," Kyros said. "He's a god."

"And you're a complete and utter asshole." She shoved him back, wanting to tear him limb from limb. "Ias came here to save you and look what you've done to him. I hope you sleep well to-night, but then people like you always do."

His face turned to stone. "You don't know anything about me."

"You're right. I don't. All I know is what Ias has told me and he's been living under the delusion that you were some kind of hero and friend. God save me from such delusions."

Shaking from the force of her anger, she sheathed her dagger, then left him to see to Alexion. He was covered in sweat as he leaned against the wall.

Her heart ached for him and for the pain he must be in. His skin was pale and clammy. He looked so lost and hurt. So tortured. She'd never seen anyone in so much pain.

"C'mon, sweetie," she whispered. "I'll get you out of here."

To her amazement, he wrapped his arm around her shoulders and leaned his weight against her. Danger staggered ever so slightly. It was a good thing that as a Dark-Hunter she was stronger than the average male. Even so, he was heavy and solid.

Kyros said absolutely nothing as they left his house. Not that she expected him to. He'd chosen his side already and she hoped he lived to regret what he'd done to a man who had come here to save him.

"No offense," she said as she staggered down the steps with Alexion. "Your taste in friends rivals my own. Now you know why I don't have any that I trust at my back."

Alexion didn't speak as she helped him into her car. His head was filled with the sound of a woman screaming for help. For direction. It echoed through him violently, making him nauseated and dizzy. He could barely focus his eyes. If only the woman inside him would stop screaming for just a few minutes so that he could think straight again.

He'd never felt anything like this before.

No wonder Acheron got so many headaches. How did he manage to cope?

Alexion only had one voice to contend with. Acheron had millions.

"It'll be okay, Alexion."

He felt Danger's hand on his hot face. That she was helping him . . . It went through him like a bullet, shattering something deep inside. No one had ever helped him like this. Not even Acheron. Of course he had never been ill like this since he'd died.

As a man, he'd only had his wife to care for him, and she'd had no use for him whenever he was ill. Having taken care of her ill parents for years before their deaths, Liora had only sought to escape him whenever he needed her.

And though Kyros would render aid in battle, he wasn't tender with it which was probably a good thing.

Yet Danger didn't shy away. She was kind and soothing. And in this moment that meant everything to him.

Danger didn't know what to do to ease Alexion's pain. She raced back to Tupelo as fast as she could, trying to think of something, anything, that might help end this.

Unfortunately, she couldn't think of anything other than finding Stryker and beating him senseless.

She pulled into her garage and quickly got out and ran to Alexion's side of the car. He looked even worse now than he had when they'd left Kyros's house.

She brushed the damp blond hair back from his forehead and wiped the sweat off his brow.

"C'mon, sweetie, we need to get you in the house."

He nodded before he pushed himself out of the car, then doubled over as if in severe pain.

She hissed in sympathetic pain for him. "I know you hurt, sweetie, but please don't hurl on my new Manolo Blahnik boots, okay? Give me a little warning first."

His groan turned into a pain-filled half-laugh that was very short-lived. He leaned against her heavily and together they made their way into her house. But it wasn't easy. He seemed unbalanced and kept staggering as they went.

They met Keller in the kitchen who was busy making what appeared to be a vat of chili. He looked at them with a stern frown. "What happened?"

"Long story," she said as she started for the hallway. "What are you doing here anyway? I thought I told you to stay home."

"Yeah, I know, but I just stopped by and there was this really hot woman watching QVC. I didn't know you had friends like that who weren't Dark-Hunters."

If it wasn't the middle of an emergency, she'd have corrected him.

"Why are you making chili?"

"Xirena was hungry. She wanted something spicy."

Alexion hissed as she accidentally bumped him into the wall. "Sorry," she said.

He didn't answer.

Keller followed them through the house, up to the guest room, where she laid Alexion down on the bed.

"He doesn't look good. He gonna puke or something?"

"I hope not." But she moved the small plastic trash can over to the bed just in case.

Keller was totally bemused. "What's wrong with him?"

"He's hearing a voice in his head."

"Is this like the one that I never listen to because it's usually telling me that getting naked with women I don't know is a bad thing?"

Danger snorted at him in disgust. "TMI, Keller. I don't want to know that much about your depraved private life."

He took her words in stride. "In that case, I have a hot babe waiting for me."

"Do yourself a favor, Keller," she called after him as he left, "and don't get too close to her."

He paused in the doorway. "Why?"

"She's not human."

"Yeah, well, neither are you and I'm around you all the time."

"No, Keller," she said, stressing the words, "she's seriously not human. Never was, never will be."

He frowned at that.

"Just keep her fed and happy," Alexion said from between clenched teeth, "and make sure you both keep your clothes on and that she doesn't leave the house."

Keller nodded, then left.

Danger turned back to Alexion who was squirming from pain. "Can I get you anything?"

"I need to be still and quiet."

She didn't think pointing out that he was being far from still would be good at this moment.

"Okay." Danger left the room to get a cold compress for him. When she returned, Alexion was still lying prone on the bed. It had been a long time since she'd ached like this for someone else. She hated the pain he was in and she wanted to kill Stryker and Kyros for it.

She touched his strong shoulder, feeling the muscles there, before she brushed the hair back from his face and placed the cloth to his forehead.

Alexion opened his eyes as soon as he felt the cold cloth on his brow. He'd never seen a more beautiful sight. She was exquisite.

Her dark eyes showed him more care and concern than he'd ever seen before and yet after tonight . . .

He dared not trust anyone. How many times in his life did he have to be betrayed before he learned his lesson? No wonder Acheron kept him away from people.

After all this time, he was still naïve.

He had to be one of the worst judges of character ever born. When would he learn?

And yet a part of him that he dared not listen to wanted to trust Danger. She'd attacked on his behalf. She'd gotten him to safety. But then so had Kyros. Countless times when they'd been human. He'd even called tonight to warn him and still he had betrayed him.

No, Danger helped him now because they'd slept together. It didn't mean that she had feelings for him. Or that tomorrow wouldn't find her siding with his enemies. How many times in the past had he thought a Dark-Hunter was safe, and then at the last minute, he or she had chosen to fight against Acheron and die?

No one could be trusted.

And still the woman's voice in his head screamed for mercy and release.

"Shut to hell up!" he snarled both mentally and audibly.

Now she started crying a piercing wail that cut through his head like a machete. The agony of it was unlike anything he'd ever experienced.

How the hell did Daimons stand this?

Alexion groaned in pain as he balled himself up into a fetal position, trying to make it stop. He held the heel of his hand against his right eye and still his head throbbed from the woman's banshee cries.

Danger crawled into bed with him and held him close, rocking him gently. She brushed her hands through his hair, making his resistance to her falter. No woman had ever held him like this. Not even his mother.

It was the tenderest moment of his life. And the most painful.

Danger leaned her cheek against the top of Alexion's blond hair. It felt so good to be this close to a man she knew. The curves of his hard masculine back pressed against her breasts and thighs, reminding her of how different their bodies were. He was all sinewy steel. Prickly flesh. Rough skin. And she loved the feel of it. The feel of him.

She just wished she knew how to help him through this.

Leaning forward, Danger inhaled his warm scent while singing an old French lullaby that her mother used to sing to her whenever she was upset. How she wished she could silence the voice inside him. She brushed her hand against his cheek, letting his whiskers tease her palm.

There was something incredibly intimate about this moment even though they were both fully dressed.

"Danger?"

She mentally cursed Keller as he swung open the door to their room, but she didn't withdraw from Alexion. "Yes?"

"You got a call from Rafael and he says you have to answer it right now. He says it's urgent."

He would. Damn that man's timing. You would think a pirate would have a better sense of when to leave someone alone. At one time, his life had depended on such instincts.

"I'll be right there." She reluctantly pulled away from Alexion. "I won't be gone long," she said softly in his ear.

She wasn't sure if he heard her or not. Her heart heavy, she left him on the bed and went to take the call.

All right," Alexion said after a few minutes, trying to talk to his newfound soul. What the hell? He didn't have anything to lose and staying here in the bed until she died didn't seem productive for either one of them. "If you want to be free, lady, you and I have to make a pact."

She continued to wail.

"Woman, listen to me," he snarled out loud. "I can't even function if you don't stop doing that. You're going to get us both killed unless you get control of yourself."

"*I want to go home. Where am I? Why am I here? Who are*

*you? Why is it so dark? I don't understand what happened to me.
I need to go home now. Why can't I go home . . . ?"*

Her questions came at him in rapid succession. So many that
he could barely focus on any one of them.

"If a Daimon can do this, I can too," he growled, forcing himself to sit up. The room swam around him.

He shook his head, trying to clear it. He had to take control
of this situation. He had to.

"Who are you?" he asked the woman.

"Carol."

The wailing lessened a degree, as if she were trying to get hold
of herself. "All right, Carol. Everything will be all right. I promise. But you have to calm down and be quiet for a little while."

"Who are you? Why are you telling me to be quiet?"

How did he answer that one? "It's a bad dream you're having. If you rest quietly for a while, it'll get better."

"I want to go home!"

"I know, but you have to trust me."

"Is it really a bad dream?"

"Yes."

"It will get better?"

"Yes."

To his relief, she settled down. Alexion took a deep breath as
his vision cleared a degree. He could hear the soul rustling around
inside him, but at least she was no longer crying or screaming.

Rubbing his eyes, he continued to breathe deeply, and hoped
that Carol stayed calm for a while.

He got up slowly from the bed and shrugged his coat off.

Stryker had given him only a few days to live or Carol's soul would die. . . .

There was no choice. He would have to kill himself to free her. But he had a lot of work to do before then. It was time he put all the foolishness with Danger behind him. He was here to do a job.

And thanks to Stryker, it would be the last thing he ever did.

After hanging up, Danger took a minute to check on Keller and Xirena, who seemed to be hitting it off famously. They were watching a movie and eating chili while Keller talked a mile a minute.

Apparently the demon didn't share Danger's need for silence while watching TV.

Satisfied the demon wasn't going to eat her Squire, Danger headed back to the guest room. She opened the door quietly, expecting to find Alexion still on the bed.

Her jaw went slack as she found him at the writing desk, making what appeared to be notes.

"You okay?" she asked, entering the room slowly.

He nodded as he continued to write.

Danger moved closer only to realize he was writing in Greek. "What are you doing?"

"Nothing."

She frowned at his curtness. There was something very different about him now. He was like he'd been the first night they'd met. Curt. Unfeeling. Distant.

Even the air around him was cold.

"Hey," she said, reaching out to stop his hand. It, too, was icy cold. "What happened?"

He looked at her, stone-faced. "I'm not here to make friends, Danger. I'm here to deliver an ultimatum. I need you to call together the Dark-Hunters on this list."

He handed her the top sheet of paper. "I can't read—" Before she could finish the words, the writing changed from Greek to English.

Whoa. That was impressive.

She saw that he was still jotting things down. "What's that over there?"

"My own personal list."

Her frown deepened, especially after she glanced over the names on her paper and found one in particular missing.

"Where's Kyros?"

Alexion didn't answer.

Danger grabbed his hand and waited until he looked at her. "What is going on with you?"

"I'm getting down to business. If Stryker was telling the truth, and in this I believe he was, I only have three days to get to the Dark-Hunters who are on the fence and convince them to side with Acheron."

"And Kyros?"

His eerie green eyes were dull and as cold as his skin. "I'm writing him off."

She shook her head in disbelief. "You can't do that. You were friends."

"Yes, we *were* friends. Now we're enemies."

She was aghast at his words. "How could you—"

"I don't have anyone in this world I can trust," he said harshly, cutting her deeply that she was included on the list after everything she had done for him. Dear Lord, she had even given *him* her trust and that was something she did for no man.

"I should never have tried to save him," Alexion said. "Artemis is right, compassion is for the weak."

"So that's it?" she asked, disgusted by his sudden turnaround. "You're going to give up on your best friend?"

"I'm not giving up. I'm dying. I have a soul inside me that will have to be freed in—"

Danger narrowed her eyes two seconds before she pulled the dagger out of her boot and plunged it straight into Alexion's heart.

He burst apart.

17

Two seconds later, Alexion was back in human form, standing before Danger, who waited with her hands on her hips.

He patted his chest as if he couldn't believe he'd returned. He reached out and placed a hand on her desk.

"Soul inside you all gone now?" she asked.

He nodded slowly.

"Good. Now you can stop being a total jerk." She turned to leave.

Alexion grabbed her and pulled her to a stop. He couldn't believe that he had his body back. "How did you know to do that?"

"I didn't. I was only guessing. But it was something I thought of while I was downstairs talking to Rafe. The first rule of being a Dark-Hunter is to stab the soul's host to free it. Stryker said that you had to kill yourself, which would cause you to die permanently—he conveniently left out what would happen if anyone else 'killed' you."

Alexion was still aghast. It was true. Whenever a Dark-Hunter stabbed a Daimon and their body burst apart, the stolen souls always returned to their resting places.

She laughed bitterly. "I'm a staunch Catholic. My mother used to excel at sins of omission. Growing up with her, I learned early on to listen to what she said, not what I heard. And most of all, to pay attention to what she didn't say. Since Stryker put the soul into you during your mid-poofing, I was betting that another poof such as the one caused by an outside person stabbing you would release it. Why else would he have said you had to stab yourself?"

Alexion was completely stunned on so many levels that he didn't even know where to begin. Part of him wanted to choke her, but another was impressed by the fact that she had correctly deduced Stryker's logic.

"I wasn't being a jerk," he said sullenly, returning to her earlier insult.

She stared at him dryly. "Yes you were."

"No," he said honestly, "I'm only being what I am. I'm here to—"

"What you are, Alexion," she said, interrupting him, "is a caring man."

He shook his head in denial. "I'm the Alexion. My only goal is to protect Acheron."

She placed her hand to his cheek. "It wasn't a cold, unfeeling entity that slept with me last night and it wasn't an unfeeling 'other' that looked hurt when Kyros betrayed him. You are still human."

"No," he insisted emphatically, "I'm not."

She stood up on her tiptoes and pulled his head down so that she could kiss him. The coldness of his skin immediately vanished as he cupped her face in his hands and kissed her blind.

She could feel his heartbeat increase as his tongue swept against hers.

Danger pulled back. "You're not unfeeling or uncaring. I doubt if you ever have been."

Alexion's head spun at her words and his reaction to her kiss. It was true. Around her he was completely different. He found himself feeling things that he hadn't felt in untold centuries. Until the moment she had entered his life, he'd begun to doubt he could ever really feel again.

With her, he did.

How could this be?

"There can never be anything between us, Danger."

"I know." He heard the pain in her voice. "I'm a big girl, Ias, and I can take care of myself. But you . . . you need to can the destroyer act around me. I don't like it."

He frowned at her words. "Why did you call me Ias?"

"Because Ias is the man who considers a demon his daughter and it was Ias who woke me up tonight with a rose tickling my cheek."

"But I'm also the Alexion."

She offered him a smile that melted the iciness of his entire existence. "There's a tough side to all of us. Be grateful; it was my tough side that nailed you with the dagger a few minutes ago."

He laughed at that, then sobered. "I don't know what to feel when I'm around you."

"Yeah, I'm confused too. I can't believe that I'm about to help you hang my friends."

"I'm not trying to hang anyone, Danger."

"No? Then what's with the list of hopeless you have over there?"

He glanced to the paper where he'd been writing. "That's not a list of names. It's a list of rules for Keller so that the demon doesn't eat him."

She laughed at him. Leave it to Alexion to think of that one. "I knew I should have studied Greek in school."

Grateful that he was almost back to "normal," she took his hand in hers. It was still warm. "Are we friends again?"

"Yeah, I think we are."

A*kri!*"

Ash rolled over in his bed as he heard Simi running down the hallway outside his room in Katoteros. She burst through the door, then launched herself at his bed.

He woofed as she landed on him then sat heavily on his chest. "I was sleeping, Sim."

"I know, but I heard Alexion calling out again. The Simi wants to go see him, *akri*. Lemme go! Please."

Ash felt the all too familiar knot in his gut as he fought himself not to allow her that wish. But he couldn't.

The last two times he'd let Simi out without him had been disastrous. In Alaska, she'd almost died, and in New Orleans . . .

That was something he still couldn't think about without his temper erupting.

"I can't, Simi."

"Why not?"

He sighed heavily. "I can't tamper with his fate. You know that. This is his time and if I answer him I will probably do whatever it is he asks. So for all our sakes, I've turned his voice off in my head and I would advise you to do the same."

She pouted as she pulled the sfora out of her pink coffin-shaped purse. "At least make this work so's I can see him."

"No."

She growled at him. "But what if he gets hurt? What if he dies?" Her face blanched. "You can't let him die, *akri*. You can't. The Simi loves her Alexion."

He reached up to brush her long black hair back from her face. "I know, *edera*," he said, using the Atlantean endearment for "precious baby." "But his fate is in his hands, not mine. I won't alter it."

Her pout increased. "You control fate. All fate. You can make everything all right. Please do it for your Simi?"

That was easier said than done. He was a living example of the disaster that came from trying to interfere with someone's destiny. His entire life both as a man and a god had been destroyed because of people who meddled with his "fate." He would *never* do such a thing to someone else. "Sim, that's not fair and you know it."

"Not fair is hearing Alexion in my head and not being able to help him. He don't sound right, *akri*. I think them peoples is being mean to him. Let the Simi go eat them."

Ash closed his eyes and tried to see the future for Alexion so that he could give Simi some peace.

But there was nothing to be seen except black mist. Damn. He hated that he couldn't see the fates of his loved ones, any more than he could see his own.

He considered calling Atropos, who was the Greek goddess in charge of cutting the thread of life that governed humans. She would be able to tell him if Alexion would die. But he knew better than to summon her. She hated him passionately.

None of the Greek Fates would ever tell him anything of the future. They had turned their backs on him centuries ago. To them, he was long dead and forgotten.

"We will just have to wait and see what happens."

Simi blew him a raspberry, then got up to leave.

She slammed the door on her way out.

Ash rubbed his head as the sound echoed in the room. Since his emotions weren't tied to the Mississippi Hunters, he knew which of them would live and who would die. That saddened him greatly, and all he could do was hope that Alexion was able to sway them away from their destinies in time.

Only their free will could alter what he saw for them.

That was why he'd sent Alexion to Danger. Since the day he'd started training her, he'd had a soft spot for her. The small French-woman covered her tender heart with a coat of arsenic to keep others away, but he knew what she hid from others. She was a good woman who'd been dealt a bad hand. The last thing he wanted was to see her dead. And yet he knew in his heart the futility of wishing for what could have been.

Danger's days were extremely numbered, and unless a miracle happened, there was nothing any of them could do to help her.

18

They were seriously batting absolute zero with no pinch hitter in sight. Danger sighed heavily as they returned to her house. They'd spent the last few hours seeking out the Dark-Hunters in the area only to find out that most of them had an ax to grind with Acheron.

Granted, there were times she got a little annoyed with his vagueness too, but this was ridiculous.

They blamed him for being stuck in Mississippi (which she personally loved). It really wasn't a bad place to live. Granted it was hot in the summer, but there was a lot of beauty to be found here.

They also blamed him for not making their immortality better. Blamed him for all kinds of stuff that was basically their decision, not his.

Worse was the fact that she knew Acheron could read their minds. No wonder he didn't visit here more often. How could he continue to let Artemis use the Dark-Hunters against him while they cursed everything about him? That man had more fortitude than anyone she'd ever known.

Personally, she'd tell them all adios, and go find her own private paradise.

The fact that he didn't . . .

He was either a saint or a masochist.

Perhaps a little of both.

"I can't believe their gall," she said to Alexion as he shut her back door. "Who knew Squid had a death wish?"

Unlike her, he took it all with nihilistic stoicism. It was true, around others he was ice-cold and without any emotion at all. Their words didn't anger him the way they did her. He just stood there and listened while they railed.

Alexion shrugged as he turned the hall light on for her. "It happens more than you'd think. If I can save ten percent, it's a good night."

She didn't want a ten percent survival rate. She wanted one hundred percent. But Squid had thrown them out the minute they'd started talking about Acheron.

Thank God she'd been able to convince Alexion not to wear his white coat over there. There was no telling what the angry ex-pirate would have done to them if he'd suspected Alexion was the destroyer Kyros prophesied him to be.

Squid had completely refused to listen. Damn him for his stubbornness.

"You know, I think we need to work on your speech."

Alexion arched a brow. "What's wrong with my speech?"

She led the way into her living room. "Well, I think it was the 'or else' part that lost us Tyrell. Have you ever noticed that Dark-Hunters aren't exactly the 'or else' kind of guys? They're the kind who will do the opposite of what you want or bust a gut trying. They'll doom themselves just to spite you because you told them not to."

He frowned. "What would you have me say to them? 'Hi, I'm here to be your friend? Let's sit, have a cup of coffee, and chat?' "

She laughed at that image. Yeah, Alexion was definitely not the type to sit and "chat."

Then again, neither were the others. For the most part, the Dark-Hunters were beer-drinking, bar-brawling kind of men. They were far more likely to slug it out than talk.

"No," she said, sobering. "But you could try to be nicer to them."

That familiar droll look came over his face. "I don't need to be nicer to them. I just need to feel them out to see what side of the fence they're going to fall on. The only ones we need to worry about are the ones who are undecided. Tyrell may yet come around."

"I don't know. He had some very creative use of the language as he told you to go blow."

"Then again, he might be a tough sell."

She shook her head at him as she went upstairs to the media room to find Xirena asleep on the couch. There was no sign of Keller.

Danger pulled the cell phone out of her pocket and called him only to discover that he'd left a couple of hours ago and gone home to bed.

"Sorry to wake you. I was just worried. Night, Keller."

He wished her good night, then hung up.

Alexion moved to stand behind her. He leaned down ever so slightly so that he could just inhale her scent of magnolias and woman. His body jerked and fired in reaction, but then he tended to keep an erection in her presence. Everything about her fired his hormones.

And it wasn't just because he was horny.

There was more to his attraction to her than that. He liked her. But more than that, he respected her. She was an intelligent, courageous woman.

In short, she was a gem.

She stepped back, into his embrace, and leaned her head against his shoulder so that she could look up at him. Her eyes were dark and searching. Something in that look tore through him, making his heart pound.

Was she his savior or his downfall?

The thought of that terrified him. But she had made him live again when nothing else had. She had reawakened his emotions, made him care. . . .

Most of all she'd made him crave.

In more than nine thousand years nothing had ever come so close to making him feel human. There were times when he was around her when he swore he could almost taste again. He wanted her to distract him.

Most of all, he wanted her to touch him.

He placed his hand against her cheek before he dipped his head down to kiss her. She moaned deep in her throat and sank her hand in his hair as she turned in his arms.

Alexion growled at the sweetness of her kiss as his heart raced out of control. Breaking away, he scooped her up in his arms and carried her to his bed.

He shouldn't be doing this again. Everything was going completely wrong with this mission and yet she made it all bearable. Somehow it didn't seem so bad with her here.

Danger sighed as he laid her down on the bed, then joined her. What was it about him that made her sizzle? Tonight had been a disaster, in more ways than one, and yet here with him it was okay.

It didn't make sense. She just wanted to be held by him, to have him chase away the entire world until there was nothing but the two of them. She'd never felt like this before.

She rose up to capture his lips as he began unbuttoning her shirt. He kneaded her breast with his hand, slow and gently. She nuzzled her cheek to his, loving the way his whiskers pricked her skin. It sent chills through her.

Unable to stand it, she jerked his turtleneck over his head so that she could run her hands over the taut muscles. She wrapped her legs around his waist and squeezed him tight.

He laughed in her ear.

"You okay?" he whispered.

"Yes. But I want to eat you up."

He laughed again. "It's a good thing you're not a Charonte. Otherwise, I might be scared."

"Yeah, but I do have fangs . . ."

His answer was another deep, passionate kiss as he unfastened her bra. He pulled back to take her breast into his mouth. Danger arched her back as she delighted in the feel of his tongue pleasing her.

Wanting to taste him too, she rolled over and pinned him to the bed.

He looked at her quizzically as she pulled back and crawled down his body.

Alexion ground his teeth at the sight of Danger making love to him. She looked predatorial and wild, and it went through him like a hot lance. She smiled wickedly as she pulled his boots and socks off.

He started to sit up, only to have her push him back.

He'd never really liked for a woman to take control, but with Danger it was different. He enjoyed the way she looked as she reached for his fly. Lying back, he watched as she undid his pants and his cock sprang forward.

She hissed at the sight of him before she ran her smooth, cool palm from his base to his tip. It was an effort not to come from the sheer beauty of that alone.

Biting her lip, she slowly pulled his pants down his legs. Still she wouldn't let him sit up. She pushed him back again. "I want to look at you," she said insistently as she pulled the rest of her clothes off.

His heart pounded at the sight of her pale beauty. She was exquisite. She picked his foot up to rub the sole of it with tender care. Ripples of pleasure went through him, until she took a nip of the flesh there.

"You're killing me, Danger," he breathed raggedly.

"There's a reason why my people call it *la petite mort*."

Alexion was beginning to understand it exactly, especially when she took him into her mouth. He couldn't remember the last time a woman had touched him like this. But one thing was certain, he'd never enjoyed it as much as he did now.

Growling in satisfaction, he cupped her face with his hand as she gave him complete satisfaction.

Danger groaned at the salty taste of him. She really did want to devour him, but she had to be careful not to hurt him with her fangs. She craved the scent and taste of this man and she didn't even know why.

But she had to have more of him.

He sat up suddenly and withdrew from her. She was confused until he rolled her over, onto her back. He positioned himself with his knees at her shoulders, then spread her legs so that he could taste her as well.

Danger dug her heels into the bed as pleasure consumed her. There was something incredible about this mutual sharing. It touched her that Alexion wasn't content to just receive pleasure. He took his time making sure that she was every bit as satisfied as he was.

There were far too many men out there who couldn't care less about a woman. She was grateful he wasn't one of them.

Alexion wished he could taste her fully. He hated having his senses dulled. But even so there was no way to get around the fact that he adored this woman. Her hands clutched his buttocks while her tongue worked magic on him.

He wanted more of her. Pulling away, he switched positions again so that he could sink himself deep inside her. She hissed the instant he did and scoured his back with her nails.

He'd barely started thrusting before she came so fiercely that she almost threw him out. Alexion laughed in her ear as he took joy in the sound of her pleasured cries. It sounded as if she were singing.

Danger wrapped her body around his as he continued to thrust against her. Each thrust went through her, heightening her orgasm even more. She pulled his lips to hers and kissed him fiercely as he moved even faster. She loved the sensation of having him inside her. The intimacy of holding him like this. He was incredible.

She felt him tense an instant before he drove himself in deep then shuddered in her arms. Smiling, she held him close as his climax claimed him. When it was over, he collapsed on top of her and held her tight.

Danger brushed his hair back from his face as they lay there lost in the aftermath of their passion. It was quiet and still in the house. But her heart ached with the thought of his leaving her. All too soon he would be gone and her life would go on for eternity without him.

"Is there any way you'll ever be able to visit me after this assignment?"

He tensed. "No." She heard the regret in his tone.

"Why not?"

"Because even if I did, you wouldn't remember me." He pulled back to look down at her. "It's the way it has to be."

Tears gathered in her throat, but she refused to let him see them. "That's not fair to you. You can never make any friends."

"No, I can't. This is all I have." He sighed wearily. "It's all *we* have."

"I don't understand how you can be so nonchalant about it. Don't you ever get mad over these stupid rules?"

He looked away and yet she saw the hurt in his eyes. "No, Danger. I don't. Believe me, this is far better than the alternative. At least this way I have moments of muted happiness."

She turned his head so that he could look at her. "Tell me the truth, Ias."

He sighed wearily. "Yes, there are times when I would give anything to be able to have one chance at being normal again. To have one moment when I was human and could eat and feel. But I'm just grateful that I have this time with you right now. You make me feel almost human. At least closer to it than I have been in a long time."

She kissed his whiskered cheek, savoring the feel of his rough shadow against her lips. "I wish this could last."

"I know, but it reminds me of a term Acheron uses a lot."

"And that is?"

"'Regret management'. You try to mitigate the regrets with the pleasure the moment brought to you."

"Does it work?"

Alexion snorted. "Not really. At least not for me. Although Acheron seems to do well with it. At least he appears to cope with his regrets most days."

She frowned. "What does Ash have to regret?"

"You'd be amazed."

"And what about you?" she asked, needing to know the answer. "What is your greatest regret?"

His gaze burned her with its intensity. "That you weren't born nine thousand years ago."

Tears welled in her eyes at words she'd never thought to hear from him or from any man. "I wish we'd met when we were both human," she whispered.

"Yeah, but you would have probably killed me then."

Huffing at him, she was offended by that. "How do you figure?"

His green eyes teased her. "You've stabbed me twice since we first met. That seems to be a bad record with me." He shook his head. "There must be something really wrong with me that all the women I love want to kill me."

Danger wasn't sure which of the two of them was most stunned by his words. "What?"

He pulled away immediately and started to get out of the bed.

Danger stopped him. "Talk to me, Ias."

"Don't call me, Ias, Danger. I'm not that man anymore."

"No, you're the man I let into my bed, and believe me, that's some feat. There haven't been many who've made it past my front door." She held him to her side even though he was trying to pull away. "Now you finish what you started."

"It doesn't matter what I feel. Or even what I think. Time is limited for both of us."

"No, Alexion, it matters to me. I want the truth from you. I deserve it."

Misery knitted his brow. "What good is the truth? Really? What good does it do us?"

But she didn't agree. She needed to know if he'd meant what he said. "Do you love me?"

He looked away and she had her answer.

Releasing him, Danger sat there with a knot in her throat as emotions swirled through her. She'd never thought to have another man say that to her. Never.

But what surprised her most was what she felt for him in return. It was warm and overwhelming and it filled her with both joy and fear.

She pulled him against her and laid her head on his shoulder. "I love you, too, Alexion."

She felt his jaw tic against her scalp.

"This is an impossible relationship. You know that, right?"

"I know," she breathed. "And when the time comes, I will kiss you on the cheek and bid you good-bye. I won't beg you to stay and I won't make this hard on you. I promise."

Alexion ground his teeth at her words. But that wasn't what he wanted.

He wanted . . .

Damn you, Acheron.

Most of all, he damned himself. Had he not been so stupid as to go to his wife so soon after making a pact with Artemis, he would still have a chance to be human again.

Acheron would be able to barter for his soul back. . . .

Then again, had he not wanted to return to his wife so desperately, Acheron wouldn't have made the pact with Artemis that allowed Dark-Hunters to go free.

None of them would have a chance for freedom from her service. His life and soul had been sacrificed for a much greater good.

One day, Danger might be free again.

Without me . . .

It was true. For him there was no way out. No future that included Danger or any woman. Not that he wanted any other woman. She was the only one he would ever love. He knew it.

"I shouldn't have come here to save Kyros," he said in a hoarse tone. "Kyros is as good as dead and all I've done is make memories that can only serve to hurt in the centuries to come." But at least she wouldn't know regret. She wouldn't feel his pain.

He clenched his hand in her hair. "I'll be able to see you, I could even pass you on the street and you'll never know who or what I am. I'll be a stranger."

Tears swam in her dark eyes. "I don't want to forget you, Alexion. Ever."

"You have no choice. You know too much about Acheron now. He'll never allow you to keep your memories intact."

Anger snapped beneath her tears. "I don't care what he does. I won't forget you. Somehow I'm going to remember you, I know it. I don't care how powerful he is, he won't make me forget you."

He wished he could believe that, but he knew better.

"You need to get some sleep, Danger. We have a long night ahead of us."

She nodded. "Are you going to sleep too?"

"In a little while. You rest."

She released him to lie back on the bed. Alexion got up and dressed while thoughts and regrets whispered through him.

Pushing them aside, he went to see Xirena, who was still asleep on the sofa.

Her feet were propped up over the back while her head dangled off the side of it. One arm was flung over her head and lay against the floor while the other was crossed over her chest. Smiling at the Simi-like pose, he grabbed the blanket off the armchair and covered her up.

His time here in Mississippi had definitely been his oddest assignment.

But at least time was on his side. Stryker would think he still had the soul within him and that it was incapacitating him.

Until the time that Stryker expected the soul to die, the Daimon should leave them alone. It gave him a few days to make contact with the other Dark-Hunters to feel them out.

He would call the Dark-Hunter meeting in three days and then the fate of them all would be decided.

His thoughts drifted back to Kyros and he wanted to curse out loud at the injustice. Kyros was lost to him.

But I found Danger.

And in the end, he would lose them both.

Life did, indeed, suck.

"Keep an eye on Dangereuse."

Alexion froze as the soft, feminine voice whispered through his head. If he didn't know better, he would swear it was . . .

"Artemis?"

"The Daimon wants you dead. If he can't take you, he will take someone else."

Alexion swallowed at her dire tone. "Why are you helping me, Artie? I know you hate me."

"I'm not Artemis. I'm just a friend who doesn't want to see Stryker hurt anyone else."

"Then how do I defeat him?"

"To defeat the invincible you can never strike at them. You must always strike at their heart."

"I've tried striking at his heart. He's a little swift on his feet."

The voice said nothing.

"Hello?" Alexion asked, but she was gone.

"Great," he said, clenching his teeth.

Stryker was going to make a move on Danger and the only way to save her would be to strike at a god who had no heart whatsoever.

"Shit, we're screwed."

19

Alexion spent the entire day watching Danger sleep. He sat in the cream jacquard padded chair beside her bed, completely absorbed by the pale beauty of her. She was without flaw. Without guile. Without cruelty inside. She would never hurt someone she loved. Indeed, she'd died trying to save her family when it would have been easy enough for her to have turned her back on them and saved herself.

It was part of why he loved her so.

"I don't want to leave her." He whispered the heartfelt words knowing that in the end he had no choice. Damn him for not being able to control his emotions where she was concerned. All he had done was ruin his own future.

Why was that?

Why did such pain have to exist in this world? Love should be easy. It should be simple. A person should be allowed to find that one person they couldn't live without and just go on their merry way to happily-ever-after.

But it didn't work that way. He was living, or dead, proof of it. Liora had sworn she loved him and look how that had turned out. It was hard to trust another person not to hurt you. There was still a part of him, even now, that wondered if he could go free, would Danger drop the medallion to save herself?

Would her own personal pain be so great that she would help herself before him?

There was no way to know the answer. Especially not now.

He sighed. He knew from Acheron that it was useless to dwell on wants or what could have been. He had to deal with the present and that meant keeping Danger safe from whatever Stryker had planned.

He had Xirena with him now. Surely the two of them were capable of protecting one woman. Weren't they?

But when dealing with a crafty god bent on vengeance, it didn't pay to get cocky.

"C'mon, boss man," he said under his breath, "talk to me."

Alexion shook his head at the irony. In the past, he'd always hated it whenever Acheron had intruded into his thoughts or space. Now that he wanted him, the Atlantean was nowhere to be found.

It figured . . .

"Alexion?"

He got up and went to the bed where Danger was stirring. She stretched and yawned as she watched him. "Do you always rise so early?"

"Yes," he said, not wanting her to know that because he was more or less a ghost, he didn't need sleep. His rest wasn't quite the same as a human's.

She yawned again before offering him a smile. "So what's on the agenda for tonight?"

He shrugged nonchalantly. "Migraine, futility, possible death. Same as every night, I guess."

Danger laughed. "That sounds like my life, all right." She glanced toward the door. "So how's our demon doing?"

"I haven't been to the media room in about two hours, but last I checked, she was knee deep in *Kirk's Folly* orders. Good thing Acheron is loaded. Then again, the way these demons shop, I'm not even sure he has enough money to cover it."

Danger was amused by his words. It was so nice to wake up to see his handsome face smiling at her.

She took his hand in hers so that she could feel the masculine roughness of it. She didn't know what it was about the sensation of a man's skin that was so appealing, but there was no denying that she enjoyed how different it was from her own.

She breathed deeply against her fingers, delighting in the warm, pleasant scent of them. His hands were powerful and yet tender. Wonderful and delectable. Opening her lips, she gently nipped his forefinger.

He hissed in response. "You keep doing that, and I won't let you out of that bed."

"Then why don't you join me?" she said, pulling back the covers so that he could see her naked body. She'd never done anything so bold with a man before, not even her husband. But for some reason, she didn't mind sharing herself with Alexion.

Her sense of modesty had flown and she wasn't really sure why.

His eyes sparked green fire. "We have a job to do."

"And we have three more days to meet with the Dark-Hunters, who are going to insult and aggravate you." She ran her tongue over the pad of his thumb, then pulled back. "They're not going anywhere. Like you said, it's just an exercise in futility. I vote we take one night off and just enjoy it." She licked the back of his knuckles.

Pure pleasure darkened his gaze, but still he resisted her. "To what purpose?"

She sat up in the bed and wrapped her legs around his lean waist, pulling him closer to her. "You've changed since you've been here, Alexion. When you first arrived, you were so cold and distant. You're not like that now. You're warm and fun. I don't want to lose that. I don't want *you* to lose that."

Alexion swallowed. She was absolutely right. She had changed him.

Danger brushed the hair back from his face. "I want you to have memories of me that will help keep you warm after you leave."

Those memories would only hurt him more, and yet his heart was thrilled by the idea of it. He hadn't had a night of normality since he'd been human, and for some reason, being with this woman made him crave it viciously.

What would it be like?

"And what will we do?"

She gave him a seductive grin that made him harden while she trailed her hand down the front of his shirt. "Have you ever been to a real movie?"

He shook his head. Acheron and Simi went all the time, but the last time he'd been in the human realm, movies hadn't been invented yet.

"Then that's what we're going to do," she said in a tone that let him know she wouldn't take no for an answer. "Dinner and a movie . . . Just like everyday Jane and Jack."

Alexion shook his head. "I think you've lost your mind."

She was slowly unbuttoning his shirt as she talked to him. Every brush of her hand against his flesh sent chills over his body. "Perhaps, but do you know what Jack and Jane would do to start off their night?"

"I have no idea."

"They'd start it off with blindingly great sex."

Alexion hissed as she sank her hand down under his waistband to stroke his hard cock. His body was already throbbing and craving hers in the worst sort of way. Or maybe it was the best sort of way.

There was truly nothing better than her hands on his body. Nothing better than the feel of Danger.

Alexion laughed as that thought went through his mind.

"What are you laughing at?" Danger asked as she stopped her sweet torture.

"I just had a bad pun go through my mind."

"And that is?"

"That I live for Danger."

Danger's heart pounded at his corny words. They shouldn't please her and yet they did. Oh, yeah, there was really something wrong with her. She was head over heels for this man and sinking in deeper by the minute.

"How do you always know the right thing to say?" she asked him.

"I didn't know that I did."

"Take my word for it, you do."

He closed his eyes as she ran her fingertips over the tip of his shaft. She loved pleasing him. But as she watched the ecstasy on his face, it fired her desire even more.

Undoing his fly, she slid his pants down his legs, then pulled his lips to hers so that she could taste him.

Her tongue danced with his as she sank her hands into his thick, soft hair. His hard shaft rubbed against her bare stomach as she took her time exploring his mouth.

Delirious from that kiss, she pulled back ever so slightly. "I love the way you touch me," she breathed against his cheek. "I love the way you smell. The way you look . . . I need to feel you inside me, Alexion."

Alexion's entire being was on fire as he watched her recline naked on the bed. Her thighs were spread open in sweet invitation, allowing him to see the tenderest part of her body. He leaned over her to take her breast into his mouth so that he could tease the taut pink tip with his tongue. Her body was absolute heaven.

Closing his eyes to better savor her, he dipped his hand down to gently stroke her. He probed the tender flesh between her thighs, separating it so that he could feel just how wet and ready she was for him. It was the sweetest sensation he'd ever known.

He massaged her as she whispered encouragements to him in French. And when he sank his finger deep inside, she arched her back with a pleasurable cry.

Unable to stand it, he moved his hand so that he could enter her.

Danger moaned at the thick fullness of Alexion inside her. He took her hand into his and held it over her head as he thrust against her hips. He moved in and out, in the sweetest rhythm that pounded through her with absolute bliss. She met him stroke for stroke, aching in bittersweet pleasure.

She wrapped her legs around his waist as their passion took her far away from the present and all her fears about the future. It'd been so long since she'd felt like this with a man. There was a connection to him. A friendship.

More than that, there was love.

How she wished that she could keep it. But at least she had this moment to remember what it was that she'd lost. This one moment to pretend that they could stay together.

He moved faster, heightening her pleasure until she couldn't stand it any longer. Crying out, she felt her body splinter in ultimate ecstasy.

Alexion watched her face as she came for him. He loved the sight of her in the throes of climax. But more than that, he loved the way her body felt under his. She was so sweet, so tormenting.

She pulled him down to kiss him while he rode her even faster, seeking his own slice of heaven.

And when he came, he cried out her name. He leaned down

over her as his body convulsed and throbbed, releasing itself deep inside her.

She ran her hands over his back, clutching him to her body. "So did I have a good thought about this, or what?"

He laughed at her question. "It was a great thought."

She wiggled her hips against his, letting him feel the wetness of their play. It was something he savored. They didn't just have sex with each other, they made love. And it had been far too long since he'd felt that.

Danger nipped his shoulder. "Anyone ever tell you that you are an incredible lay?"

He laughed. "Well, they never phrased it quite that way."

She hugged him close to her, then kissed his cheek. "You are the best, Alexion. I mean that."

"I'm only as good as my partner is."

She offered him a smile that made his stomach jerk. And the kiss she gave him for those words set his entire body back on fire. "You keep this up and I won't let you out of the bed tonight."

She nibbled his chin. "Would that be so bad?"

No, it would be heaven.

Alexion gently cupped her breast, delighting in the softness of the skin, before he pulled back. How he wished he could love her the way she deserved. But even if he were able to be human again, he wasn't sure he would ever be able to trust fate with her by his side.

He was so tired of regretting the past. So tired of knowing that for him there could never be normality.

"What's wrong?" she asked, smoothing his frown with her fingers.

"Nothing."

Danger pulled back. He wasn't being honest with her, she knew it. His mood had turned around completely. There was such a deep sadness in his eyes that it tore through her.

She watched as his eyes turned to a dark emerald again. It was weird how they changed color. "Do you control your eye color?"

He appeared surprised by her question. Maybe he didn't realize they did that. "Huh?"

"They change colors constantly," she explained. "Kind of like a mood ring. Whenever we're around other Dark-Hunters and on the night you arrived they were black. Now they're a vibrant green. Do you decide or do they do that on their own?"

He squeezed her hand lightly. "The black I control. The green does what it wants to."

"Ew!" she said, wrinkling her nose. "That's kind of gross."

He laughed. "Good thing I have a strong ego, huh?"

She kissed him on the top of his nose and squeezed him between her thighs. "Like cast iron. Now let me up so that we can get our date started."

Date. There was a word Alexion had never thought to hear in relation to himself. Moving back, he let her get up to go shower as he thought over the strangeness of all this.

He was going on a date? He'd seen such things in movies and read about them in books, but to actually be on one . . .

How completely odd.

None of this is real. Don't get any more involved with her. You'll regret it later. There were only three more days until he'd have to return.

And then he'd never see her again.

Danger popped her head back in the bedroom door. Alexion was still lying naked on her bed. She had to admit that he looked incredible like that. Michelangelo would have a field day painting that divine Greek body. It was absolutely perfect in proportion. She'd never seen anyone with a better set of abs or a nicer rump. And when it came to his pecs and shoulders . . .

She was already getting turned on again.

Except that he continued to look sad and forlorn. "Hey? Want to join me?"

He looked startled by her question. "Really?"

She laughed at his shock. "It's not like you haven't already seen me naked . . . a lot."

He smiled, then scooted off the bed to join her. Before she could move out of his way, he scooped her up and carried her to the shower.

She yelped as he turned on the water, which was freezing cold.

"Sorry," he said. The water turned warm so quickly that she knew he'd intervened with the temperature.

His thoughtfulness never ceased to amaze her. *Don't, Danger.* She couldn't afford to let herself fall for him more than she already had.

Then again, why not? If he was to be believed, and she certainly did believe him, she wouldn't recall him at all by week's end.

And that made her want to cry. How could she forget someone who meant so much to her? That thought alone was terrifying.

Just my luck. After all these centuries I finally find the one person I actually want to be around only to find out that it really is impossible.

La vie n'est pas juste. How many times had her mother told her that? And unfortunately, her mother was right. Life wasn't fair. It was cruel and sad, but at times it was fun and miraculous.

And tonight it would be miraculous. She refused to let herself or anyone else ruin it. She might not remember him, but he would remember her and she didn't want his memories to be of a sullen-faced crybaby. He deserved one perfect night.

Everyone did.

Alexion picked up the cloth and soaped it before he turned to Danger. Her eyes were closed, her arms raised, as she parted her hair to let the water saturate it. To his amazement, he felt himself starting to harden again as he watched her. What was it about this woman that left him so hard and needful all the time?

She opened her eyes and pinned him with a tender gaze that left him breathless and aching. He kissed her before he started bathing her.

Danger sighed at the sensation of Alexion's hands on her body, soaping her skin.

"There has to be some way around this." She hadn't realized she'd spoken out loud until he straightened.

"There isn't, Danger. When I leave, it's over."

She wanted to curse in frustration. "I can't believe that we can't make it work. Surely there's some way we can fix this."

"I'm not real. I'm not even human anymore."

He kept saying that, but everything about him refuted those words. How could someone let go of the best thing they'd ever found simply because . . . Well, there was a lot of "becauses" in this relationship. Still, love could conquer all, right?

But she knew better. Love couldn't conquer death. Ever.

Sighing, she didn't say anything else as they bathed and dressed.

After they were ready, Alexion opened the door to the hallway to find Xirena there.

Standing in the hallway, she had her head cocked as she gave him a look reminiscent of a hawk sighting prey. "I have been thinking much this last day. I know you care for my sister and I want to stay with her. But I don't want to bond myself to the cursed god for it. His mother is unkind and vicious, and no matter what you say, I don't trust her son to be any better. But if I don't bond, the bitchtress can reclaim me and make me go back to Kalosis and serve her. My brother has left there and gone I know not where, and my sister was sent away countless centuries ago."

Her eyes were troubled and sad, and they showed the full depth of her heart. "I only want to be with my family, Alexion. Will you let me bond to you so that Xirena can't be forced back to Kalosis?"

Alexion exchanged a shocked look with Danger as Xirena's words rang in his head. That was one hell of a request she was making.

To bond with a demon was irreversible. At least as far as he knew. Xirena would become a part of him in much the same way that Simi was part of Acheron. She would live on his body and be his to command.

Could he even do that?

"I'm not human or a god," he said to her. "I don't really even have a body for you to bond to."

"We bond to the *ousia*. Not the flesh."

He looked back at Danger. If he took Xirena up on her offer, he would have one more entity who could guard her at all times. No matter when or where Stryker attacked, Xirena would be with him.

But he couldn't take advantage of the demon for his own peace of mind. That would be selfish and cruel, and there was no way he would ever be like that to another living being. "Are you sure you want to do this?"

Xirena nodded. "I have to. Please don't make me go back there. The bitchtress will kill me and I only want to stay with my sister. Please."

"Will Ash be mad?" Danger asked.

Xirena hissed like a cat. "I don't care what the cursed god says. He doesn't control me."

Truthfully, Alexion didn't know how Acheron would react, but he couldn't imagine him getting angry over this, especially not if it made Simi happy.

In a weird way, it made total sense. The last thing he wanted was to see Xirena pulled back into Kalosis where she might be punished for helping him. He didn't know much about Acheron's mother, other than the fact that she wasn't known for her under-standing or compassion. Alexion had already had Simi for nine thousand years—at least *this* one was an adult.

"I guess it's okay," he said.

Danger gaped. He was bonding with a demon? She didn't know what that was, but it didn't sound good. "Are you two get-ting married?"

He laughed. "No."

Still not sure, she watched as Xirena's body became a bizarre shadow that shrank in size until it was no larger than half a foot. She took on the shape of a dragon.

Alexion lifted his shirt and she laid herself across his ribs to form a brightly colored tattoo there.

Completely stunned, Danger reached out to touch the demon tattoo. "Does that hurt?"

"Burns a little," he said as he looked down at the demon on his skin.

"What did she do?"

"I'm not exactly sure how they do it, but she's now a part of me. She can feel my emotions. If she senses I'm in danger, she'll manifest back into her demon form and protect me."

Wow, that was impressive . . . and scary. "Can she hear us?"

"No," he assured her. "I can hear her thoughts, though, and if I allow her to, she can hear mine."

"That's just so weird."

"I know. Apparently, the ancient Atlantean gods used to pick one demon they favored above all others to become their companions."

"So Simi is Ash's?"

"Yes."

Her face lightened as if she finally understood something. "So that's why Ash's tattoo changes shapes and positions? It's not really a tattoo. It's his demon."

He nodded.

"Well, that's just a total freak. So what happens if one of you dies? Does it kill the other?"

He felt the color drain from his face. "Now there's something I never thought about. Let's hope we never find out."

"Yeah, it could seriously stink, huh?"

Before Alexion could answer, Xirena started crawling up his chest, toward his shoulder. He jumped as her path burned him and caused him to shiver. "Xirena, stop moving!"

"*Sorry*, akri."

"*Don't call me* akri, *Xirena. I'm not a control freak.*"

"*You are good, quality people, Alexion. Xirena will sleep now.*"

"You two talking?" Danger asked.

"For only a second. She's going to sleep for a while." He rubbed his chest where Xirena now rested as a permanent part of his being. "Now I understand why Acheron jumps every now and again for no reason. Simi must be twitching on him."

Danger laughed. "I hope you don't start doing that. People around here might think you're having a seizure. Next thing you know, they'll be throwing you down on the ground and putting a stick in your mouth."

"Really?"

She laughed again. "No. C'mon, gullible. Let's go eat."

So why aren't you eating this time?" Danger asked as they sat in a small family-owned Italian restaurant down the street from her house, looking over the menu.

"I told you, I can't taste anything."

She gave him a piercing glare. "C'mon, Alexion, don't lie to me. With the exception of the popcorn, you haven't eaten anything since you've been here, have you?"

He looked away from her.

Danger reached across the table and took his hand. She wanted an answer to this. "Please tell me the truth."

Alexion considered the ramifications of being honest with her. But then she wouldn't remember it, so why not? She already knew more than she should.

But what if it disgusted her?

Then again, that might be beneficial. She might find the truth so repellent that she'd leave him to do this alone, and not be in danger anymore.

He didn't know, but in the end, he found himself confiding in her. "Have you ever studied Greek myth at all?"

"A little."

Good, that would make this a little easier on him. "Do you remember when the heroes would travel to the Underworld what they had to do to be able to speak with Shades?"

She thought it over for a few minutes before she answered. "They made a blood sacrifice."

He braced himself mentally for her possible reaction. "And what did the Shade do with their sacrifice?"

Her face went pale as she realized the truth of him. "It drank the blood so that it could speak."

He nodded.

Danger sat there horrified at what he was telling her. "You live on blood?"

Again he nodded.

She went completely cold at the next thought that entered her mind. There was only one person he could feed from. Only one person he was ever around. "You drink Ash's blood?"

"Yes."

"Ew!" she said, scooting her chair back. She had a horrible image in her head of the two of them feeding each other. "So you suck on Ash's neck?"

"Hell, no!" he said in an offended tone. "A, never in a million years—I'd rather be dead and tortured, and B, you go near that man's neck and you better have a will made out. He can't stand for anything to touch his neck."

"Then how do you feed?"

"He literally opens a vein, drains his blood into a cup, and gives it to me to drink. I know it's disgusting. I know you're horrified. But if I don't feed, I return to what I was and I don't know if it's true or not, but Artemis claims that if I return to a Shade, there's no way to bring me back again."

She thought about that until she remembered something he had told her yesterday. "But you said you were different from the other Shades. Do they drink blood too?"

"No. Acheron brings them back another way."

"And that would be?"

"I don't know. Acheron never shared that secret with me, probably because he knows I'd want to kill him for the injustice of it."

She couldn't blame Alexion there. Ash really had screwed him up. "So how did he learn this other way?"

He sighed. "About three hundred years after he brought me back, he met a . . ."—he hesitated as if searching for the right word—"teacher who taught him how to use his god powers. Savitar is the one who showed Acheron how to bring back the dead without using blood for it. But it was too late for me. Because I live off his blood, he and I are bonded much like two classic Holly-wood vampires."

Now they were back to being gross again. "So he has to feed from you too?"

"No. Well, actually I guess, in theory, he could. But I think he'd rather die than feed from a man."

Oh, yeah, like the alternative was any better. "So he feeds off women? Stryker was right, he is a Daimon."

"Calm down," Alexion said, taking her hand in his. "He's not a Daimon or an Apollite. And he doesn't prey on people. He only feeds from one person and she's not human either."

And in that instant she understood who. "Artemis."

He nodded.

Everything made sense now. No wonder Acheron put up with all of them. He really had no choice. "So neither one of you can eat?"

"We can eat. We just don't have to. I don't eat out of habit. Since I can't taste food, it's rather futile."

"Then why are we here?"

"Because you do need food to fuel your body, and I want you to live a long and happy immortality."

You summoned me, *akri*?"

Stryker turned away from his window, which looked out onto the city in Kalosis where daylight never shone. The lights there sparkled like diamonds in the darkness, while his people lived in fear of the gods who had cursed them and the one god who had saved them.

Being one of the first who was cursed, he, unlike the majority of the others here, knew what it had once felt like to have sun on his skin. He remembered the time when he'd loved his father, Apollo, when he would have given his life for him.

And then in a fit of anger over a Greek whore, his father had cursed the entire race he'd created. Every Apollite adult, every Apollite child . . . even Apollo's own son and grandchildren had been cursed so that they could never walk in daylight again.

Stryer's wife, who had been Greek, had been spared the curse. But his sons and daughter hadn't.

Strange how after eleven thousand years he couldn't remember what Dyana had sounded like, but he still recalled his daughter's precious face. She'd been lovely until the day she had died on her twenty-seventh birthday, cursing her grandfather's name as she disintegrated into dust. To his eternal pain, she had refused to turn Daimon and be saved.

His sons hadn't. They had followed in his footsteps and had sworn allegiance to Apollymi, the Atlantean god who had shown them how to feed on human souls so that they didn't have to die. For centuries his family had been virtually intact.

Until his aunt Artemis had created her damned Dark-Hunters.

One by one, his sons, her blood nephews, had been destroyed by the Dark-Hunters she sanctioned.

Except for Urian . . .

The pain of that thought was enough to drive him insane. He wanted his son back with a need and grief so strong that it was crippling.

Now it was just him. He, alone, was left. So much for his dreams of eternity spent with his family.

But life seldom turned out the way one planned.

"*Akri?*" Trates said again, drawing Stryker's attention back to his second-in-command.

Stryker focused his gaze on the tall Daimon. "I want you to gather together the Illuminati." They were the strongest and bravest of the warrior Spathi Daimons. "Tell them they are going to have a treat."

Trates looked confused by that. "A treat?"

He nodded. "If I know the Alexion, and I do, he will pull all the Dark-Hunters together to deliver his ultimatum before he dies. I think we should have a little surprise waiting for him when he does."

"But if all the Dark-Hunters are together . . . they'll kill us."

Stryker laughed evilly as he patted Trates on the shoulder. The poor fool was not half the strategist Urian had been. "You forget, Trates, that when they are together, the Dark-Hunters weaken each other. In that form, they will be easy pickings for us."

Still Trates didn't join his humor. "What if the Alexion doesn't kill himself? He has the power to kill us even without Artemis's servants."

Stryker clenched the hand on Trates's shoulder, digging his fingers into the Daimon's flesh.

Trates pulled away with a hiss.

"Don't you think I've thought of that?" he asked Trates, who stood rubbing his bruised shoulder. "The Alexion has one major weakness."

"And that is?"

"The Dark-Huntress he travels with. She is our key to destroying him."

He looked horrified. "She's a Dark-Hunter, she'll kick our ass."

"I don't think so."

"And why is that?"

Stryker went to his desk where a black wooden box sat. He opened the box and pulled out the deep red stone medallion, then cradled it in his palm. "Because I have something I think she'll want returned to her."

The Daimon's eyes widened at the sight of what should never have fallen into Stryker's hands. "How did you get her soul?"

"I have my ways." Stryker laughed again. "If she interferes or if the Alexion refuses to do the right thing, then they can both suffer eternal torment."

20

It was one of the most incredible nights of Alexion's extremely long life—but then all of his time with Danger was special.

Even so, he'd never seen anything like this. To be sitting in the middle of people as if he were no different from them . . . there were no words that could describe that miracle. He'd heard them laugh at the movie, take a deep breath at tense parts, and even talk around him. Unlike the other moviegoers, the talking hadn't bothered him in the least.

For a time, he'd been one of them.

No wonder Acheron sought this out. Now he understood completely.

Hell, he even liked his feet sticking to the floor of the theater. But the best part was when Danger pulled the armrest up so that they could share her tub of popcorn. She'd leaned her head against his chest and there in the dark they had cuddled.

"So this is what being normal feels like, huh?" he asked as they left the theater in the middle of the crowd.

"Yeah. Kind of nice, isn't it?"

Alexion nodded as he watched groups of young adults and teenagers veer off together. He draped his arm over Danger's shoulders. A touch of magnolias filled his head—he adored this woman's scent.

"Do you see a lot of movies at the theater?" he asked her.

She wrapped her arm around his waist as they left the building. There was something unbelievably intimate about this. "Not too many. I spend most nights at home when I'm not culling the Daimon herd."

He couldn't understand such forced solitude when she, unlike him, had a choice in the matter. "Why?"

"It makes me lonely to come out." She indicated a couple to the side of the building who were kissing in the parking lot. "It reminds me of what I don't have anymore, and what I won't have again after you leave."

Alexion pulled her to a stop and held her close. He cradled her body with his and closed his eyes, wishing both their lives were different. "If I could, I would give you what you want."

"Thanks. I appreciate it."

He tilted her chin up so that she was looking at him. "I will always be with you, Danger."

Danger could see the sincerity of his words in his eyes. That meant a lot to her. Yet it wasn't enough. "But I won't know it, will I?" His eyes darkened with remorse, making her regret her words. The last thing she wanted to do was hurt him. "It's okay, Alexion. I didn't mean to bring the moment down. I'm just grateful we had tonight."

"Me too." He gave her a squeeze before taking her hand and leading her toward her car.

They didn't say much as they headed back to her house. It was an average, quiet night. As they drove past the tiny white house where Elvis Presley was born, Danger glanced over at him. "Do you know who Elvis is?"

Alexion smiled. "King of rock and roll, baby. Of course I know him. Simi adores him."

She laughed. "One day I have to meet this Simi." She indicated the house with a tilt of her head. "He was born right there, and I rode past this house a dozen times when he was only a few weeks old, never realizing the infant inside would have so much impact on American culture."

"Yeah. That's the weirdest of Acheron's gifts. He would have known exactly what was coming for the child."

What she wouldn't give for that ability. It would be the best, to be able to see into the future "Can you tell?"

"Not without the sfora. Acheron doesn't let me channel powers that he thinks I can't handle."

Danger frowned. "Why doesn't he think you can handle that one?"

"Because there are times when even he can't."

"How so?"

Alexion expelled a long breath and was quiet a few seconds before he answered. "It's hard to know that serious ill-fortune is about to strike someone and not intervene to make it better for them."

"Then why doesn't he intervene?"

"Because people learn from their mistakes, Danger. Pain and failure are a natural part of life. It's kind of like a parent who watches their child fall down while learning to walk. Instead of coddling the child, you set them back on their feet and let them try again. They have to stumble before they can run."

She shook her head in denial. It seemed callous to her. "I don't know about that. It seems cruel to me. Most people get a little more injured than just a skinned knee."

"Life is cruel sometimes."

True. She knew that better than anyone. Her heart clenched as she saw the faces of her family.

They had been on their way to Germany when her husband's garrison had overtaken them.

Danger closed her eyes as she saw that day so clearly in her mind.

"No, Michel! He is my father."

There had been no mercy on his face, no compassion in his steel-blue eyes. "He is an aristo. Death to them all."

"Then kill me too. I will not let you take them while I breathe."

And so he had shot her . . . straight in the heart that had loved him so dearly.

"Aristo whore," he had snarled as she lay dying while her father held her. "Death to you all."

The last sound she'd heard had been the shot that took her father's life as well.

Anger and pain swelled inside her as those old memories coalesced with her rage over what would happen with Alexion. She still couldn't believe she had learned to trust another man. But now that she had, she didn't want to let him go.

"Do you really believe that we need to have our hearts ripped out?"

His answer was automatic. "A flower can't grow without rain."

"Too much rain and it drowns."

"And yet the most beautiful of the lotus flowers are the ones that grow in the deepest mud."

She snorted at his words. "You're not going to let me win this one, are you?"

"There's nothing to win, Danger. As John Lennon once said, 'life is what happens while you're making other plans.' It is messy and heartbreaking, but at the same time, it's a thrill ride."

She shook her head. "It amazes me that you know so much about our culture and icons."

He shrugged. "I have a lot of time on my hands."

Danger felt for him. There were times when her life was monotonous. . . . She could only imagine how more so his was. But since it was obvious that the two of them had differing views about how much strife humanity needed, she returned to their original topic.

"You know, I've always wanted to go in and see Elvis's birth-place museum."

"Why haven't you?"

"They close before dark. But they do have an Elvis Festival in June. That's a lot of fun and there's usually a Daimon or two in the crowd."

He laughed. "The way you say that it makes me wonder which part is business and which is pleasure."

She smiled. "I like being a superhero. Not many people are lucky enough to help others."

"Very true."

As she drove, Danger got a strange feeling. "Are we being watched again?"

Alexion shook his head. "I don't know why, but Stryker seems to be on hiatus."

Still, her precognitive powers kept ringing, telling her some-thing weird was going to happen.

It wasn't until they reached her house that she understood why. In her driveway, waiting for them, was a black Aston Mar-tin Vanquish.

That was a car she'd never seen in her neck of the woods before.

"What in the world is Viper doing here?" she asked.

Alexion frowned. Viper was a Dark-Hunter assigned to Mem-phis, Tennessee—two hours from Tupelo. "That's a good question."

As Danger pulled in and parked beside the Aston Martin, a tall, handsome black-haired man got out of the car. Even though they were banned from sunlight, Viper still had an olive complexion that looked nicely bronzed—something he'd inherited from his mother's Moorish background.

One of the original Thirteen of Glory who had gone with Pizarro to the Inca city of Tumbez, he'd come to America almost five hundred years ago in search of gold and fame. The Incas had written of Viper and his party, "These men were so bold that they did not fear dangerous things. . . . The strangers traveled across the sea in large wooden houses."

To this day, Viper feared nothing.

Danger couldn't imagine what had brought him so far from home. She'd only met him once in person, but had spoken with him online and over the phone a few times.

Like most Dark-Hunters, the Spaniard was dressed all in black. He had on a pair of pleated black slacks and a skin-tight T-shirt. His hair was short and stylishly trimmed. As he waited for them to leave the car, he pulled his sunglasses off and tossed them into his seat.

"*Hola,* Viper," she said in greeting as they left the car. "*Cómo está?*"

He didn't answer her. Instead, he headed straight for Alexion. Without a word, he buried his fist into Alexion's stomach, then backhanded him.

"Stop!" Danger snapped as she ran to them.

Alexion straightened with a look on his face that threatened Viper's life. For an instant, she half expected him to kill the Spaniard.

Luckily, his restraint held.

But when Viper moved to hit Alexion again, he was thrown

back by nothing at all. Xirena came out from under Alexion's sleeve in her shadow form as if ready to kill.

"No, Xirena," Alexion said forcefully. "It's all right."

The demon glared at Viper, who crossed himself. "What are you?" he asked, his tone threatening.

"She's a demon," Danger explained. "And what the hell are you doing? Why did you attack him?"

Viper turned on her with a glare. "He killed Euphemia tonight."

Danger covered her mouth at the mention of the Greek slave woman who was stationed in Memphis with Viper. Euphemia was a beautiful blond woman who'd been viciously funny and smart.

"Efie's dead?" Alexion asked. "When?"

Viper's hate-filled gaze narrowed on him. "Don't play stupid with me. Stryker has told me all about you." He turned on her with a curled lip. "And you're helping him."

"Yes, I'm helping him because he's not killing anyone. Stryker is."

But Viper wasn't listening. He tried again to reach Alexion, but Xirena went after him with a hiss.

"Xirena, return to me."

The demon now hissed at Alexion. She looked less than pleased before she returned to shadow form and drifted back beneath his clothes.

Danger cocked her brow. That was an interesting talent.

"You know I didn't kill her," Alexion said in a calm voice to Viper. "You're upset and you want to blame someone, I respect that. But you know Danger would never be a part of hurting another Dark-Hunter."

She saw the anguish in Viper's eyes. The grief. He'd known Euphemia a long time and this was obviously killing him emotionally. "They cut her head off."

Danger pulled him into her arms to offer him comfort. "I'm so sorry, Viper. I am."

His arms were tense around her as his grief reached out to her and brought tears to her eyes. "How could they do that to her?"

Danger didn't understand it. She never had. "I don't know."

Alexion moved to stand within striking distance. "Do you really believe we're responsible, Viper? Honestly?"

She could see the indecision on his face as he pulled away. He cut a venomous look at her. "Danger, tell me the truth. Did you have anything to do with this?"

She knew he knew the answer to that. But she could understand and respect his need for confirmation. No doubt he felt betrayed enough. "When did Efie die?"

"Three hours ago."

Danger reached into her jacket pocket and pulled out her receipt for the restaurant and the movie stubs. "As you can see, we were here in town the whole time. There's no way we could have been in Memphis."

He looked at the tickets and nodded. "Then Stryker is lying to us. Why?"

"He's a Daimon," she said simply. "He wants us all dead."

Viper shook his head. "I've known Kyros for centuries. I trusted him."

"Kyros isn't thinking straight right now," Danger said. "But we have all got to get our heads on straight or we'll lose them."

He nodded. "I didn't believe them when they started their crap. Ash has been too helpful to me over the years. I don't often misjudge someone."

"And you didn't," Alexion said.

Tears brightened Viper's eyes as a muscle worked in his lean jaw. "Efie didn't deserve what she got. Man, it's a waste of a good woman." His agonized gaze came back to hers. "I want the ones who are responsible. I want to feel their blood on my hands."

"We'll get them," Danger assured him.

Viper looked at Alexion. "I'm sorry I attacked you."

Alexion shrugged it off. "It's understandable, given the circumstances, and forgiven."

Danger offered him a smile. That was part of why she loved him so. He understood people in a way few did.

Viper took a deep breath as he looked Alexion over. "I only have one question. If you're not Ash's destroyer, why are you here?"

Alexion's answer was dry and sarcastic. "To make friends and influence people."

Viper frowned as Danger laughed.

"The influencing people is true," Alexion said stoically. "But I really don't care about friends. What I do care about are the Dark-Hunters. Kyros and Stryker are right about—"

Danger cleared her throat, interrupting him as she recognized from previous Dark-Hunter encounters where this particular speech was heading: disaster.

Alexion might understand people's emotions and actions, but

he didn't know how to talk to them. "Did we not have a discussion about the 'or else' bit?" she asked him.

He gave her a peeved stare. "Okay, then what do you suggest I say?"

She patted him playfully on the stomach. "Watch and learn." She turned toward Viper. "How long have you known Ash?"

"Like you, since the night I was made a Dark-Hunter."

She nodded. "Right, and what did Ash tell you the night you met him?"

Viper fell silent for a minute as if he were reliving the event in his head. "Basically, he said that he was there to show me how to survive."

"Right. And if he meant that then why would he send someone out to kill you now?"

She saw the truth in Viper's eyes as he realized it. "He wouldn't."

"No, he wouldn't." She touched his arm sympathetically. "Don't feel bad. I forgot that part myself, but that is the spiel Ash gives every Dark-Hunter when he first meets them. Then he spends the next few weeks teaching us how to fight and how to live. More than that, we get all the money we can spend, great homes, and servants. If we were just his expendable pawns, in his army, why take such good care of us?"

Viper laughed darkly at that. "You're right. I gave my loyalty, blood, and sweat to the Spanish armada and they didn't give a damn what I ate or where I slept. And my pay stunk."

She nodded.

"The only Dark-Hunters I have ever killed were the ones who preyed on humans," Alexion said emphatically. "That is the only thing Acheron will not stand for. And it's the reason I'm sent in. If you're willing to leave the humans alone and let bygones be bygones, so is Acheron. You can go home in peace. But if you think that he's lying to you and that you can do whatever you want to the humans without fear of retribution, then you go home in pieces."

Danger saw Viper's eyes flash at the threat. She half expected him to attack Alexion again.

To her relief, he didn't.

After a few tense seconds, Viper stepped back. "Kyros is calling together the Dark-Hunters in the area the night after tomorrow. He says he has something to show us about Acheron that will prove his guilt above everything else. . . ." He looked at Alexion. "I won't be there."

Danger smiled. "Good man."

"I try most nights." Viper inclined his head to them. "I better go. We're now short one DH in Memphis, and Danger is draining the shit out of my powers. Not to mention, the last thing I need is to breeze the dawn."

She nodded. *"Vaya con Dios, Sebastian,"* she said, using Viper's real name.

"Hasta la vista, francés." He looked at Alexion. *"Y tu,* weirdo."

Alexion laughed. *"Adiós, mi amigo."*

Danger watched as Viper returned to his car. As he drove away, a deep sadness claimed her.

Euphemia was dead. . . .

The pain of the thought ached deep inside her. "How many more Dark-Hunters are they going to kill?"

Alexion came to her and held her close. "It'll be all right."

"Will it?" She held on to him as morbid thoughts and grief for her comrades poured through her. "What bothers me most is that they got to her in Memphis. How could Stryker attack there and be here to—"

"Bolt-hole," Alexion said, interrupting her. "He can command them any place and any time. One minute he can be here at your house and in the next, Moscow."

"Then how do we stop him?"

He gave her a tough stare. "You don't. That's my job."

"And if you fail?"

"Not an option. We'll get him. I promise."

And yet even as he said those words, Danger had an awful premonition that they wouldn't. She felt something cold and sinister deep down inside.

Good didn't always win. She knew that better than anyone.

Ash paced the floor of his throne room restlessly. His emotions in turmoil, he tried to block out the images that haunted him.

"I will not interfere." It was a mantra he'd been chanting all day, and yet how could he not?

The lives and well-being of people he cared about hung in the balance.

He held his hand out and the monitors on his left flashed images of his human life. The horror of it all. The humiliation. The pain and terror. And all because two women had sought to "save" him.

He wouldn't do that to Ias. To interfere with fate or human free will . . .

It was disastrous.

"*Acheron?*"

The monitors went blank and he froze as he heard a voice in his head that he wasn't expecting. "Savitar?"

"*How many people you got in this head of yours that you have to ask that question?*"

He laughed at the man's dry humor. Savitar knew better than anyone else exactly how many voices Acheron heard at any given time.

An eerie blue mist hissed in front of him. Two seconds later, it coalesced into a man who stood almost even in height to him. Only Savitar would dare enter his domain without an invitation . . . well, he and Artemis, but Artemis was a whole other nightmare.

Physically appearing around the age of thirty, Savitar stood before him with a wry grin and his arms crossed over his chest. Dressed in a pair of white beach pants and a short-sleeved blue shirt that was worn over a white T-shirt, he looked nothing like what he really was. Nothing like a being who held the wisdom of the ages and enough power to give Ash a good run for his money. Then again, Savitar might actually be even more powerful.

There was only one way to know for sure, but Ash respected him too much to find out.

Lean and muscular, Savitar hadn't changed much since the day they'd first crossed paths—except for his wardrobe, but Ash's had changed a lot more.

Colorful tattoos covered Savitar's forearms. His wavy black hair hung just past his ears, and he wore it in a casual, easy style. His eyes were a vibrant shade of lavender. Those eyes were timeless, powerful, and even a little corrupt.

No, they were a lot corrupt.

Ash was never sure which side Savitar would fall on. Only Savitar knew that one and he didn't always share it.

"How's Simi?" Savitar asked.

Ash pulled a corner of his formesta back to show him Simi's tattoo. "Fine. She's resting now. I kept her out too late."

"You shouldn't abuse your demon so. She needs her rest."

Ash ignored his comment. They both knew he would never really abuse Simi.

Savitar walked around the room, his gaze seeking out every corner and crevice. "Very sterile place you have here."

"I'm sure yours is a study in hedonism."

Savitar laughed, then sobered. "You can't go to them, Atlantean. If you do you will kill Stryker."

Ash closed his eyes, wishing he could see his own future as easily as Savitar did. But at least Savitar was willing to share his visions for once. "Are you sure?"

"As sure as I'm standing here." Savitar flashed from before the throne to stand directly behind Ash's back. "Maybe I'm not there after all."

Ash immediately turned around so that Savitar wasn't at his back—more than anyone, Savitar knew how much he hated for anyone to come up behind him. "Don't push me, Savitar," he growled. I've long ceased being a neophyte."

"No, you're not. But if you want to attack me, so be it. I can't interfere with your free will any more than you can interfere with theirs."

Savitar held his hand up and spread out his fingers. Colors danced and swirled in vibrant patterns in the air around it. They danced around his fingers. "Everything in the universe is changing right now. Realigning. But then you know that. I know you can feel it."

Ash ground his teeth as pain swept through him. He knew exactly why the universe was still shifting to accommodate what never should have happened. "I made a mistake."

"Nick Gautier."

Ash nodded. "I cursed him to die and I altered numerous other lives in the process. Lives of people I love."

Savitar gave him a hard stare. "And now you know why I love no one. Why I never have and never will." He lowered his voice. "Heed my words well, little brother. Love only destroys."

Ash refused to believe it. He knew better. "Love saves."

Savitar scoffed. "Love has destroyed you how many times now?"

Ash smiled bitterly at those memories. "That wasn't love. It was stupidity."

"You still haven't learned your lesson, Atlantean. So long as you feel like a human and love, you are crippled. That is why, eleven thousand years later, the Greek bitch still has her claws into you. Scrape her off and seize your destiny."

"No," Ash said emphatically. "My compassion is what keeps me from doing something even more imbecilic. Without it . . . You don't want to live in the world that would exist if I ever seized my destiny."

"Are you so sure?"

No, he wasn't. Savitar could be brutal and callous at times. "Love is always salvation."

"Then you can keep it. I have better things to do than pace a room, debating what to do." His form started to fade.

"Wait," Ash said.

He reappeared. "Yes?"

Ash hesitated, but he needed to know. "How's Nick doing?"

Savitar shrugged nonchalantly. "He's away from all he has ever known. He's scared and grieving. I think it's safe to say he has had better days."

Ash didn't want to think about that. It was all his fault that Nick was dead and suffering. And it was why he'd sent the Cajun to Savitar for training. The Cajun needed compassion right now that Ash wasn't sure he could give him.

"Thank you for training him."

"There's no need to thank me, Atlantean. One day, I'll ask you for a favor."

"And I will return it."

"I know." Suddenly the stoic veil dropped from Savitar's face. "I don't mean this to be patronizing, Acheron, but I am proud of what you have become. You have learned much and used it wisely, unlike some people I know. . . ."

Ash nodded. Savitar had his own demons that he hid. But then everyone did.

"I hope you find peace, my brother," he said to Savitar.

Savitar scoffed. "Peace walks hand in hand with a quiet conscience."

"Then we're both seriously screwed."

Savitar laughed. "Yes, we are."

Ash fell silent for a minute as thoughts and scenarios played through his mind. "Question?"

"Answer?"

He gave Savitar an irritated grimace. There were times when Savitar enjoyed provoking him. "Would killing Stryker be such a bad thing?"

"Only you can answer that."

"I hate it when you play prophet with me. But I suppose I deserve it."

Savitar shrugged. "All of us answer to someone."

Those words surprised Ash. He found it hard to believe that Savitar would allow anyone to have any power over him. "And who holds your chain?"

"If I told you that, you'd know too much about me."

"You already know too much about me."

Savitar didn't comment on that. "Life is what *we* make it," he said slowly. "You don't need me to tell you what would happen if you killed Stryker. You know that answer." He moved to stand to Ash's side. "You let your emotions control you in New Orleans and what happened?"

Complete and utter disaster.

Ash bit his tongue to keep from asking if Alexion would survive the coming battle with Stryker. If the answer was no, then there was no way he could not interfere.

I have to stay out of this.

"Don't worry, Atlantean," Savitar said quietly. "The one thing

I can assure you . . . through your own actions, you will be saved."

"And Alexion?"

"Through his, he will be damned. But then you already knew that."

21

Alexion spent the next two days getting used to Xirena being a part of him, and popping off his body at inopportune moments because his blood was racing and his blood pressure was elevated. It seemed his demon couldn't tell the physical difference between when he was in danger and when he was "in" Danger.

To which Xirena often commented, "Naked human sex, ew!"

That was okay with him since the idea of naked demon sex was equally repugnant to him.

Meanwhile he continued to grapple with fears about Danger's future. Part of him wanted the voice back in his head that had warned him originally to watch over her. Who had it been and where had she gone?

How could he get her back?

Damn. There were never voices in his head when he needed them.

And tonight was the night. He would deliver his ultimatum to the Dark-Hunters and then he would channel Acheron's powers.

In the past, he'd always been ready to return home. This time, he wasn't. The thought of leaving Danger brought a pain to his chest the likes of which he'd never known before.

"I can't do this."

And yet what choice did he have? He couldn't live in this body. His time was so finite as to be ridiculous. There was no choice here. He couldn't stay.

It was over.

He looked up as Danger entered the room. Dressed in a pair of black jeans with a long-sleeved black shirt, she looked good enough to eat.

She crossed the room to stand in front of him. And the kiss she gave him set his entire body on fire. "When do you leave?"

He looked away as his heart sank, unable to face her with the truth. "Tonight. Once judgment is rendered, I'll be taken back."

He returned to her gaze to see sadness flash in her dark eyes a moment before she hid it. "If I don't get a chance to say it later, I'm glad you came here. And I'm really sorry I stabbed you . . . twice."

He smiled at her words, but his chest tightened as pain over-whelmed him. He was going to miss her more than he would have ever thought possible.

"Danger—"

"Don't," she said, placing her finger over his lips to stop him from speaking. "I know what you're thinking. I can see it in your eyes. I'll miss you too, but let's not make this any harder on either one of us, okay?"

She was so strong that it never ceased to amaze him. There were times when he thought she might even be stronger than he was. "Okay."

She took a deep breath as she dropped her hand to his shoulder. "You know, we might still be able to reach Kyros and save him."

"I'm not counting on that one."

"But you might," she said with a hope he'd long stopped feeling. "Let's not give up on him yet. People can sometimes surprise you."

He frowned at her insistence. "Why is it so important to you that we give him another shot?"

Her dark gaze scorched him. "Because if not for Kyros, I wouldn't have met you. And as wonderful as you are, I keep thinking that he would have to be too, otherwise you wouldn't have believed in him in the first place."

Alexion had to give her credit, she made a convincing argument. How could any man in his right mind find fault with that?

Even more, he didn't want to hurt or disappoint her. For her, he would do anything.

"All right, I'll try."

Kyros paced his dark office, which was lit only by candles, as thoughts drifted through his mind. It was three hours and ticking. The great showdown was coming.

And it was unavoidable.

Every time he thought about it, the hairs on the back of his neck rose in warning. Something wasn't right about tonight and it wasn't just that Ias was here.

There was something else. Something he couldn't see but he could feel it with every fiber of his being. Tonight was going to be unlike anything he'd ever seen before.

"You need anything before I leave?" his Squire, Rob, asked.

Kyros turned to see the young man in the doorway. The man was only five feet seven and dressed in a T-shirt and jeans. By his appearance, the dark-haired boy didn't look any older than Kyros, but at twenty-nine, he was just a baby compared to the centuries that marked Kyros's time on this earth.

"No. You can go on."

In case things went bad, he didn't want his Squire anywhere near this area. At his behest, Rob was heading to Nashville to visit his family.

Rob nodded. "Okay, I'll see you next week."

"I hope so," Kyros breathed as the boy left. He was about to make a betrayal tonight that would most likely get him killed. But he'd known what he was doing from the beginning.

At least he hoped he had.

Danger lay naked in bed, wrapped in Alexion's arms. She had her head resting on his chest while he played with her hair. Time was slipping away for them. Speeding by so fast that it left her bereft and dizzy.

She wanted to scream for it to stop. She wanted to hold on to

Alexion through this night and through the next day and every day that followed after it.

But it wasn't meant to be.

I won't cry. I won't.

It wouldn't be fair to him or to her. But inside she was sobbing uncontrollably. She was torn to pieces. How could she get through this night?

How could she say good-bye to the best thing she'd ever found?

How did people leave their loved ones behind?

But she knew. She'd been forced against her will to leave hers so many times in the past that it made her wonder how she had ever allowed herself to care for someone else.

Then again, not loving a man like Alexion would be an impossibility.

She heard the grandfather clock down the hall striking ten o'clock.

"We have to go," Alexion said, his voice deep and husky.

"I know."

Reluctantly, she pulled away and forced herself to concentrate on anything and everything other than Alexion.

Neither of them spoke as they showered and dressed.

What was there to say? Even worse, she was afraid one of them would say something to set off her tears. It was much easier to keep herself together if she were silent.

She couldn't even tell him that she wouldn't forget him. And that hurt most of all.

"I don't want to forget . . ."

She didn't realize she'd spoken aloud until Alexion gathered her into his arms. "It's better if you do. I couldn't leave you if I knew you were in pain because of me. The only thing that makes this bearable to me is knowing that tomorrow your life will be back to normal."

A tear fled past her control. "I'm sorry," she said, brushing it quickly away. But it was too late. That one tear started an avalanche of sobbing.

Her mind and heart shattered at the thought of the days to come, when she would never even know he existed. She'd no longer know his touch . . . his scent. . . .

God, how she loved the smell of his skin. The caress of his hand on her face. The feel of his body under and over hers. . . .

How could she live without him?

"Don't leave me," she said, her voice breaking.

Alexion closed his eyes as he felt his own tears swelling. If he could have one wish. . . .

But all the wishes in the world couldn't make him human and they couldn't keep them together.

"I won't leave you, Danger. I will be here for you anytime you need me."

She looked up at him with pain in her eyes that made him ache all the way through his being. "But I won't see you."

"No. But I won't ever leave you alone. I swear it."

Danger tightened her hold on him. She didn't know who had it worse. The one who had no memory at all or the one who knew and couldn't speak of it.

She didn't want the night to end. Unable to stand it, she captured his lips to taste him one last time. To inhale his warm, masculine scent and to let it carry her away from this moment of pain.

Not even love could save them. Nothing could.

"I love you, Alexion. I love you, Ias. With all that is within me and more."

"*Je t'aime pour toujours.*"

"*Moi aussi.*"

And then she did the hardest thing she'd ever done in her life. . . .

She let go of him and stepped back even though every fiber of her being screamed at her to hold on regardless.

Unable to look at him without falling apart again, she turned, took a deep breath as she wiped away her tears, and headed for the garage.

Alexion cursed as he watched her leave. *I'm stronger than this.* But the problem was, he wasn't. Not even his powers and Acheron's combined could alleviate the ragged misery that engulfed him.

Danger had unleashed something inside him and set it free. He would never be the same again.

He just wanted one more day with her.

No, that was a lie and he knew it. One day would never content him.

He wanted it all.

He took a deep breath and expelled it. *If wishes were horses, even beggars would ride.* It was a saying he'd learned from a Dark-Hunter three hundred or so years ago.

In every incarnation, he'd learned something new.

In this one, he'd learned how to love. . . . No, that wasn't true. He'd finally learned how to live.

And tonight he would learn how to leave.

Grinding his teeth, he forced himself to follow Danger. And with every step he took, he reminded himself of the greater good.

That was what sustained Acheron. It was what had kept his boss going for thousands and thousands of years. It was what made the unbearable tolerable.

Closing his eyes, he summoned the numbing calm. Later, he would weep for what he had lost. But tonight, he would keep Danger safe and do his job.

May the gods show their mercy to Kyros and Stryker. The Alexion would not.

22

Danger paused outside the building where the Dark-Hunters were gathering. By the cars in the parking lot, the total cost of which would amount to the GNP for a small nation, she would say they were already here and yet . . .

"I don't feel my powers draining," she said to Alexion. "How can that be?"

"It's a trick. Somehow Stryker must be disguising it."

She shook her head. "I don't think so. Maybe he knows some way to keep us from draining each other's powers."

The look on his face chilled her. "Trust me, Danger," Alexion said as he paused to look at her. "There is no way a group of Dark-Hunters are together without draining each other. Stryker would never be able to gain that ability. The only way for it to happen would be if Acheron were here himself. Since he's not . . . it's not possible. The gods would never allow it."

She wasn't so sure, but she trusted him. If anyone knew the truth, it was Alexion.

As they walked in the front door, she half expected someone to stop them. But there were no guards, no Squires. . . .

Nothing.

Since it had been vacant for a number of years, the building wasn't the cleanest thing in the world. There were cobwebs and other things she didn't want to think about littering the floor. The air was stale with a rancid quality to it that left her breathing through her mouth in an effort not to pinch her nose closed.

She found it strange that there were working lights in the building.

But then Stryker was a god. . . .

"Where's the light coming from upstairs?" she asked Alexion.

"I don't know. Maybe they have a generator hooked up, or again, Stryker is using his powers to light it."

They found the stairs in the back and started up. As they headed up, they could hear faint voices, but the words were unintelligible.

Danger tried not to breathe deeply as she wondered what lies Kyros and Stryker were telling the others.

How many of them would buy into it?

As they reached the door at the end of the upstairs hall where the others seemed to be gathered, she pulled Alexion to a stop to listen to what was going on inside before they entered. She was only now beginning to feel a pull on her powers, but it was still very mild.

"So how do we defeat Acheron?"

Danger winced as she recognized Squid's voice. That little rat-bastard. But she'd suspected as much. He'd been vehement in his hatred of Acheron.

She looked up to see a cold, determined look on Alexion's face.

"He is a Daimon," Stryker said. "You kill him as you would any of our people."

Kyros was the next to speak. His voice rang out. "Are you with us, brothers and sisters?"

She cringed as she heard the sound of unanimous agreement.

Alexion pulled her back. "I'll take it from here." He kissed her lightly on the lips before he turned, held his hand out, and blasted the steel door into oblivion.

Alexion strode confidently into the room, even though he knew Stryker probably had some means to kill him. Let the bastard try. If he did, then he was in for a fight.

It was time now to do his job.

There were twenty Dark-Hunters in the room—eighteen men and two women, along with several dozen Daimons. It was a good thing Dark-Hunter blood was poisonous to the Daimons, otherwise they would most likely be feasting by now on the fools who had gathered here to die like sheep being led blithely to the butcher.

But it was Kyros who held his attention. He stood before the group, his eyes burning with hatred.

Sighing, Alexion shook his head. "What fools these immortals be," he said. "To listen to a Daimon and fall victim to his lies."

"We fell victim to those centuries ago," Squid snarled. "There's not a one of us here who hasn't been used by Acheron."

Alexion pitied him. "I'm not here to argue with any of you anymore. I'm here to give you your last chance to save yourselves. Those of you who want to live to see another night, step to the right. Those of you who wish to believe in Stryker's bullshit and die tonight stay where you are."

"Don't be afraid of him," Stryker said. "What can one man do to all of you?"

Alexion gave him a wry grin. "If I'm so little a threat, Stryker, why haven't you killed me?"

He looked around at the gathered crowd of Dark-Hunters. "Don't throw your lives away so needlessly. All of you have survived too much to be so damned stupid."

He paused to stare at Kyros. "And you, *adelfos,* I carried you on my back when you were wounded. I gave you bread when it was the last bite I had to sustain me. Look me in the eyes now and tell me that you are willing to back a Daimon over me."

Kyros looked to Stryker, who began clapping sarcastically. "Great speech. Practice long?"

Alexion raised his hand and threw Stryker back against a wall. "Decide, Hunters. Now!"

The Daimons rushed at him, only to rebound off the wall he raised around himself. Still, they continued to attack as if seeking some way to break through his hold.

He watched as the Dark-Hunters exchanged nervous looks

with each other. Then, to his relief, sixteen of them moved to the right.

The instant they did, he saw the confusion on their faces.

"What the hell?" Eleanore, one of the Dark-Huntresses, said. "I feel so weak suddenly."

No doubt the break in Stryker's hold allowed them to feel the fact that their powers had been significantly drained.

Kyros took one step, then paused as Stryker broke Alexion's hold and shot a blast at him. It pierced the force field and sent him flying backward.

Alexion hissed as pain cut through him. Stryker blasted him again and again. The pain was searing. He tried to push himself up only to find Danger by his side, helping him.

A bad premonition struck him hard. "Get the Dark-Hunters and get out of here," he said to her.

But before she could move, Stryker attacked her with the bolt as well.

Alexion turned on the demigod with a curse as he returned fire with fire.

"Spathis!" Stryker snapped to his men as he ducked Alexion's blast. "Kill the Dark-Hunters! All of them."

The Daimons attacked en masse. Danger drew the dagger from her boot as she ran to join the fray.

"Danger, stay back!" Alexion shouted as he blasted the Daimons away.

He tried to shatter them with his powers, but couldn't.

Stryker laughed at him. "They're stronger than you are, Alexion. We're not the wimpy little Daimons you normally fight. We are so much more."

Alexion's gaze narrowed on him before he called out, "Xirena, take human form."

The demon came off him and transformed.

Danger smiled at their ace in the hole. The Daimons would never be able to stand against Xirena.

"You traitorous bitch," Stryker snarled at the demon as he raked a disgusted sneer over her.

Xirena flew at him only to have Stryker slash at her wings with his dagger. The demon shrieked, then fell to the ground where she lay, unable to get up, as Stryker continued to stab at her. Whimpering, Xirena tried to crawl away from him before he could kill her.

Danger didn't know what had happened. She ran to the demon to try and help her.

Alexion's heart stopped as he realized what Stryker had used against the demon . . . an Atlantean dagger. The only thing that could kill Charontes. But more to the point, it could also kill Danger, even with her Dark-Hunter powers.

Shit! He could flash out of here with one of them, but not both. If he used his powers, he would have to choose between Danger or the demon. . . .

But more than that, he couldn't leave the Dark-Hunters who were drained. They were having an almost impossible time fighting the Daimons who were attacking them.

"What's going on here?" Squid asked an instant before a Daimon killed him.

"Run!" Kyros shouted at the others. "They've weakened us so that they can kill us."

"Danger," Alexion said as he shielded the demon, "grab Xirena and get out."

As she moved to obey, Stryker pulled out a red medallion. "Touch the demon and I'll destroy your soul."

Everyone in the room froze at those words. Alexion noted the horror on the faces of the Dark-Hunters who realized just what the Daimon held. If Danger's soul was destroyed, she would never be able to go free.

More than that, it would turn her into a Shade.

Her expression one of terror, Danger held Xirena close.

Alexion cocked his head at the strangeness of Stryker's threat. The momentary panic that he held her soul lasted for only a few seconds, before he realized something. "Run with Xirena, Danger. He doesn't have your soul."

Stryker laughed at him as he passed a pitying look to Danger. "How wonderful. Your lover thinks to call my bluff."

"It's not a bluff," Alexion said assuredly as he faced the Daimon coldly. "I don't know what you have, but it's not her soul."

Stryker's gaze was cold, sinister, and if he'd actually had Danger's soul, Alexion might have been scared. "Are you willing to take that chance?"

Alexion didn't blink. "Yes."

"Alexion!" Danger snapped, her voice filled with fear. "If it is my soul—"

"It's not," he said, looking at her. "Trust me in this. Artemis holds those souls too closely and there's only one man alive who can get them from her. You can bet your life, your *ousia,* and everything else you have that Stryker's not him."

"Are you so sure?" Stryker asked as he toyed with the medallion in his hand. He tightened his grip around it. "Artemis is my aunt, after all."

Alexion scoffed. "Yeah, and she hates your guts with a blazing passion. The only way for you to get a soul is for Acheron to hand it over to you and we both know the chances of that."

Cursing, Stryker threw the medallion down and crushed it under his heel.

Danger cringed until she realized that nothing had happened to her.

She felt her chest just to make sure. . . .

Nope, she was still intact. Breathing in relief, she returned to Xirena, who was still holding her chest where Stryker had stabbed her.

"I told you to kill them all," Stryker commanded his Daimons.

Danger stood before the demon to protect her. As the Daimons attacked and she fought them, she realized something terrifying. Her powers weren't there in full strength.

With every strike and blow, she seemed to weaken.

The Daimon she was fighting kicked her backward. Danger hit the ground so hard, it knocked the breath from her. She rolled, trying to get away, only to find herself at the feet of another Daimon. He laughed as he raised a sword to behead her.

Just as she was sure she was dead, the Daimon was thrown back. She looked up expecting to see Alexion.

Instead, it was Kyros who stood over her.

He had killed the Daimon, and was holding his hand out to

her. "I've been a stupid fool," he breathed as he pulled her to her feet. "I'm sorry."

"I'm not the one you need to apologize to."

He glanced to Alexion who was fighting Stryker. "I know." He pushed her toward the door. "C'mon. We have to get the other Dark-Hunters out of here before it's too late."

Before she could say anything, he bent over and picked Xirena up to carry her away from the Daimons.

Alexion paused as he saw Kyros and Danger working together to get the others to safety. She'd been right—he had come around in the end. Gods, he owed that woman more than could ever be repaid.

He did a quick head count of the Dark-Hunters who were leaving and realized that only three Dark-Hunters had been killed by the Daimons so far.

They'd been the ones who hadn't moved to the right.

Kyros and Danger were fighting the Daimons as the rest of them rushed to make it out of the room.

To buy them more time, he lunged at Stryker again.

The Daimon turned with a snarl. "You can't stop me," Stryker said ominously.

He tossed the dagger at Danger.

Alexion threw his hand out to deflect the dagger's path. The dagger should have shot to his hand. It didn't.

Just as it started for him, one of the Daimons hit him in the chest. He staggered forward, then regained his balance. Before he could reclaim the dagger, it returned to Stryker who tossed it faster than he could blink.

It buried itself deep into Danger's chest.

Alexion couldn't breathe for a full heartbeat as he saw it hit her so hard it knocked her off her feet before sending her twisting to the floor.

Kyros turned with a curse as he ran for her.

No! Alexion's mind screamed in denial.

It couldn't be. . . .

"You should have backed off," Stryker said between clenched teeth as the dagger flew back into his outstretched hand. "But that's all right. The best way to kill someone is to always aim for their heart. She dies because of you and you die because of Acheron."

The Daimon threw the dagger at him.

Strike at the heart . . .

Catching the dagger in his fist an instant before it would have embedded itself in his chest, Alexion finally understood what the unknown feminine voice had been trying to tell him. He felt his powers surging at those words.

He turned on Stryker with a snarl. "You want a heart, Stryker? I'll give you yours. . . ."

He knew his eyes were glowing green as he shouted, "Urian!"

"Don't you dare defile my son's name with—" Stryker's words broke off as the air around them stirred.

Two seconds later, Urian appeared. Tall and blond, the man looked eerily similar to his father except Stryker dyed his hair black while Urian's was white-blond. As always, he kept it long, and in a ponytail that was secured with a black leather cord.

Urian looked less than pleased to have been summoned. His

jaw went slack as he glanced around the room at the Daimons who were staring at him in disbelief.

"Nice way to keep me incognito, Lex," Urian said, until his gaze fell on his father.

His eyes narrowed in hatred.

"Urian?" Stryker breathed the name like a sacred prayer.

"You bastard!" Urian snarled.

"Kill him," one of the Daimons shouted.

"No!" Stryker said. "He's my son."

Urian shook his head. "No, old man. I'm your enemy." Urian grabbed the dagger from Alexion's hand and ran at his father with it while Alexion went for Danger.

"Retreat!" Stryker ordered his Daimons an instant before five bolt-holes appeared.

Stryker hesitated, looking at Urian for a long minute, before he jumped through and vanished.

His heart broken, Alexion gathered Danger into his arms while Xirena stared at them from where Kyros had set her down. Alexion pressed a cloth to Danger's chest to stop the blood flow from her injury.

The demon was wounded but, unlike Danger, not fatally. Stryker hadn't stabbed the demon in the heart.

Urian turned on him. "What the hell was that action, Shade? My life was supposed to be kept secret."

"Shut up, Urian," Alexion growled as he held Danger and fought against the tears that wanted to blind him. Fought against the debilitating pain that overwhelmed him.

His entire being was screaming out in pain as it refused to believe what had happened to her.

"Come on, baby," he whispered to her as he gently rocked her in his arms. "Don't die on me."

"It should heal," Danger whispered softly in a voice that belied her pain. "Why isn't the wound healing?"

"I'm sorry, *akri*," Xirena whispered. "Xirena didn't mean to get stabbed and let your woman die."

Urian joined them, his face pale as he noted her chest wound. "Did Stryker stab her with his personal dagger?"

"Yes," Alexion choked, noting the haunted look behind Urian's eyes. No doubt the man was reliving the death of his own beloved wife at Stryker's hands.

"Is there any way to save her?" he asked the Daimon.

"Acheron!" Urian called.

Alexion tensed as he heard a summons he knew Acheron wouldn't heed. He knew the rules of his mission. Acheron wouldn't interfere.

Danger was going to die.

The pain of that thought lacerated his chest and shredded his heart.

It brought tears to his eyes that he couldn't stop.

"I wish he would have had your soul," Alexion whispered against her cheek. "At least then I could have made you human."

"Can't you call on Ash's powers to heal her?" Urian asked.

Alexion shook his head. The power over life and death wasn't one Acheron was willing to share.

Kyros fell to his knees beside them. "I'm so sorry, Danger. None of the Dark-Hunters were supposed to be hurt tonight. Dammit, this is all my fault."

Alexion glared at him and his stupidity as his anger swelled, wanting to kill his so-called friend. "How do you figure? You were trying to turn them against Acheron."

"I know," Kyros said with a sincere gaze. "I screwed up. I'm so sorry. Stryker was so convincing. At first he turned Marco, and the next thing I knew, Marco was dead. Stryker swore it was you who killed him. I should never have listened to him."

But Alexion wasn't really listening to Kyros at the moment. All he could hear was Danger's breathing getting lighter and lighter.

She choked as she struggled to continue breathing. She reached up and touched his cheek with a cold hand. "If anything is left of me, will you take it to France? There's a mass grave in a park in Paris—"

"I know that park," Alexion said. It was where the victims of the guillotine had all been buried.

Danger took a deep breath. "My father, his wife, and my brother and sister are there. If I can't be with you, I want to be with them."

Alexion nodded as tears choked him. "I promise, Danger. I won't let you be alone."

She offered him a wan smile. "We had fun, didn't we, *mon coeur*?" She stroked his cheek with her thumb. "I'm so going to miss you."

Then he felt it . . . that last expulsion of breath from her body.

She went limp in his arms as her hand fell away from his face.

Alexion threw his head back and cried out as pain tore through him. In that moment, he hated Acheron. He hated Kyros. He hated Stryker, but most of all he hated himself for not being able to protect her.

Xirena and Kyros stayed back, their faces pale as they watched him, but Alexion didn't care. Nothing mattered except the woman who lay limply in his arms.

A woman whose vibrancy had shown him how to live again. More than that, she had shown him how to love. She had reached inside his heart and made it beat for the first time in more than nine thousand years.

Now she was gone.

And his heart would never beat again.

No! his heart screamed in denial. She couldn't die. Not like this. Not someone who had loved to live so much. Someone who had spent her life helping others.

She had believed in him and he had let her die. . . .

Urian paced back and forth between Kyros and Xirena, and Danger and Alexion. "I can't believe Ash just let her die," he growled. He looked up at the ceiling. "You are a fucking asshole!"

"No," Alexion said as tears fell, while he held her cold, pale body to his chest. "It has to be this way. He can't change fate."

"The fuck he can't," Urian snarled angrily. "He brought me back and I was a Daimon. Why would he save me and not her?"

Alexion had no answer to that. He didn't have any answers at the moment. All he could feel was the pain of her loss. The agony. It was raw and consuming.

How could she be dead?

How could he have allowed this to happen? *Damn me, damn me, damn me!*

"I'm sorry I failed you, *akri*," Xirena said.

Alexion didn't speak. He couldn't.

Suddenly, a bright light appeared in the room.

Acheron flashed into a corner, where he stood with a stoic expression.

Urian turned on him with a curled lip.

"Don't even, Daimon." Acheron zapped him out of there before Urian could speak.

"Kyros," Acheron said gently. "Go home and rest."

Then he, too, was gone.

Acheron hesitated as the demon stared at him as if he were an apparition.

Her face was ghostly pale from her fear of him. "Will you kill Xirena now?"

"No." Ash knelt by her side and healed her wounds. "Return to your master for a little while and you will meet your sister soon."

The demon nodded, then ran up Alexion's sleeve, to his chest.

Alexion still hadn't moved as he cradled Danger to him.

Acheron cocked his head as he watched them with those all-powerful, swirling silver eyes. "Why don't you question me?"

Alexion swallowed against the bitter lump in his throat that was choking him. "Because I know better." He looked up at Acheron so that he could see the sincerity in his eyes. "But I hate you right now."

"I know."

And then it happened. . . .

Danger's body evaporated into a shiny gold powder.

Alexion cried out again as he felt her loss completely. "No!" he growled as he tried to scoop the powder up so that he could take it to Paris for her as he'd promised.

"Don't," Acheron said gently as he reached out for him.

Alexion shoved him away. "Damn you, you bastard, I promised her. I promised—"

He covered his eyes with his hands as he sobbed, realizing it was hopeless. "There's nothing left to bury. Nothing left to gather even."

Oh, gods, how could she be gone like this? How? It wasn't right. It wasn't fair.

"We have to go, Alexion."

He nodded even though what he wanted to do was attack Acheron himself. He knew it wasn't Acheron's fault, but it didn't matter. He wanted to strike out and hurt someone. Anything to ease the burning, aching hole inside him.

There was nothing left to stay for.

Danger was gone. . . .

His heart shattered, he felt his human body melting as it shifted from the human realm to Katoteros. He found himself back in the throne room where Simi was waiting.

"Alexion!" she shrieked happily, running at him before she launched herself into his arms. "You're back!"

She pulled away and frowned when he didn't return her enthusiasm. Cocking her head, she scowled at him. "But you're so sad. Why are you sad, Lexie? Was them Daimons mean to you? The Simi will eat them if they hurt you."

Acheron gently pulled her away. "He needs to be alone for a little while, Sim."

"But . . ."

"It's okay." Acheron took her hand and gave him the space he needed.

Alexion didn't speak as he walked the back hallway toward

his chambers. He was so cold inside that he didn't think he could ever be warm again.

For the first time ever, he hated this place. He hated everything about it. Most of all, he hated Acheron.

At least he did until he opened the doors to his room. He stopped short, his breath catching, as he saw the impossible.

It couldn't be, yet it was. . . .

There in the center of his room, dressed in a red chiton, was Danger.

He couldn't speak as he caught sight of her there.

She was looking around as if disoriented. "Where am I?"

No words would come out of his mouth as he rushed to her and scooped her up in his arms. She felt real.

She felt alive. . . .

Could it be? Did he dare believe that this was real?

Holding her close, he buried his head against her neck, inhaled her scent and wept.

"Alexion, you're starting to freak me out."

He pulled back with a laugh. "How did you get here?"

"I have no idea. One minute I was in a lot of pain, then everything was dark, and then I was here." She leaned toward him. "Where is here?"

"My chambers. You're in Katoteros."

She frowned up at him. "I don't understand."

Neither did he.

"You didn't really think I was going to let this end badly, did you?"

Alexion turned to find Acheron standing in the doorway, watching them with a smile.

"We learn from our pain," he said, using the words Acheron so often quoted to him.

Acheron shrugged. "But we are rewarded with pleasure." His gaze shifted to Danger before it returned to meet his levelly. "You've served me too long and too well for me to turn my back on you, Alexion. I couldn't save her life without altering too much of the universe. But I can give you this."

Alexion was grateful and at the same time stunned by it. He had never expected Acheron to do something like this . . . ever. "You hate people in your house."

Acheron let out a weary breath. "What the hell? I got used to you. I'll get used to Danger in time too."

Danger gaped. "I get to stay? Here? With Alexion? Really?"

"Only if you want to," Alexion said.

Danger swallowed as her eyes filled with tears. She wrapped herself around Alexion and held him tight. "I can't believe this."

"I'm sorry for what you lost, Danger," Acheron said quietly. "This existence is far from perfect."

Alexion saw a panicked look darken her eyes. "Do I have to drink blood to live?"

Acheron shook his head. "Only Einstein over there has to do that. But like him, you won't be able to taste food anymore."

Danger laughed. "That's all right. Who needs taste buds anyway? I'll just eat a lot of popcorn."

Acheron's gaze softened. "If you want to release your demon, Alexion, I'll go introduce her to Simi and give you two some time alone."

Alexion frowned. "How is it that you're not stunned she has a sister?"

"I've known for a long time that she wasn't the only demon out there. It wasn't too big a leap of faith to figure she probably had some family too."

Still, Alexion was shocked that Acheron had kept such a secret from them. "Then why didn't you tell us?"

"Simi likes the idea of being the only one. I was going to tell her the truth once she got a little older. But I guess now's the time."

Alexion agreed. "Xirena, I summon you to human form."

The demon popped off his body and stood back, reserved. "Am I in trouble?"

"No," Alexion assured her. "You're going to meet Simi."

Her eyes sparked with happiness.

"Come, Xirena," Acheron said. "I'll take you to her."

She hesitated. "You're not trying to trick Xirena, are you?"

"No."

"It'll be all right," Alexion said. "You can trust him."

Xirena went to Ash hesitantly before the two of them left the room.

Danger waited until they were alone before she turned back to Alexion and pulled him into her arms. "Is this really real?"

"Yeah," he breathed as he held her close. "I still can't believe you're here."

"You can't? I thought I had lost you forever."

"At least I didn't die on you."

"No, but that's not a problem for either one of us again, is it?"

Alexion smiled as he savored the sight of her bright brown eyes shining up at him. "Not unless we piss off a Charonte."

"Then I will make sure I never do."

He hugged her tight and picked her up in his arms, grateful

that he had her back. This time, he was going to make damn sure that nothing happened to her again. "I love you, Danger."

Danger kissed him as her heart swelled with joy. "I love you too," she breathed.

And though this life with him wasn't going to be perfect, it would be really, really close. So long as they were together, nothing else mattered.

EPILOGUE

Standing in the throne room, Simi stared at the other demon suspiciously as she moved her head back and forth much like a snake eyeing something it wanted to strike at. "What do you mean, she's my sister?" she asked Ash.

"Xiamara, do you not—"

"I am the Simi," she said, stomping her foot. "Xiamara is my mother."

Xirena was so confused that Ash actually felt sorry for her.

Simi came up to her slowly and poked at her. "You look real."

"I am real."

"Then why did you not come see me?"

Xirena was aghast at the question. "I couldn't. The bitch-goddess wouldn't let me."

"Artemis?" Simi squealed. "I hate her."

"No," Xirena corrected her, "the other bitch-goddess, Apollymi."

"Hey!" Ash snapped simultaneously with Simi.

Xirena looked even more confused.

"She a goddess, that Apollymi," Simi said reverently. "She always good to the Simi. She makes me horney-warmers to keep my horneys warm and she gives me lots of cookies when I come see her."

Xirena's jaw dropped. "She does what?"

Simi put her hands on her hips. "You heard me, deaf demon. She a good lady, that Apollymi, and the Simi will hurt anyone who says otherwise."

Xirena stepped forward and whispered loudly. "Will your *akri* let me talk to you alone?"

Simi blew a raspberry and waved her hand at Ash. "Like I care if he says no. He don't control me."

Xirena appeared horrified by her words. "He's your *akri*."

Simi blew her another raspberry. "He's my daddy."

"He's your *akri*," she said from between clenched fangs.

Simi frowned at Ash. "There's something seriously wrong with my sister. Why she keep saying you my lord and master when you're just my daddy, *akri*?"

Ash shrugged. "I have no idea, Sim. You need to set her straight."

"Hmmm." Simi wrapped her arm around her sister's shoulders and led her over to the corner where she had her own television monitors. "See, in this world, Xirena, the Simi does what she wants and *akri*, he say, 'Okay, Simi, whatever you want, Simi.' Unless it involves eating people; then he usually says no, but that's the only time. Other than that, he do what the Simi says. See how that works?"

Xirena appeared completely baffled by her sister.

Simi popped her head up to look at Ash. "Where she staying anyway?"

"You could share a room with—"

"No," she said immediately. "The Simi don't share her room, *akri*. Ever. I don't care that she is my sister. My room has all my special mementos in there. I think you should make her one of her own."

Ash knew better than to argue with his demon. Not to mention the fact that it didn't bother him to humor her. He actually enjoyed spoiling her. "Okay. Where do you want it?"

"Kind of next to mine, but not so close that she blocks the view to my Travis Fimmel billboard that the Simi has on the great wall."

"Your what?" Xirena asked. "What's a Travis Fimmel?"

Simi's jaw dropped as she looked stunned. "You don't know about Travis Fimmel? Oh, sister, you are deprived. He the finest man alive."

Xirena shuddered. "You lust for men?"

"Well, I certainly don't lust for women."

"No," Xirena corrected, "I mean, you lust for humans?" The way she said that you could tell it was the most disgusting thing the demon could imagine.

"Well, don't you?" Simi asked.

"Ew!" Xirena looked at Ash. "What have you done to her? You have corrupted a good demon!" She looked back at Simi. "You need to see Drakus."

"Who that?"

"He the finest demon to ever live. He can breathe fire out his nose and mouth at the same time."

Simi's face beamed. "Ooo!"

Ash cringed as he saw where this was going. "Simi's too young for that."

"No she's not," they said in unison.

"I think you're outnumbered, boss."

Ash turned to see Alexion behind him. Danger was entering the room just behind him. Her eyes widened as she took in the opulence of the Atlantean throne room.

He sighed as Alexion stopped beside him. "Forget Armageddon, this is the scariest thing I've ever seen." Ash watched in horror as the two demons sat down and started comparing notes on "hot" men and male demons.

Alexion turned to Danger and smiled. "I think it's a good thing we have a woman in the house now. Maybe she can talk some sense into them."

Danger snorted. "The demons are your domain, not mine. I'm not even going there."

Ash actually whimpered as Xirena began telling Simi the correct mating habits of the Charontes. "This is going to get ugly. Thanks, Lex."

Alexion smiled as he pulled Danger in his arms and held her close. "No, boss, thank you."

Ash glanced at the two of them and saw the love that they had for each other.

It went a long way in soothing the part of him that hated to have strangers in his home.

And as he looked into Danger's future, he saw absolutely nothing. For the first time in his long life, he found it comforting.

It meant only one thing.

Danger would definitely be an integral part of their future lives.